The Voyage of the Space Beagle, as the immense rocket leaps from galaxy to galaxy, vertiginously hurtling ever deeper into space, is one of the most enthralling 'outward bound' stories ever written.

On some planets they find traces of long vanished alien civilisations. On other worlds the aliens have by no means vanished!

And one terrifying race they come upon needs no planet: it exists and lives after its fashion in space itself.

But the final aliens that van Vogt brilliantly and disturbingly conjures up are discovered in the rocket – Man himself.

The Voyage of the Space Beagle is an SF classic.

W0027787

Also by A. E. van Vogt

Slan
The Mind Cage
Away and Beyond
Destination : Universe!
Moonbeast
The Book of Ptath
The War Against the Rull
Rogue Ship

A. E. van Vogt

The Voyage of the Space Beagle

Panther

Granada Publishing Limited
Published in 1959 by Panther Books Ltd
Frogmore, St Albans, Herts AL2 2NF
Reprinted 1963, 1968, 1970, 1973, 1975, 1977

First published in Great Britain by
Grayson and Grayson Ltd 1951
Made and printed in Great Britain by
Hunt Barnard Printing Ltd
Aylesbury, Bucks
Set in Monotype Plantin

This book is sold subject to the condition that it shall not, by way of trade or otherwise, be lent, re-sold, hired out or otherwise circulated without the publisher's prior consent in any form of binding or cover other than that in which it is published and without a similar condition including this condition being imposed on the subsequent purchaser.
This book is published at a net price and is supplied subject to the Publishers Association Standard Conditions of Sale registered under the Restrictive Trade Practices Act, 1956.

to Ford McCormack

CHAPTER ONE

ON and on Coeurl prowled. The black, moonless, almost starless night yielded reluctantly before a grim reddish dawn that crept up from his left. It was a vague light that gave no sense of approaching warmth. It slowly revealed a nightmare landscape.

Jagged black rock and a black, lifeless plain took form around him. A pale red sun peered above the grotesque horizon. Fingers of light probed among the shadows. And still there was no sign of the family of id creatures that he had been trailing now for nearly a hundred days.

He stopped finally, chilled by the reality. His great forelegs twitched with a shuddering movement that arched every razor-sharp claw. The thick tentacles that grew from his shoulders undulated tautly. He twisted his great cat head from side to side, while the hair-like tendrils that formed each ear vibrated frantically, testing every vagrant breeze, every throb in the ether.

There was no response. He felt no swift tingling along his intricate nervous system. There was no suggestion anywhere of the presence of the id creatures, his only source of food on this desolate planet. Hopelessly, Coeurl crouched, an enormous catlike figure silhouetted against the dim, reddish sky line, like a distorted etching of a black tiger in a shadow world. What dismayed him was the fact that he had lost touch. He possessed sensory equipment that could normally detect organic id miles away. He recognized that he was no longer normal. His overnight failure to maintain contact indicated a physical breakdown. This was the deadly sickness he had heard about. Seven times in the past century he had found coeurls, too weak to move, their otherwise immortal bodies emaciated and doomed for lack of food. Eagerly, then, he had smashed their unresisting bodies, and taken what little id was still keeping them alive.

Coeurl shivered with excitement, remembering those meals. Then he snarled audibly, a defiant sound that quavered on the air, echoed and re-echoed among the rocks, and shuddered back along his nerves. It was an instinctive expression of his will to live.

And then, abruptly, he stiffened.

High above the distant horizon he saw a tiny glowing spot. It came nearer. It grew rapidly, enormously, into a metal ball. It became a vast, round ship. The great globe, shining like polished silver, hissed by above Coeurl, slowing visibly. It receded over a black line of hills to the right, hovered almost motionless for a second, then sank down out of sight.

Coeurl exploded from his startled immobility. With tigerish speed, he raced down among the rocks. His round, black eyes burned with agonized desire. His ear tendrils, despite their diminished powers, vibrated a message of id in such quantities that his body felt sick with the pangs of his hunger.

The distant sun, pinkish now, was high in the purple and black sky when he crept up behind a mass of rock and gazed from its shadows at the ruins of the city that sprawled below him. The silvery ship, in spite of its size, looked small against the great spread of the deserted, crumbling city. Yet about the ship was leashed aliveness, a dynamic quiescence that, after a moment, made it stand out, dominating the foreground. It rested in a cradle made by its own weight in the rocky, resisting plain which began abruptly at the outskirts of the dead metropolis.

Coeurl gazed at the two-legged beings who had come from inside the ship. They stood in little groups near the bottom of an escalator that had been lowered from a brilliantly lighted opening a hundred feet above the ground. His throat thickened with the immediacy of his need. His brain grew dark with the impulse to charge out and smash these flimsy-looking creatures whose bodies emitted the id vibrations.

Mists of memory stopped that impulse when it was still only electricity surging through his muscles. It was a memory of the distant past of his own race, of machines that could destroy, of energies potent beyond all the powers of his own body. The remembrance poisoned the reservoirs of his strength. He had time to see that the beings wore something over their real bodies, a shimmering transparent material that glittered and flashed in the rays of the sun.

Cunning came, understanding of the presence of these creatures. This, Coeurl reasoned for the first time, was a scientific expedition from another star. Scientists would investigate, and not destroy. Scientists would refrain from killing him if he did not attack. Scientists in their way were fools.

Bold with his hunger, he emerged into the open. He saw the creatures become aware of him. They turned and stared. The three nearest him moved slowly back toward larger groups. One individual, the smallest of his group, detached a dull metal rod from a sheath at his side, and held it casually in one hand.

Coeurl was alarmed by the action, but he loped on. It was too late to turn back.

Elliott Grosvenor remained where he was, well in the rear, near the gangplank. He was becoming accustomed to being in the background. As the only Nexialist aboard the *Space Beagle*, he had been ignored for months by specialists who did not clearly understand what a Nexialist was, and who cared very little anyway. Grosvenor had plans to rectify that. So far, the opportunity to do so had not occurred.

The communicator in the headpiece of his space suit came abruptly to life. A man laughed softly, and then said. "Personally, I'm taking no chances with anything as large as that."

As the other spoke, Grosvenor recognized the voice of Gregory Kent, head of the chemistry department. A small man physically, Kent had a big personality. He had numerous friends and supporters aboard the ship, and had already announced his candidacy for the directorship of the expedition in the forthcoming election. Of all the men facing the approaching monster, Kent was the only one who had drawn a weapon. He stood now, fingering the spindly metalite instrument.

Another voice sounded. The tone was deeper and more relaxed. Grosvenor recognized it as belonging to Hal Morton, Director of the expedition. Morton said, 'That's one of the reasons why you're on this trip, Kent – because you leave very little to chance."

It was a friendly comment. It ignored the fact that Kent had already set himself up as Morton's opponent for the directorship. Of course, it could have been designed as a bit of incidental political virtuosity to put over to the more naïve listeners the notion that Morton felt no ill will towards his rival. Grosvenor did not doubt that the Director was capable of such sublety. He had sized up Morton as a shrewd, reasonably honest, and very intelligent man, who handled most situations with automatic skill.

Grosvenor saw that Morton was moving forward, placing himself a little in advance of the others. His strong body bulked the transparent metalite suit. From that position, the Director watched the catlike beast approach them across the black rock plain. The comments of other departmental heads pattered through the communicator into Grosvenor's ears.

"I'd hate to meet that baby on a dark night in an alley."

"Don't be silly. This is obviously an intelligent creature. Probably a member of the ruling race."

"Its physical developments," said a voice, which Grosvenor recognized as that of Siedel, the psychologist, "suggest an animal-like adaptation to its environment. On the other hand, its coming to us like this is not the act of an animal but of an intelligent being who is aware of our intelligence. You will notice how stiff its movements are. That denotes caution, and consciousness of our weapons. I'd like to get a good look at the end of those shoulder tentacles. If they taper into handlike appendages or suction cups, we could start assuming that it's a descendant of the inhabitants of this city." He paused, then finished, "It would be a great help if we could establish communication with it. Off-hand, though, I'd say that it has degenerated into a primitive state."

Coeurl stopped when he was still ten feet from the nearest beings. The need for id threatened to overwhelm him. His brain drifted to that ferocious edge of chaos, where it cost him a terrible effort to hold back. He felt as if his body were bathed in molten liquid. His vision kept blurring.

Most of the men walked closer to him. Coeurl saw that they were frankly and curiously examining him. Their lips moved inside the transparent helmets they wore. Their form of intercommunication – he assumed that was what he sensed – came to him on a frequency that was well within his ability to receive. The messages were meaningless. In an effort to appear friendly, he broadcast his name from his ear tendrils, at the same time pointing at himself with one curving tentacle.

A voice Grosvenor didn't recognize drawled, "I got a sort of static in my radio when he wiggled those hairs, Morton. Do you think –"

Morton's use of the man's name identified the other. Gourlay, chief of communications. Grosvenor, who was recording the conversation, was pleased. The coming of the beast might enable him to obtain recordings of the voices of all the rest of the important men aboard the ship. He had tried to do that from the beginning.

"Ah," said Siedel, the psychologist, "the tentacles end in

suction cups. Provided the nervous system is complex enough, he could with training operate any machine."

Director Morton said, "I think we'd better go inside and have lunch. Afterwards, we'll have to get busy. I'd like a study made of the scientific development of this race, and particularly I want to know what wrecked it. On Earth, in the early days before there was a galactic civilization, one culture after another reached its peak and then crumbled. A new one always sprang up in its dust. Why didn't that happen here? Each department will be assigned its special field of investigation."

"What about pussy?" somebody said. "I think he wants to come in with us."

Morton chuckled, then said seriously, "I wish there were some way we could take it in with us, without forcibly capturing it. Kent, what do you think?"

The little chemist shook his head decisively. "This atmosphere has a higher chlorine than oxygen content, though actually not much of either. Our oxygen would be dynamite to his lungs."

It was clear to Grosvenor that the catlike being had not considered that danger. He watched the monster follow the first men up the escalator and through the great door.

The men glanced back towards Morton, who waved a hand at them and said, "Open the second lock and let him get a whiff of the oxygen. That'll cure him."

A moment later the Director's amazed voice was loud on the communicator. 'Well, I'll be damned! He doesn't notice the difference! That means he hasn't any lungs, or else the chlorine is not what his lungs use, You bet he can go in! Smith, here's a treasure house for a biologist – harmless enough if we're careful. What a metabolism!"

Smith was a tall, thin bony man with a long, mournful face. His voice, unusually forceful for his appearance sounded in Grosvenor's communicator. "In the various exploring trips I've been on, I've seen only two higher forms of life. Those dependent on chlorine, and those who need oxygen – the two elements that support combustion. I've heard vague reports of a fluorine-breathing life form, but I've yet to see an example. I'd almost stake my reputation that no complicated organism could ever adapt itself to the actual utilization of both gases. Morton, we mustn't let this creature get away if we can help it."

Director Morton laughed, then said soberly, "He seems anxious enough to stay."

He had been riding up the escalator on one side of the gangplank. Now he moved into the air lock with Coeurl and the two men. Grosvenor hurried forward, but he was only one of a dozen men who also entered the large space. The great door swung shut, and air began to hiss in. Everybody stood well clear of the catlike monster. Grosvenor watched the beast with a growing sense of uneasiness. Several thoughts occurred to him. He wished he could communicate them to Morton. He should have been able to. The rule aboard these expeditionary ships was that all heads of departments should have easy access to the director. As head of the Nexial department – though he was the only one in it – that should have applied to him also. The communicator of his space suit should have been fitted so that he could talk to Morton as did the heads of the other departments. But all he had was a general receiver. That gave him the privilege of listening in to the great men when they were doing field work. If he wanted to talk to anyone, or if he were in danger, he could throw a switch that would open a channel to a central operator.

Grosvenor did not question the general value of the system. There were just under one thousand men aboard, and it was obvious that all of them could not talk to Morton whenever they pleased.

The inner door of the lock was opening. Grosvenor pushed his way out with the others. In a few minutes they were all standing at the bottom of a series of elevators that led up to the living quarters. There was a brief discussion between Morton and Smith. Finally, Morton said, "We'll send him up alone if he'll go."

Coeurl offered no objection until he heard the door of the elevator clang shut behind him, and the closed cage shot upward. He whirled with a snarl. Instantly, his reason twisted into chaos. He pounced at the door. The metal bent under his plunge, and the desperate pain maddened him. Now he was all trapped animal. He smashed at the metal with his paws. He tore the tough welded panels loose with his thick tentacles. The machinery screeched in protest. There were jerks as the magnetic power pulled the cage along in spite of projecting pieces of metal scraping against the outside walls. Finally, the elevator reached its destination and stopped. Coeurl snatched off the rest of the door and hurtled into the corridor. He waited there until the men came up with drawn weapons.

Morton said, "We're fools. We should have shown him how

it works. He thought we'd double-crossed him, or something."

He motioned to the monster. Grosvenor saw the savage glow fade from the beast's coal-black eyes as Morton opened and closed the door of a near-by elevator several times. It was Coeurl who ended the lesson. He trotted into a large room that led off from the corridor.

He lay down on the carpeted floor and fought down the electric tautness of his nerves and muscles. He was furious at the fright he had shown. It seemed to him that he had lost the advantage of appearing a mild and placid individual. His strength must have startled and dismayed them.

It meant greater danger in the task he must accomplish: to seize this ship. On the planet from which these beings had come, there would be unlimited id.

CHAPTER TWO

WITH unwinking eyes, Coeurl watched two men clear away loose rubble from the metal doorway of a huge, old building. The human beings had eaten lunch, had again donned their space units, and now he could see them, singly and in groups, wherever he looked. Coeurl assumed that they were still investigating the dead city.

His own interest was entirely in food. His body ached with the hunger of his cells for id. The craving put a quiver in his muscles, and his mind burned with the desire to be off after the men who had gone deeper into the city. One of them had gone alone.

During the lunch period, the human beings offered him a variety of their own food, all valueless to him. They apparently did not realize that he must eat living creatures. Id was not merely a substance but a configuration of a substance, and it could be obtained only from tissues that still palpitated with the flow of life.

The minutes went by. And still Coeurl restrained himself. Still he lay there watching, aware that the men knew he watched. They floated a metal machine from the ship to the rock mass that blocked the great door of the building. His fierce state noted all their movements. Even as he shivered with the intensity of his hunger, he saw how they operated the machinery, and how simple it was.

He knew what to expect finally when the flame ate incandescently at the hard rock. In spite of his preknowledge, he deliberately jumped and snarled as if in fear.

From a small patrol ship, Grosvenor observed the action. It was a role he had assigned himself, watching Coeurl. He had nothing else to do. No one seemed to feel the need of assistance from the one Nexialist aboard the *Space Beagle*.

As he watched, the door below Coeurl was cleared. Director Morton and another man came over together. They went inside, and disappeared from view. Presently their voices came through Grosvenor's communicator. The man with Morton spoke first.

"It's a shambles. There must have been a war. You can catch the drift of this machinery. It's secondary stuff. What I'd like to know is, how was it controlled and applied?"

Morton said, "I don't quite understand what you mean."

"Simple," said the other. "So far, I've seen nothing but tools. Almost every machine, whether it's a tool or a weapon, is equipped with a transformer for receiving energy, altering its form, and applying it. Where are the power plants? I hope their libraries will give us a clue. What could have happened to make a civilization crash like this?"

Another voice broke through the communicators. "This is Siedel. I heard your question, Mr Pennons. There are at least two reasons why a territory becomes uninhabited. One is lack of food. The other is war."

Grosvenor was glad that Siedel had used the other's name. It was another voice identified for his collection. Pennons was chief ship's engineer.

Pennons said, "Look, my psychological friend, their science should have enabled them to solve their food problems, for a small population at least. And failing that, why didn't they develop space travel and go elsewhere for their food?"

"Ask Gunlie Lester." It was Director Morton. "I heard him expounding a theory before we landed."

The astronomer answered the first call. 'I've still got to verify all the facts. But one of them, you'll agree, is significant by itself. This desolate world is the only planet revolving around that miserable sun. There's nothing else. No moon. Not even a planetoid. And the nearest star system is nine hundred light-years away. So tremendous would have been the problem of the ruling race of this world that in one jump they would have had to solve not only interplanetary but interstellar-space flight. Consider for comparison how slow our own development was. First, we reached the moon. The planets followed. Each success led to the next, and after many years the first long journey was made to a near-by star. Last of all, man invented the anti-accelerator drive which permitted galactic travel. With all this in mind, I maintain it would be impossible for any race to create an interstellar drive without previous experience."

Other comments were made, but Grosvenor did not listen. He had glanced towards where he had last seen the big cat. It was not in sight. He cursed under his breath for having let himself be distracted. Grosvenor swung his small craft over the whole area in a hasty search. But there was too much confusion, too much rubble, too many buildings. Everywhere he looked there were obstacles to his vision. He landed and questioned several hard-working technicians. Most recalled having seen the cat "about twenty minutes ago." Dissatisfied, Grosvenor climbed back into his lifeboat and flew out over the city.

A short while before, Coeurl had moved swiftly, seeking concealment wherever he found it. From group to group he sped, a nervous dynamo of energy, jumpy and sick from his hunger. A little car rolled up, stopped in front of him, and a formidable camera whirred as it took a picture of him. Over on a mound of rock, a gigantic drilling machine was just going into operation. Coeurl's mind became a blur of images of things he watched with half-attention His body ached to be off after the man who had gone alone into the city.

Suddenly he could stand it no longer. A green foam misted his mouth. For a moment, it seemed, no one was looking at him. He darted behind a rocky embankment and began to run in earnest. He floated along with great, gliding leaps. Everything but his purpose was forgotten, as if his brain had been wiped clean by some magic, memory-erasing brush. He followed deserted streets, taking short cuts through gaping holes in time-weakened walls and through long corridors of mouldering buildings. Then he slowed to a crouching lope as his ear tendrils caught the id vibrations.

Finally, he stopped and peered from a scatter of fallen rock. A two-legged being was standing at what must once have been a window, directing the beams of his flashlight into the gloomy interior. The flashlight clicked off. The man, a heavy-set, powerful individual, walked off swiftly, turning his head alertly this way and that. Coeurl didn't like that alertness. It meant lightning reaction to danger. It presaged trouble.

Coeurl waited until the human being had disappeared around a corner, then he padded into the open, faster than a man could walk. His plan was clearly made. Like a wraith he slipped down a side street and past a long block of buildings. He turned the first corner at great speed, leaped across an open space, and then, with dragging belly, crept into the half-darkness between the building and a huge chunk of debris. The street ahead was a channel between two unbroken hills of loose rubble. It ended in a narrow bottleneck, which had its outlet just below Coeurl.

In the final moment he must have been too eager. As the human being started to pass by below, Coeurl was startled by a tiny shower of rocks that streamed down from where he crouched. The man looked up with a jerk of his head. His face changed, twisted, distorted. He snatched at his weapon.

Coeurl reached out and struck a single crushing blow at the shimmering, transparent headpiece of the space suit. There was a sound of tearing metal and a gushing of blood. The man doubled up as if part of him had been telescoped. For a moment his bones and legs and muscles combined almost miraculously to keep him standing. Then he crumpled with a metallic jangling of his space armour.

In a convulsive movement, Coeurl leaped down upon his victim. He was already generating a field that prevented the id from being released into the blood. Swiftly, he smashed the metal and the body within it. Bones cracked. Flesh spattered. He plunged his mouth into the warm body and let the lacework of tiny suction cups strain the id out of the cells. He had been at this ecstatic task about three minutes when a shadow flicked across his eye. He looked up with a start, and saw that a small ship was approaching from the direction of the lowering sun. For one instant, Coeurl froze, then he glided into the shelter of a great pile of debris.

When he looked again, the small vessel was floating lazily off to the left. But it was already circling, and he saw that it might come back toward him. Almost maddened by the interruption of his feeding, Coeurl nevertheless deserted his kill and headed back towards the space ship. He ran like an animal fleeing danger, and slowed only when he saw the first group of workers. Cautiously, he approached them. They were all busy, and so he was able to slip up near them.

In his search for Coeurl, Grosvenor grew progressively dissatisfied. The city was too large. There were more ruins, more places of concealment than he had first thought. He headed back finally to the big ship. And was considerably relieved when he found the beast comfortably sprawled on a rock sunning himself. Carefully, Grosvenor stopped his ship at a vantage height behind the animal. He was still there twenty minutes later when the chilling announcement came over the communicator that a group of men who were exploring the city had stumbled over the smashed body of Dr. Jarvey of the chemistry department.

Grosvenor took down the direction given, and then headed for the scene of the death. Almost immediately he discovered that Morton was not coming to look at the body. He heard the Director's solemn voice on the communicator. "Bring the remains to the ship."

Jarvey's friends were present, looking sober and tense in their space suits. Grosvenor stared down at the horror of tattered flesh and blood-sprayed metal and felt a tightening in his throat. He heard Kent say, "He would go alone, damn him!"

The chief chemist's voice was husky. Grosvenor recalled having heard that Kent and his principal assistant, Jarvey, were very good friends. Somebody else must have spoken on the private band of the chemistry department, for Kent said, "Yes, we'll have to have an autopsy." The words reminded Grosvenor that he would miss most of what was going on unless he could tune in. Hastily, he touched the man nearest him and said, "Mind if I listen in to the chemistry band through you?"

"Go ahead."

Grosvenor kept his fingers lightly on the other's arm. He heard a man say in a shuddering tone, "The worst part of it is, it looks like a senseless murder. His body is spread out like so much jelly, but it seems to be all there."

Smith, the biologist, broke in on the general wave. His long face looked gloomier than ever. "The killer attacked Jarvey, possibly with the intention of eating him, and then discovered that his flesh was alien and inedible. Just like our big cat. Wouldn't eat anything set before him – " His voice trailed into thoughtful silence. He went on finally, slowly, "Stay, what about that creature? He's big enough and strong enough to have done this with his own little paws."

Director Morton, who must have been listening, interrupted: "That's a thought that has probably already occurred to a lot of us. After all, he's the only living thing we've seen. But, naturally, we can't execute him just on suspicion."

"Besides," said one of the men, "he was never out of my sight."

Before Grosvenor could speak, the voice of Siedel, the psychologist, came over the general wave. "Morton, I've been talking by touch to a number of the men, and I get the following reaction: Their first feeling is that the beast was never out of their sight. And yet, when pinned down, they admit that maybe he was for a few minutes. I, also, had the impression that he was always around. But, thinking back over it, I find gaps. There were moments, probably long minutes, when he was completely out of sight."

Grosvenor sighed, and deliberately remained silent now. His point had been made by somebody else.

It was Kent who broke the silence, He said in a fierce voice, "I say, take no chances. Kill the brute on suspicion before he does any more damage."

Morton said, "Korita, are you around?"

"Right here at the body, Director."

"Korita, you've been wandering around with Cranessy and Van Horne. Do you think pussy is a descendant of the dominant race of this planet?"

Grosvenor located the archaeologist standing slightly behind Smith and partly surrounded by colleagues from his department.

The tall Japanese said slowly, almost respectfully, "Director Morton, there is a mystery here. Take a look, all of you, at that majestic sky line. Notice the architectural outline. In spite of the megalopolis which they created, these people were close to the soil. The buildings are not merely ornamented. They are ornamental in themselves. Here is the equivalent of the Doric column, the Egyptian pyramid, and the big Gothic cathedral, growing out of the ground, earnest, big with destiny. If this lonely, desolate world can be regarded as a mother earth, then the land had a warm, a spiritual place in the hearts of the inhabitants. The effect is emphasized by the winding streets. Their machines prove they were mathematicians, but they were artists first. And so they did not create the geometrically designed cities of the ultra-sophisticated world metropolis. There is a genuine artistic abandon, a deep, joyous emotion written in the curving and unmathematical arrangements of houses, buildings, and avenues; a sense of intensity, of divine belief in an inner certainty. This is not a decadent hoary-with-age civilization but a young and vigorous culture, confident, strong with purpose. There it ended. Abruptly, as if at this point the culture had its Battle of Tours and began to collapse like the ancient Mohammedan civilization. Or as if in one leap it spanned centuries of adjustment and entered the period of contending states.

"However, there is no record of a culture anywhere in the universe making such an abrupt jump. It is always a slow development. And the first step is a merciless questioning of all that was once held sacred. Inner certainties cease to exist. Previously unquestioned convictions dissolve before the ruthless probings of scientific and analytical minds. The sceptic becomes the highest type of human being. I say that this culture ended suddenly in its most flourishing age. The sociological effects of such a catastrophe would be an end of morality, a reversion of bestial criminality unleavened by a sense of ideal. There would be a callous indifference to death. If this – if pussy is a descendant of such a race, then he will be a cunning creature, a thief in the night, a cold-blooded murderer who would cut his own brother's throat for gain."

"That's enough!" It was Kent, his voice curt. "Director, I'm willing to act as executioner."

Smith interrupted sharply. "I object. Listen, Morton, you're not going to kill that cat yet, even if he is guilty. He's a biological treasure house."

Kent and Smith were glaring angrily at each other. Smith said slowly, "My dear Kent, I appreciate the fact that in the chemistry department they would like to put pussy into retorts and make chemical compounds out of his blood and his flesh. But I regret to inform you that you're getting ahead of yourself. In the biology department we want the living body, not the dead one. I have a feeling the physics department would like to have a look at him, also, while he's still alive. So I'm afraid you're last on the list. Adjust yourself to that thought, please. You may see him a year from now, certainly not sooner."

Kent said thickly, 'I'm not looking at this from the scientific point of view."

"You should be, now that Jarvey is dead and nothing can be done for him."

"I'm a human being before I'm a scientist," Kent said in a harsh voice.

"You would destroy a valuable specimen for emotional reasons?"

"I would destroy this creature because he is an unknown danger. We cannot take the risk of having another human being killed."

It was Morton who interrupted the argument. He said thoughtfully, "Korita, I'm inclined to accept your theory as a working basis. But one question. Is it possible that his culture is a later one on this planet than ours is in the galactic-wide system we have colonized?"

"It is definitely possible," said Korita. "His could be the middle of the tenth civilization of his world; while ours, as far as we've been able to discover, is the end of the eighth sprung from Earth. Each of his ten will, of course, have been built on the ruins of the one before it."

"In that case, pussy would not know anything about the scepticism that made us suspect him as a criminal and a murderer?"

"No, it would be literally magic to him."

Morton's grim laugh sounded on the communicator. He said, "You get your wish, Smith. We'll let pussy live. And if there are any fatalities, now we know him, it will be due to carelessness. There's a possiblity, of course, that we're wrong. Like Siedel, I also have the impression that the creature was always around. We may be doing him an injustice. There may be other dangerous creatures on this planet." He broke off. "Kent, what are your plans for Jarvey's body?"

The chief chemist said in a bitter voice, "There'll be no immediate funeral. The damned cat wanted something from the body. It looks to be all there, but something must be missing. I'm going to find out what, and pin this murder on that beast, so you'll have to believe it beyond a shadow of a doubt."

CHAPTER THREE

BACK on the ship, Elliott Grosvenor headed for his own department. The sign on the door read, "SCIENCE OF NEXIALISM." Beyond it were five rooms measuring altogether forty by eighty feet of floor space. Most of the machines and instruments that the Nexial Foundation had asked the goverment for had been installed. As a result, space was rather cramped. Once through the outer door, he was alone in his private preserve.

Grosvenor seated himself at his work desk and started his brief to Director Morton. He analysed the possible physical structure of the catlike inhabitant of this cold and desolate planet. He pointed out that so virile a monster should not be regarded merely as a "biological treasure house". The phrase was dangerous in that it might make people forget that the beast would have its own drives and needs based on a non-human metabolism. "We have enough evidence now," he dictated into the recorder, "to make what we Nexialists call a Statement of Direction."

It took him several hours to complete the Statement. He carried the wire to the stenography section and put in a requisition for an immediate transcription. As head of a department, he got prompt service. Two hours later, he delivered the brief to Morton's office. An under-secretary gave him a receipt for it. Grosvenor ate a late dinner in the commissary, convinced that he had done what was possible to him. Afterwards, he inquired of the waiter where the cat was. The waiter wasn't sure, but he believed the beast was up in the general library.

For an hour, Grosvenor sat in the library watching Coeurl. During that time, the creature lay stretched out on the thick carpet, never once moving his position. At the end of the hour, one of the doors swung open, and two men came in carrying a large bowl. Following close behind them was Kent. The chemist's eyes were feverish. He paused in the middle of the room, and said in a weary yet harsh voice, "I want you all to watch this!"

Though his words included everyone in the room, he actually faced a group of top scientists who sat in a special reserved section. Grosvenor stood up and had a look at what was in the bowl carried by the two men. It contained a brownish concoction.

Smith, the biologist, also climbed to his feet. "Wait a minute, Kent. Any other time I wouldn't question your actions. But you look ill. You're overwrought. Have you got Morton's permission for this experiment?"

Kent turned slowly. And Grosvenor, who had seated himself again, saw that Smith's words had conveyed only a part of the picture. There were dark circles under the chief chemist's eyes. And his cheeks seemed sunken. He said, "I invited him to come up here. He refused to participate. His attitude is that if this being does willingly what I want, no harm will be done."

Smith said, "What have you got there? What's in that bowl?"

"I've identified the missing element," Kent said. "It's potassium. There was only about two-thirds or three-quarters of the normal amount of potassium left in Jarvey's body. You know how potassium is held by the body cells in connection with a large protein molecule, the combination providing the basis for the electrical charge of the cell. It's fundamental to life. Usually, after death the cells release their potassium into the blood stream, making it poisonous. I proved that some potassium is missing from Jarvey's cells but that it did not go into the blood. I'm not sure of the full significance of that, but I intend to find out."

"What about the bowl of food?" somebody interrupted. Men were putting away magazines and books, looking up with interest.

"It's got living cells with potassium in suspension. We can do that artificially, you know. Maybe that's why he rejected our food at lunch time. The potassium was not in a useable form for him. My idea is he'll get the scent, or whatever he uses instead of scent – "

"I think he gets the vibrations of things," Gourlay interjected with a drawl. "Sometimes when he wiggles those tendrils, my instruments register a distinct and very powerful wave of static. And then, again, there's no reaction. My guess is he moves on to a point higher or lower on the wave scale. He seems to control the vibrations at will. I'm assuming the actual motion of the tendrils does not in itself generate these frequencies."

Kent waited with obvious impatience for Gourlay to finish, then he went on. "All right, so it's vibrations that he senses. We can decide what his reaction to this vibration proves when he starts reacting." He concluded in a mollifying tone, "What do you think, Smith?"

"There are three things wrong with your plan," the biologist replied. "In the first place, you seem to assume that he is only animal. You seem to have forgotten he may be surfeited after having fed on Jarvey – if he did. And you seem to think he will not be suspicious. But have the bowl set down. His reaction may tell us something."

Kent's experiment was reasonably valid, despite the emotion behind it. The creature had already shown that he could respond violently when suddenly stimulated. His reaction to being locked up in the elevator could not be dismissed as unimportant. So Grosvenor analysed.

Coeurl stared with unblinking eyes as the two men set the bowl before him. They retreated quickly, and Kent stepped forward. Coeurl recognized him as the one who had held the weapon that morning. He watched the two-legged being for a moment, then gave his attention to the bowl. His ear tendrils identified the thrilling emanation of id from the contents. It was faint, so faint as to have been unnoticeable until he concentrated on it. And it was held in suspension in a manner that was almost useless to him. But the vibration was strong enough to point at the reason for this incident. With a snarl, Coeurl rose to his feet. He caught the bowl with the suction cups at the end of one looping tentacle, and emptied its contents into the face of Kent, who shrank back with a yell.

Explosively, Coeurl flung the bowl aside and snapped a hawser-thick tentacle around the cursing man's waist. He didn't bother with the gun that hung from Kent's belt. It was only a vibration gun, he sensed – atomic powered, but not an atomic disintegrator. He tossed the squirming Kent into a corner, and then realized with a hiss of dismay that he should have disarmed the man. Now he would have to reveal his defensive powers.

Kent furiously wiped the gruel from his face with one hand, and with his other hand reached for his weapon. The muzzle snapped up, and the white beam of the traced light flashed at Coeurl's massive head. Ear tendrils hummed as they automatically cancelled out the energy. Round black eyes narrowed as he caught the movement of men reaching for their vibrators.

From near the door, Grosvenor said sharply, "Stop! We'll all regret it if we act hysterically."

Kent clicked off his weapon and half turned to send a puzzled glance at Grosvenor. Coeurl crouched down, glowering at this man who had forced him to reveal his ability to control energies outside his body. There was nothing to do now but wait alertly for repercussions.

Kent looked again at Grosvenor. This time his eyes narrowed "What the hell do you mean by giving orders?"

Grosvenor made no reply. His part of the incident was finished. He had recognized an emotional crisis, and he had spoken the necessary words in the right tone of peremptory command. The fact that those who had obeyed him now questioned his authority to give the command was unimportant. The crisis was over.

What he had done had no relation to the guilt or innocence of Coeurl. Whatever the eventual result of his interference, any decision made about the creature must be made by the recognized authorities, not by one man.

"Kent," said Siedel coldly, "I don't believe you actually lost control of yourself there. You deliberately tried to kill pussy, knowing that the Director has ordered him kept alive. I have a good mind to report you, and to insist that you suffer the penalties. You know what they are. Loss of authority in your department, ineligibility for any of the dozen elective offices."

There was a stirring and murmur in a group of men whom Grosvenor recognized as Kent supporters. One of them said, "No, no, don't be foolish, Siedel." Another was more cynical. "Don't forget there are witnesses for Kent as well as against him."

Kent stared grimly at the circle of faces. "Korita was right when he said ours was a highly civilized age. It's positively decadent." He went on passionately. "My God, isn't there a man here who can see the horror of the situation? Jarvey dead only a few hours, and this creature, whom we all know to be guilty, lying here unchained, planning his next murder. And the victim is probably here in this room. What kind of men are we? Are we fools, cynics, or ghouls? Or is it that our civilization is so steeped in reason that we can contemplate even a murderer sympathetically?" He fixed his brooding eyes on Coeurl. "Morton was right. That's no animal. That's a devil from the deepest hell of this forgotten planet."

"Don't go melodramatic on us," Siedel said. "Your analysis is psychologically unstable. We're not ghouls or cynics. We're simply scientists, and pussy here is going to be studied. Now that we suspect him, we doubt his ability to corner any of us. One against a thousand hasn't got a chance." He glanced around. "Since Morton isn't here, I'll put this to a vote here and now. Do I speak for all of you?"

"Not for me, Siedel." It was Smith who spoke. As the psychologist stared in astonishment, Smith continued. "In the excitement and momentary confusion no one seems to have noticed that when Kent fired his vibration gun, the beam hit this creature squarely on his cat head, and didn't hurt him!"

Siedel's amazed glance went from Smith to Coeurl, and back again to Smith. "Are you certain it hit him? As you say, it all happened so swiftly – when pussy wasn't hurt I simply assumed that Kent had missed him."

"I was pretty sure it hit him in the face," Smith said. "A vibration gun, of course, can't even kill a man quickly, but it can injure him. Pussy is showing no sign of injury; he's not even trembling. I don't say that's conclusive, but in view of our doubts – "

Siedel was briefly distracted. "Perhaps his skin is a good insulation against heat and energy."

"Perhaps. But in view of our uncertainty, I think Morton should be requested to order him locked in a cage."

While Siedel frowned doubtfully, Kent spoke up. "Now you're talking sense, Smith."

Siedel said swiftly, "Then you would be satisfied, Kent, if we put him in a cage?"

Kent considered, then said reluctantly, "Yes. If four inches of micro-steel can't hold him, we'd better give him the ship."

Grosvenor, who had remained in the background, said nothing. He had discussed the problems of imprisoning Coeurl in his brief to Morton, and found the cage inadequate, principally because of its lock mechanism.

Siedel walked to a wall communicator, talked in a low voice to someone, and then returned. "The Director says if we can get him into the cage without violence, it's fine with him. Otherwise, just lock him up in any room that he's in. What do you think?"

"The cage!" A score of voices spoke in unison.

Grosvenor waited for a moment of silence, then said, "Put him outside for the night. He'll stay around."

Most of the men ignored him. Kent glanced at him and said sourly, "You don't seem to be able to make up your mind, do you? One moment you save his life, the next you recognize him as dangerous."

"He saved his own life," said Grosvenor shortly.

Kent turned away, shrugging. "We'll put him in the cage. That's where a murderer ought to be."

Siedel said, "Now that we've made up our minds, how are we going to do this?"

Grosvenor said, "You definitely want him in the cage?" He didn't expect an answer to that, and he didn't get one. He walked forward and touched the end of the nearest of Coeurl's tentacles.

It shrank away from him slightly, but Grosvenor was

determined. He grasped the tentacle again firmly, and indicated the door. The animal hesitated a moment longer, and then started silently across the room.

Grosvenor called, "There's got to be exact timing here. Get set!"

A moment later Coeurl trotted docilely after Grosvenor through another door. He found himself in a square metal room, with a second door on the opposite wall. The man went through that. As Coeurl started to follow, the door slid shut in his face. Simultaneously, there was a metallic clang behind him. He whirled, and saw that the first door was shut also. He felt the flow of power as an electric lock clicked into place. His lips parted in a grimace of hate as he realized the intent of the trap, but he gave no other outward indication. He was aware of the difference between his earlier reaction to a small enclosure and his present one. For hundreds of years he had been intent on food, and food only. Now a thousand memories of the past were reawakening in his brain. There were powers in his body that he had long since ceased using. In remembering them, his mind automatically fitted their possibilities to his present situation.

He sat back presently on the thick, lithe haunches into which his body tapered. With his ear tendrils he examined the energy content of his surroundings. Finally he lay down, his eyes glowing with contempt. The fools!

It was about an hour later when he heard the man – Smith – fumbling with some mechanism on top of the cage. Coeurl leaped to his feet, startled. His first feeling was that he had misjudged these men, and that he was to be killed out of hand. He had counted on being given time, and on being able to do what he planned.

The danger confused him. And when he suddenly sensed radiation far below the level of visibility, he stimulated his entire nervous system against possible peril. Several seconds went by before he realized what was happening. Somebody was taking pictures of the inside of his body.

After a while the man went away. For a time, then, there were noises of men doing things far away. These died away gradually. Coeurl was patient as he waited for the silence to envelop the ship. In the long ago, before they had achieved relative immortality, coeurls also had slept at night. Watching some of the men dozing in the library, he had remembered the habit.

There was one sound that did not fade away. Long after the great ship was generally silent, he could hear the two pairs of feet. They paced rhythmically past his cell, receded to some remote distance, and then came back. The trouble was, the guards were not together. First one pair of footsteps walked past. Then, about thirty feet behind, came the second pair.

Coeurl let them come by several times. Each time he estimated how long it took them. Finally, he was satisfied. Once again he waited for them to make their round. This time, the moment they were past, he switched his senses from concentration on human-made vibrations to a vastly higher range. The pulsating violence of the atomic pile in the engine room stammered its soft story to his nervous system. The electric dynamos hummed their muffled song of pure power. He felt the whisper of that flow through the wires in the walls of his cage, and through the electric lock of his door. He forced his quivering body into straining immobility, while he tried to tune in on that sibilant tempest of energy. Abruptly, his ear tendrils vibrated in harmony.

There was a sharp click of metal on metal. With a gentle touch of one tentacle, Coeurl pushed open the door. Then he was out in the corridor. For a moment he felt a return of contempt, a glow of superiority, as he thought of the stupid creatures who dared to match their wits against a coeurl. And in that moment he suddenly remembered that there were a few other coeurls on this planet. It was a strange and unexpected thought. For he had hated them and had fought them ruthlessly. Now he saw that vanishing small group as his kind. If they were given a chance to multiply, no one – least of all these men – would be able to stand against them.

Thinking of that possibility, he felt weighted down by his limitations, his need for other coeurls, his aloneness – one against a thousand, with the galaxy at stake. The starry universe itself beckoned his rapacious, vaulting ambition. If he failed, there would never be a second chance. In a foodless world he could not hope to solve the secret of space travel. Even the builders had not freed themselves from their planet.

He padded along through a large salon and into the adjoining corridor. There he came to the first bedroom door. It was electrically locked, but he opened it noiselessly. He pounced inside and smashed the throat of the sleeping man in the bed. The lifeless head rolled crazily. The body twitched once. The id emanations from it almost overwhelmed him, but he forced himself to go on.

Seven bedrooms; seven dead men. Then, silently, he returned to the cage and locked the door behind him. His timing was beautifully precise. Presently, the guards came along, peered through the audioscope, and went on their way. Coeurl emerged for his second foray, and within minutes had invaded four more bedrooms. Then he came to a dormitory with twenty-four men sleeping in it. He had been killing swiftly, aware of the exact moment when he must again return to the cage. The opportunity to destroy a whole roomful of men confused him. For more than a thousand years he had slain all the living forms he could capture. Even in the beginning, that had yielded him no more than one id creature a week. And so he had never felt the necessity for restraint. He went through that room like the great cat he was, silent but deadly, and emerged from the sensuous joy of the kill only when every man in the dormitory was dead.

Instantly, he realized he had overstayed his time. The tremendousness of the blunder made him cringe. For he had planned a night of murder, each wave of deaths timed exactly so that he would be able to return to his prison and be there when the guards glanced in at him, as they had done on every round. That hope of seizing this monster ship during one sleep period was now jeopardized.

Coeurl caught at the vanishing remnants of his reason. Frantically, careless now of the accidental sounds, he raced through the salon. He came out into the cage corridor, tense, half expecting to be met by energy blasts too powerful for him to handle.

The two guards were together, standing side by side. It was obvious that they had just discovered the open door. They looked up simultaneously, briefly paralysed by the nightmare of claws and tentacles, the ferocious cat head and hate-filled eyes. Far too late, one of the men reached for his blaster. But the other was physically frozen by the doom he could not avoid. He uttered a shriek, a shrill cry of horror. The eerie sound floated along the corridors, awakening a shipload of men. The sound ended in a frightful gurgle as Coeurl flung the two corpses with one irresistible motion the full length of that long corridor. He didn't want the dead bodies found near the cage. That was his one hope.

Shaken to the depths, conscious of his terrible mistake, unable to think coherently, he plunged into the prison. The door clicked softly shut behind him. Power flowed once more through the electric lock. He crouched down on the floor, simulating sleep, as he heard the rush of many feet and caught the sound of excited voices. He knew when someone actuated the cage audioscope and looked in at him. The crisis would come when the other bodies were discovered.

Slowly, he stiffened himself for the greatest struggle of his life.

CHAPTER FOUR

"SIEVER gone!" Grosvenor heard Morton say. The Director's voice sounded numb. "What are we going to do without Siever? And Breckenridge! And Coulter and – horrible!"

The corridor was packed with men. Grosvenor, who had come some distance, stood at the tail end of one overflow. Twice he tried to jostle through, but he was effectively jostled back by men who did not even glance around to identify him. They blocked his passage impersonally. Grosvenor gave up the futile effort, and realized that Morton was about to speak again. The Director looked out grimly over the throng. His heavy chin seemed more prominent than usual. He said, "If anybody's got so much as a germ of an idea, bring it out!"

"Space madness!"

The suggestion irritated Grosvenor. It was a meaningless phrase, still current after all these years of space travel. The fact that men had gone insane in space from loneliness, fear, and tension did not make a special sickness of it. There were certain emotional dangers on a long voyage like this – they were among the reasons why he had been put aboard – but insanity from loneliness was not likely to be one of them.

Morton was hesitating. It seemed clear that he also regarded the remark as valueless. But it was not a moment to argue subtle points. These men were tense and afraid. They wanted action and reassurance and the feeling that adequate countermeasures were being taken. At such moments, directors of expeditions, commanders in chief, and others in authority had been known to lose permanently the confidence of their followers. It seemed to Grosvenor that those possibilities were in Morton's mind when he spoke again, so careful were his words.

The Director said, "We've thought of that. Dr. Eggert and his assistants will examine everybody, of course. Right now, he's looking at the bodies."

A thunderous baritone bellowed almost in Grosvenor's ear. "Here I am, Morton. Tell these people to make way for me!"

Grosvenor turned and recognized Dr. Eggert. Men were already crowding aside for him. Eggert plunged forward. Without hesitation, Grosvenor pushed after him. As he had expected, each individual took it for granted that he was with the doctor. As they came up near Morton, Dr. Eggert said, "I heard you, Director, and I can tell you right now the space-madness theory won't fit. The throats of these men were smashed by something with the strength of ten human beings. The victims never had a chance to cry out."

Eggert paused, then asked slowly, "What about our big cat, Morton?"

The Director shook his head. "Pussy is in his cage, Doctor, pacing back and forth. I'd like to ask the opinion of the experts on him. Can we suspect him? That cage was built to hold four beasts four or five times as large as he is. It seems hard to believe that he can be guilty, unless there's a new science here, beyond anything we can imagine."

Smith said grimly, "Morton, we have all the evidence we need. I hate to say this; you know that I'd rather keep the cat alive. But I used the telefluor camera on him, and tried to take some pictures. They were all blanks. Remember what Gourlay said. This creature can apparently receive and send vibrations of any wave length. The way he dominated the power of Kent's gun is adequate proof for us – after what has happened – that he has a special ability to interfere with energy."

A man groaned. "What in the name of all the hells have we got here? Why, if he can control that energy and send it out on any wave length, there's nothing to stop him killing all of us."

"Which proves," said Morton, "that he isn't invincible, or he would have done it long ago."

In a deliberate fashion, he walked over to the mechanism that controlled the cage.

"You're not going to open the door!" Kent gasped, and reached for his blaster.

"No, but if I pull this switch, electricity will flow through the floor and electrocute whatever is inside. We had that built into all our specimen cages as a precaution."

He unlocked the special electrocution switch and jerked the switch itself hard over. For a moment the power was full on. Then blue fire flashed from the metal, and a bank of fuses above Morton's head went black. Morton reached up, took one of them out of its socket, and frowned down at it.

"That's funny," he said. "Those fuses shouldn't have blown!" He shook his head. "Well, we can't even look inside the cage now. That wrecked the audio, also."

Smith said, "If he could interfere with the electric lock enough to open the door, then he very likely probed every possible danger and was ready to interfere when you threw the switch."

"At least it proves he's vulnerable to our energies," Morton said grimly. "Because he had to render them harmless. The important thing is, we've got him behind four inches of the toughest of metals. At worst, we can open the door and turn a semi-portable blaster on him. But, first, I think we'll try to feed electricity in there through the telefluor power cable."

A sound from inside the cage interrupted his words. A heavy body crashed against a wall. That was followed by a sustained thudding, as if many objects were collapsing to the floor. Grosvenor mentally compared it to a small landslide.

"He knows what we're trying to do," Smith said to Morton. "And I'll bet it's a very sick pussy in there. What a fool he was to go back in the cage, and does he realize it!"

The tension was relaxing. Men were smiling nervously. There was even a ripple of humourless laughter at the picture Smith had drawn of the monster's discomfiture. Grosvenor was puzzled. He didn't like the sounds he had heard. Hearing was the most deceptive of senses. It was impossible to identify what had happened or was happening in the cage.

"What I'd like to know," said Pennons, the chief engineer, "is why did the telefluor-meter dial jump and waver at full power when pussy made that noise? It's right here under my nose, and I've been trying to guess what happened."

There was silence both within and without the cage. Abruptly, there was a stir in the doorway behind Smith, Captain Leeth and two officers in their military uniforms stepped into the corridor.

The commander, a wiry man of fifty, said, "I think I'd better take charge here. There seems to be some conflict between the scientists as to whether or not this monster should be killed – is that right?"

Morton shook his head. "The conflict is over. We all feel now he should be executed."

Captain Leeth nodded. "That was the order I was about to give. I believe the security of the ship is threatened, and that's my province." He raised his voice. "Make room here! Get back!"

It took several minutes to ease the pressure in the corridor. Grosvenor was glad when it was done. If the creature had come out while those in the foreground were unable to move back quickly, he'd have been able to destroy or injure many men. That danger wasn't completely over, but it was alleviated.

Somebody said, "That's funny! The ship seemed to move just then!"

Grosvenor had felt it, also, as if for an instant the drive had been tested. The big ship trembled as it settled back from that moment of straining.

Captain Leeth said sharply, "Pennons, who's down in the engine room?"

The chief engineer was pale. "My assistant and his helpers. I don't see how they – "

There was a jerk. The big ship careened, and threatened to fall on its side. Grosvenor was flung with cruel violence to the floor. He lay stunned, and then in alarm fought back to consciousness. Other men were sprawled all around him. Some of them were groaning in pain. Director Morton yelled something, an order Grosvenor didn't hear. Then Captain Leeth was struggling to his feet. He was cursing. Grosvenor heard him say savagely, "Who the devil started those engines!"

The frightful acceleration continued. It was at least five, possibly six gravities. Having assessed its tremendous force as being within his capabilities, Grosvenor climbed agonizingly to his feet. He fumbled with the nearest wall communicator, and punched the engine-room number, not really expecting that it would work. Behind him, a man let out a bass bellow. Grosvenor turned in surprise. Director Morton was peering over his shoulder. The big man called out, "It's pussy! He's in the engine room. And we're heading out into space."

Even as Morton spoke, the screen went black. And still the pressure of acceleration continued. Grosvenor staggered through the door into the salon, and across the great room into a second corridor. There was, he remembered, a space-suit store-room there. As he approached it, he saw that Captain Leeth was ahead of him and was in the act of fumbling his body into a suit. As Grosvenor came up, the commander closed up the suit and manipulated its anti-acceleration unit.

Quickly he turned to help Grosvenor. A minute later, Grosvenor sighed with relief as he reduced the gravity of his suit to one G. There were two of them now; and other men were stumbling up. It took only a few minutes to exhaust the supply of space suits in that store-room. They went down to the next floor and brought up suits from there. But now dozens of the crew members were available for the job. Captain Leeth had already disappeared; and Grosvenor, guessing the next step to be taken, hurried back to the cage where the big cat had been imprisoned. He found a score of scientists assembled at the door, which had apparently just been opened.

Grosvenor pressed forward and peered over the shoulders of those who were ahead of him. There was a gaping hole in the rear wall of the cage. The hole was big enough for five men to have squeezed through at one time. The metal looked bent, and had numerous jagged edges. The hole opened on to another corridor.

"I'll swear," whispered Pennons through the unclosed headpiece of his space suit, "that it's impossible. The ten-ton hammer of the machine shop couldn't more than dent four inches of micro-steel with one blow. And we heard only one. It would take at least a minute for the atomic disintegrator to do the job, but the whole area would be poisonously radio-active for several weeks at least. Morton, this is a super-being!"

The Director made no reply. Grosvenor saw that Smith was examining the break in the wall. The biologist glanced up. "If only Breckenridge weren't dead. We need a metallurgist to explain this. Look!"

He touched the broken edge of the metal. A piece crumbled between his fingers and slithered away in a fine shower of dust to the floor. Grosvenor pushed his way in.

"I know something of metallurgy," he said.

Several men automatically made way for him. And presently he was standing beside Smith. The biologist frowned at him. "One of Breck's assistants?" he asked pointedly.

Grosvenor pretended not to hear. He bent down and ran the fingers of his space suit through the pile of metallic debris on the floor. He straightened quickly. "No miracle here," he said. "As you know, such cages as this are made in electro-magnetic moulds, and we use a fine metallic powder for the job. The creature used his special powers to interfere with the forces holding the metal together. That would account for the drain on the telefluor power cable that Mr Pennons noticed. The thing used the electric energy, with his body as a transforming engine, broke down the wall, ran along the corridor, and so down into the engine room."

He was surprised that he was allowed to complete the hurried analysis. But it seemed clear that he had been accepted as an assistant of the dead Breckenridge. It was a natural error in so big a ship, where men had not yet had time to identify all the lower-rank technicians.

"In the meantime, Director," Kent said quietly, "we are faced with a super-being in control of the ship, completely dominating the engine room and its almost unlimited power, and in possession of the main section of the machine shops."

It was a simple statement of the situation. And Grosvenor felt its impact upon the other men. Their anxiety showed on their faces.

A ship's officer spoke up. "Mr. Kent is wrong," he said. "The thing doesn't dominate the engine room completely. We've still got the control bridge, and that gives us first control of all the machines. You gentlemen, being super-numeraries, may not know the mechanical set-up we have. Undoubtedly, the creature could eventually disconnect us, but right now we could cut off all the switches in the engine room."

"For God's sake!" said a man, "why didn't you just shut off the power instead of putting a thousand men into space suits?"

The officer was precise. "Captain Leeth believes we are safer within the force fields of our space suits. It is probable that the creature has never before been subjected to five or six gravities of acceleration. It would be unwise to give up that and other advantages in panicky moves."

"What other advantages have we got?"

Morton spoke up. "I can answer that. We know things about him. And right now I'm going to suggest to Captain Leeth that we make a test." He turned to the officer. "Will you ask the commander to authorize a little experiment I want to make?"

"I think you'd better ask him yourself, sir. You can reach him by communicator. He's up on the bridge."

Morton came back in a few minutes. "Pennons," he said, "since you're a ship's officer and head man in the engine room, Captain Leeth wants you to take charge of this test."

It seemed to Grosvenor that there was a hint of irritation in Morton's tone. Evidently, the commander of the ship had been in earnest when he had said that he was taking charge. It was the old story of partially divided commands. The dividing line had been defined as precisely as possible, but obviously the authorities could not predict all contingencies. In the final issue, much depended on the personality of the individuals. Until now, the ship's officers and crew, all military people, had meticulously carried out their ship duties, subordinating themselves to the purpose of the tremendous voyage. Nevertheless, past experience on other ships had proved to the government that for some reason military men did not have a high opinion of scientists. In moments such as this, the hidden hostility showed itself. Actually, there was no reason why Morton should not be in charge of his own experimental attack.

Pennons said, "Director, there isn't time for you to explain the details to me. You give the orders! If I disagree with any of them, we'll talk it over."

It was a graceful surrender of prerogative. But then Pennons, as chief engineer, was a fully-fledged scientific man in his own right.

Morton wasted no time. "Mr. Pennons," he said crisply, "detail five technicians to each of the four approaches to the engine room. I'm going to lead one group. Kent, you take number two. Smith, number three. And Mr. Pennons, of course, number four. We'll use mobile heaters and blast through the big doors. They're all shut, I noticed. He's locked himself in.

"Selenski, you go up to the control bridge and shut off everything except the drive engines. Gear them to the master switch, and cut them all off at the same time. One thing, though. Leave the acceleration on full blast. No anti-acceleration must be applied to the ship. Understand!"

"Yes, sir!" The pilot saluted, and started along the corridor.

Morton called after him, "Report to me through the communicators if any of the machines start to run again!"

The men selected to assist the leader were all members of the fighting crew. Grosvenor, with several others, waited to watch the action from a distance of about two hundred feet. He felt an empty sense of waiting for disaster as the mobile projectors were brought up and the protective screens arranged. He appreciated the forcefulness and the purpose of the attack that was about to be made. He could even imagine that it might be successful. But it would be a hit-or-miss success, not actually predictable. The affair was being handled on the basis of an old, old system of organizing men and their knowledge. Most irritating was the fact that he could only stand by and be negatively critical.

Morton's voice came over the general communicator. "As I've said, this is largely a test attack. It's based on the presumption that he hasn't been in the engine room long enough to do anything. That gives us an opportunity to conquer him now, before he's had time to prepare against us. But aside from the possibility that we can destroy him immediately, I have a theory. My idea is this: Those doors are built to withstand powerful explosions, and it will take fifteen minutes at least for the heaters to burn them down. During that period, the creature will have no power. Selenski is about to shut it off. The drive, of course, will be on, but that's atomic explosion. My guess is he can't touch stuff like that. In a few minutes you'll see what I mean – I hope."

His voice went up in pitch as he called, "Ready, Selenski?"

"Ready."

"Then cut the master switch!"

The corridor – the whole ship, Grosvenor knew – was abruptly plunged into darkness. He clicked on the light of his space suit. One by one, the other men did the same. In the reflections from the beams, their faces looked pale and tense.

"Blast!" Morton's command was clear and sharp in the communicator.

The mobile units throbbed. The heat that sprayed out of them, though not atomic, was atomic generated. It poured upon the hard metal of the door. Grosvenor could see the first molten drops let go of the metal and begin to flow. Other drops followed until a dozen streams moved reluctantly out of the path of the energy. The transparent screen began to mist, and presently it was harder to see what was happening to the door. And then, through the misted screen, the door began to shine with the light of its own hotness. The fire had a hellish look to it. It sparkled with a gemlike brightness as the heat of the mobile units ate at the metal with slow fury.

Time went by. At last Morton's voice came, a husky sound. "Selenski!"

"Nothing yet, Director."

Morton half whispered, "But he must be doing something. He can't just be waiting in there like a cornered rat, Selenski!"

"Nothing, Director."

Seven minutes, then ten, then twelve went by.

"Director!" It was Selenski's voice, taut. "He's got the electric dynamo running."

Grosvenor drew a deep breath. And then Kent's voice sounded on the communicator. "Morton, we can't get any deeper. Is this what you expected?"

Grosvenor saw Morton peering through the screen at the door. It seemed to him, even from the distance, that the metal was not as white-hot as it had been. The door grew visibly redder, and then faded to a dark, cool colour.

Morton was sighing. "That's all for now. Leave the crew men to guard each corridor! Keep the heaters in place! Department heads come up to the control bridge!"

The test, Grosvenor realized, was over.

CHAPTER FIVE

To the guard at the entrance of the control bridge, Grosvenor handed his credentials. The man examined them doubtfully.

"I guess it's all right," he said finally. "But so far I haven't admitted anyone in here who's under forty. How did you rate?"

Grosvenor grinned. "I got in on the ground floor of a new science."

The guard looked again at the card, and then said as he handed it back, "Nexialism? What's that?"

"Applied whole-ism," said Grosvenor, and stepped across the threshold.

When he glanced back a moment later, he saw that the man was gazing after him blankly. Grosvenor smiled, and then put the incident out of his mind. It was the first time he had been on the bridge. He gazed around him with curious eyes, impressed and fascinated. In spite of its compactness, the control board was a massive structure. It was built in a series of great curving tiers. Each arc of metal was two hundred feet long, and a full sweep of steps led steeply from one tier to the next. The instruments could be manipulated from the floor, or, more swiftly, from a jointed control chair that hung from the ceiling at the end of a power-driven, upside-down crane structure.

The lowest level of the room was an auditorium with about a hundred comfortable chairs. They were big enough to hold men wearing space suits, and nearly two dozen men so dressed were already sitting in them. Grosvenor settled himself unobtrusively. A minute later, Morton and Captain Leeth entered from the captain's private office, which opened from the bridge. The commander sat down. Morton began without preamble.

"We know that of all the machines in the engine room, the most important to the monster was the electric dynamo. He must have worked in a frenzy of terror to get it started before we penetrated the doors. Any comments on that?"

Pennons said, "I'd like to have somebody describe to me just what he did to make those doors impregnable."

Grosvenor said, "There is a known electronic process by which metals can be temporarily hardened to an enormous degree, but I've never heard of it being done without several tons of special equipment, which doesn't exist on this ship."

Kent turned to look at him. He said impatiently, "What's the good of knowing how he did it? If we can't break through those doors with our atomic disintegrators, that's the end. He can do as he pleases with this ship."

Morton was shaking his head. "We'll have to do some planning, and that's what we're here for." He raised his voice. "Selenski!"

The pilot leaned down from the control chair. His sudden appearance surprised Grosvenor. He hadn't noticed the man in the chair. "What is it, sir?" Selenski asked.

"Start all the engines!"

Selenski swung his control seat skilfully toward the master switch. Gingerly, he eased the great lever into position. There was a jerk that shook the ship, an audible humming sound, and then for several seconds a shuddering of the floor. The ship steadied, the machines settled down to their work, and the humming faded into a vague vibration.

Presently, Morton said, "I'm going to ask various experts to give their suggestions for fighting pussy. What we need here is a consultation between many different specialized fields and, however interesting theoretical possibilities might be, what we want is the practical approach."

And that, Grosvenor decided ruefully, effectively disposed of Elliott Grosvenor, Nexialist. It shouldn't have. What Morton wanted was integration of many sciences, which was what Nexialism was for. He guessed, however, that he would not be one of the experts whose practical advice Morton would be interested in. His guess was correct.

It was two hours later when the Director said in a distracted tone, "I think we'd better take half an hour now to eat and rest. This is the big push we're coming to. We'll need everything we've got."

Grosvenor headed for his own department. He was not interested in food and rest. At thirty-one, he could afford to dispense with the occasional meal or a night of sleep. It seemed to him he had half an hour in which to solve the problem of what should be done with the monster that had taken control of the ship.

The trouble with what the scientists had agreed on was that it was not thorough enough. A number of specialists had pooled their knowledge on a fairly superficial level. Each had briefly outlined his ideas to people who were not trained to grasp the wealth of association behind each notion. And so the attack plan lacked unity.

It made Grosvenor uneasy to realize that he, a young man of thirty-one, was probably the only person aboard with the training to see the weaknesses in the plan. For the first time since coming aboard six months before, he had a sharp appreciation of what a tremendous change had taken place in him at the Nexial Foundation. It was not too much to say that all previous education systems were outdated. Grosvenor took no personal credit for the training he had received. He had created none of it. But as a graduate of the Foundation, as a person who had been put aboard the *Space Beagle* for a specific purpose, he had no alternative but to decide on a definite solution, and then use every available means to convince those in authority.

The trouble was he needed more information. He went after it in the quickest possible fashion. He called up various departments on the communicator.

Mostly, he talked to subordinates. Each time he introduced himself as a department head, and the effect of that was considerable. Junior scientists accepted his identification of himself and were usually very helpful though not always. There was the type of individual who said, "I'll have to get authority from my superiors." One department head – Smith – talked to him personally, and gave him all the information he wanted. Another was polite and asked him to call again after the cat was destroyed. Grosvenor contacted the chemistry department last and asked for Kent, taking it for granted – and hoping –

that he would not get through. He was all ready to say to the subordinate, "Then you can give me the information I want." To his annoyance and amazement he was connected with Kent at once.

The chemist chief listened to him with ill-concealed impatience, and abruptly cut him off. "You can obtain the information from here through the usual channels. However, the discoveries made on the cat's planet will not be available for some months. We have to check and countercheck all our findings."

Grosvenor persisted. "Mr. Kent, I ask you most earnestly to authorize the immediate release of information regarding the quantitative analysis of the cat-planet atmosphere. It may have an important bearing on the plan decided upon at the meeting. It would be too involved at the moment to explain fully, but I assure you – "

Kent cut him off. "Look, my boy," and there was a sneer in his tone, "the time is past for academic discussion. You don't seem to understand that we're in deadly danger. If anything goes wrong, you and I and the others will be physically attacked. It won't be an exercise in intellectual gymnastics. And now, please don't bother me again for ten years."

There was a click as Kent broke the connection. Grosvenor sat for several seconds, flushing at the insult. Presently, he smiled ruefully, and then made his final calls.

His high-probability chart contained, among other things, check marks in the proper printed spaces showing the amount of volcanic dust in the atmosphere of the planet, the life history of various plant forms as indicated by preliminary studies of their seeds, the type of digestive tracts animals would have to have to eat the particular plants examined and, by extrapolation, what would be the probable ranges of structure and type of the animals who lived off the animals who ate such plants.

Grosvenor worked rapidly, and since he merely put marks on an already printed chart, it was not long before he had his graph. It was an intricate affair. It would not be easy to explain it to someone who was not already familiar with Nexialism. But for him it made a fairly sharp picture. In the emergency it pointed at possibilities and solutions that could not be ignored. So it seemed to Grosvenor.

Under the heading of "General Recommendations," he wrote, "Any solution adopted should include a safety valve."

With four copies of the chart, he headed for the mathematics department. There were guards, which was unusual and an obvious protection against the cat. When they refused to let him see Morton, Grosvenor demanded to see one of the Director's secretaries. A young man emerged finally from another room, politely examined his chart, and said that he would "try to bring it to Director Morton's attention."

Grosvenor said in a grim tone, "I've been told that kind of thing before. If Director Morton does not see that chart, I shall ask for a Board of Inquiry. There's something damn funny going on here in connection with the reports I make to the Director's office, and there's going to be trouble if there's any more of it."

The secretary was five years older than Grosvenor. He was cool and basically hostile. He bowed, and said with a faintly satirical smile, "The Director is a very busy man. Many departments compete for his attention. Some of them have long histories of achievement, and a prestige that give them precedence over younger sciences and – " he hesitated – "scientists." He shrugged, "But I shall ask him if he wishes to examine the chart."

Grosvenor said, "Ask him to read the 'Recommendations'. There isn't time for any more."

The secretary said, "I'll bring it to his attention."

Grosvenor headed for Captain Leeth's quarters. The commander received him and listened to what he had to say. Then he examined the chart. Finally, he shook his head.

"The military," he said in a formal tone, "has a slightly different approach to these matters. We are prepared to take calculated risks to realize specific goals. Your notion that it would be wiser in the final issue to let this creature escape is quite contrary to my own attitude. Here is an intelligent being that has taken hostile action against an armed ship. That is an intolerable situation. It is my belief that he embarked on such an action knowing the consequences." He smiled a tight-lipped smile. "The consequences are death."

It struck Grosvenor that the end result might well be death for people who had inflexible ways of dealing with unusual danger. He parted his lips to protest that he did not intend that the cat should escape. Before he could speak, Captain Leeth climbed to his feet. "I'll have to ask you to go now," he said. He spoke to an officer. "Show Mr. Grosvenor the way out."

Grosvenor said bitterly, "I know the way out."

Alone in the corridor, he glanced at his watch. It was five minutes to attack time.

Disconsolately, he headed for the bridge. Most of the others were already present as Grosvenor found a seat. A minute later, Director Morton came in with Captain Leeth. And the meeting was called to order.

Nervous and visibly tense, Morton paced back and forth before his audience. His usually sleek black hair was rumpled. The slight pallor of his strong face emphasized rather than detracted from the out-thrust aggressiveness of his jaw. He stopped walking abruptly. His deep voice was crisp to the point of sharpness as he said, "To make sure that our plans are fully co-ordinated, I'm going to ask each expert in turn to outline his part in the over-powering of this creature. Mr. Pennons first!"

Pennons stood up. He was not a big man, yet he looked big, perhaps because of his air of authority. Like the others, his training was specialized, but because of the nature of his field he needed Nexialism far less than anyone else in the room. This man knew engines, and the history of engines. According to his file record – which Grosvenor had examined – he had studied machine development on a hundred planets. There was probably nothing fundamental that he didn't know about practical engineering. He could have spoken a thousand hours and still only have touched upon his subject.

He said, "We've set up a relay in the control room here which will start and stop every engine rhythmically. The trip lever will work a hundred times a second. And the effect will be to create vibrations of many kinds. There is just a possibility that one or more of the machines will shatter, on the same principle as soldiers crossing a bridge in step – you've heard that old story, no doubt – but in my opinion there is no real danger of a break from that cause. Our main purpose is simply to interfere with the interference of the creature, and smash through the doors!"

"Gourlay next!" said Morton.

Gourlay climbed lazily to his feet. He looked sleepy, as if he were somewhat bored by the proceedings. Grosvenor suspected that he liked people to think him lackadaisical. His title was chief communications engineer, and his file record chronicled a sustained attempt to acquire knowledge in his chosen field. If his degrees were any evidence, then he had an orthodox educational background second to none. When he finally spoke, he drawled in his unhurried fashion. Grosvenor noticed that his very deliberateness had a soothing effect on the men. Anxious faces relaxed. Bodies leaned back more restfully.

Gourlay said, "We've rigged up vibration screens that work on the principle of reflection. Once inside, we'll use them so that most of the stuff he can send will be reflected right back at him. In addition, we've got plenty of spare electric energy that we'll just feed him from mobile copper cups. There must be a limit to his capacity for handling power with those insulated nerves of his."

"Selenski!" called Morton.

The chief pilot was standing by the time Grosvenor's gaze flicked over to him. It was so swiftly done that he seemed to have anticipated Morton's call. Grosvenor studied him, fascinated. Selenski was a lean-bodied, lean-faced man with startlingly vivid blue eyes. He looked physically strong and capable. According to his file record, he was not a man of great learning. He made up for it in steadiness of nerve, in lightning response to stimuli, and in a capacity for sustained clocklike performance.

He said, "The impression I've received of the plan is that it must be cumulative. Just when the creature thinks that he can't stand any more, another thing happens to add to his trouble and confusion. When the uproar's at its height, I cut in the anti-acceleration. The Director thinks with Gunlie Lester that this creature will know nothing about anti-acceleration. It's a development of the science of interstellar flight and wouldn't have been likely to come about in any other way. We think when the creature feels the first effects of the anti-acceleration – you all remember the caved-in sensation you had the first time it happened to you – it won't know what to think or do." He sat down.

Morton said, "Korita next!"

"I can only offer you encouragement," said the archaeologist, "on the basis of my theory that the monster has all the characteristics of the criminal of the early ages of any civilization. Smith has suggested that his knowledge of science is puzzling. In his opinion, this could mean that we are dealing with an actual inhabitant, and not the descendant of the inhabitants, of the dead city we visited. This would ascribe a virtual immortality to our enemy, a possibility which is partly borne out by his ability to breathe both oxygen and chlorine – or neither. But his immortality in itself would not matter. He comes from a certain age in his civilization; and he has sunk so low that his ideas are mostly memories of that age. In spite of his ability to control energy, he lost his head in the elevator when he first entered the ship. By becoming emotional when Kent offered him food, he placed himself in such a position that he was forced to reveal his special powers against a vibration gun. He bungled the mass murders a few hours ago. As you can see, his record is one of the low cunning of the primitive, egotistical mind, which has little or no understanding of its own body processes in the scientific sense, and scarcely any conception of the vast organization with which it is confronted.

"He is like the ancient German soldier who felt superior to the elderly Roman scholar as an individual, yet the latter was part of a mighty civilization of which the German of that day stood in awe. We have, then, a primitive, and that primitive is now far out in space, completely outside of his natural habitat. I say, let's go in and win."

Morton stood up. There was a twisted smile on his heavy face. He said, "According to my previous plan, that pep talk by Korita was to be a preliminary to our attack. However, during the past hour I have received a document from a young man who is aboard this ship representing a science about which I know very little. The fact that he is aboard at all requires that I give weight to his opinions. In his conviction that he had the solution to this problem, he visited not only my quarters but also those of Captain Leeth. The commander and I have accordingly agreed that Mr. Grosvenor will be allowed a few minutes to describe his solution and to convince us that he knows what he is talking about."

Grosvenor stood up shakily. He began, "At the Nexial Foundation we teach that behind all the grosser aspects of any science there is an intricate tie-up with other sciences. That is an old notion, of course, but there is a difference between giving lip service to an idea and applying it in practice. At the Foundation we have developed techniques for applying it. In my department I have some of the most remarkable educational machines you have ever seen. I can't describe them now, but I can tell you how a person trained by those machines and techniques would solve the problem of the cat.

"First, the suggestions so far made have been on a superficial level. They are satisfactory so far as they go. They do not go far enough. Right now, we have enough facts to make a fairly clear-cut picture of pussy's background. I will enumerate them. About eighteen hundred years ago, the hardy plants of this planet suddenly began to receive less sunlight in certain wave lengths. This was due to the appearance of great quantities of volcanic dust in the atmosphere. Result: Almost overnight, most of the plants died. Yesterday, one of our exploring lifeboats flying around within a hundred miles of the dead city detected several living creatures about the size of a terrestrial deer but apparently more intelligent. They were so wary they couldn't be captured. They had to be destroyed; and Mr. Smith's department made a partial analysis. The dead bodies contained potassium in much the same chemical-electrical arrangement as is found in human beings. No other animals were seen. Possibly: This could be at least one of the potassium sources of the cat. In the stomachs of the dead animals the biologists found parts of the plants in various stages of being digested. That seems to be the cycle: vegetation, herbivore, predator. It seems probable that when the plant was destroyed, the animal whose food it was must have died in proportionate numbers. Overnight, pussy's own food supply was wiped out."

Grosvenor sent a quick glance over his audience. With one exception everyone present was watching him intently. The exception was Kent. The chief chemist sat with an irritated expression on his face. His attention seemed to be elsewhere.

The Nexialist continued swiftly. "There are many examples in the galaxy of the complete dependency of given life forms on a single type of food. But we have met *no* other example of the intelligent life form of a planet being so exclusive about diet. It does not seem to have occurred to these creatures to farm their food and, of course, the food of their food. An incredible lack of foresight, you'll admit. So incredible, indeed, that any explanation which does not take that factor into account would *ipso facto*, be unsatisfactory."

Grosvenor paused again, but only for breath. He did not look directly at anyone present. It was impossible to give his evidence for what he was about to say. It would take weeks for each department head to check the facts that involved his particular science. All he could do was give the end conclusion, something which he had not dared to do in his probability chart or in his conversation with Captain Leeth. He finished hurriedly. "The facts are inescapable. Pussy is not one of the builders of that city, nor is he a descendant of the builders. He and his kind were animals experimented on by the builders.

"What happened to the builders? We can only guess. Perhaps they exterminated themselves in an atomic war eighteen hundred years ago. The almost levelled city, the sudden appearance of volcaniclike dust in the atmosphere in such quantities as to obscure the sun for thousands of years, are significant. Emotional man almost succeeded in doing the same thing, so we must not judge this vanished race too harshly. But where does this lead us?"

Once more, Grosvenor took a deep breath and went on quickly. "If he had been a builder, we would by now have had evidence of his full powers and would know precisely what we are up against. Since he is not, we are at the moment dealing with a beast who can have no clear understanding of his powers. Cornered, or even if pressed too hard, he may discover within himself a capacity not yet apparent to him for destroying human beings and controlling machines. We must give him an opportunity to escape. Once outside this ship, he will be at our mercy. That's all, and thank you for listening to me."

Morton glanced around the room. "Well, gentlemen, what do you think?"

Kent said sourly, "I never heard such a story in my life. Possibilities. Probabilities. Fantasies. If this is Nexialism, it will have to be presented much better than that before I'll be interested."

Smith said gloomily, "I don't see how we could accept such an explanation without having pussy's body for examination."

Chief physicist von Grossen said, "I doubt if even an examination would definitely prove him a beast who has been experimented upon. Mr. Grosvenor's analysis is distinctly controversial, and will remain so."

Korita said, "Further exploration of the city might uncover evidence of Mr. Grosvenor's theory." He spoke cautiously. "It would not completely disprove the cyclic theory, since such an experimental intelligence would tend to reflect the attitudes and beliefs of those who taught him."

Chief engineer Pennons said, "One of our lifeboats is in the machine shop right now. It is partly dismantled and occupies the only permanent repair cradle available below. To get a usable lifeboat in to him would require as much effort as the all-out attack we are planning. Of course, if the attack should fail, we might consider sacrificing a lifeboat, though I still don't know how he could get it out of the ship. We have no air locks down there."

Morton turned to Grosvenor. "What is your answer to that?"

Grosvenor said, "There is an air lock at the end of the corridor adjoining the engine room. We must give him access to it."

Captain Leeth stood up. "As I told Mr. Grosvenor when he came to see me, the military mind has a bolder attitude in these matters. We expect casualties. Mr. Pennons expressed my opinion. If our attack fails, we will consider other measures. Thank you, Mr. Grosvenor, for your analysis. But now, let's get to work!"

It was a command. The exodus began immediately.

CHAPTER SIX

IN the blazing brilliance of the gigantic machine shop, Coeurl laboured. Most of his memories were back, the skills he had been taught by the builders, his ability to adjust to new machines and new situations. He had found the lifeboat resting in a cradle. It had been partly dismantled.

Coeurl slaved to repair it. The importance of escaping grew on him. Here was access to his own planet and to other coeurls. With the skills he could teach them, they would be irresistible. This way, victory would be certain. In a sense, then, he felt as if he had made up his mind. Yet he was reluctant to leave the ship. He was not convinced that he was in danger. After examining the power sources of the machine shop, and thinking back over what had occurred, it seemed to him that these two-legged beings didn't have the equipment to overcome him.

The conflict raged on inside him even as he worked. It was not until he paused to survey the craft that he realized how tremendous a repair job he had done. All that remained was to load up the tools and instruments he wanted to take along. And then – would he leave, or fight? He grew anxious as he heard the approach of the men. He felt the sudden change in the tempestlike thunder of the engines, a rhythmical off-and-on hum, shriller in tone, sharper, more nerve-racking than the deep-throated, steady throb that had preceded it. The pattern had an unnerving quality. Coeurl fought to adjust to it and, by dint of concentrating, his body was on the point of succeeding when a new factor interfered. The flame of powerful mobile projectors started its hideous roaring against the massive engine-room doors. Instantly, his problem as whether to fight the projectors or counter the rhythm. He couldn't, he quickly discovered, do both.

He began to concentrate on escape. Every muscle of his powerful body was strained as he carried great loads of tools, machines, and instruments, and dumped them into any available space inside the lifeboat. He paused in the doorway at last for the penultimate act of his departure. He knew the doors were going down. Half a dozen projectors concentrating on one point of each door were irresistibly, though slowly, eating away the remaining inches. Coeurl hesitated, then withdrew all energy resistance from them. Intently, he concentrated on the outer wall of the big ship, toward which the blunt nose of the forty-foot lifeboat was pointing. His body cringed from the surge of electricity that flowed from the dynamos. His ear tendrils vibrated that terrific power straight at the wall. He felt on fire. His whole body ached. He guessed that he was dangerously close to the limit of his capacity for handling energy.

In spite of his effort, nothing happened. The wall did not yield. It was hard, that metal, and strong beyond anything he had ever known. It held its shape. Its molecules were monatomic but their arrangement was unusual – the effect of close packing was achieved without the usual concomitant of great density.

He heard one of the engine-room doors crash inward. Men shouted. Projectors rolled forward, their power unchecked now. Coeurl heard the floor of the engine-room hiss in protest as those blasts of heat burned the metal. Closer came that tremendous, threatening sound. In a minute the men would be burning through the flimsy doors that separated the engine room from the machine shop.

During that minute, Coeurl won his victory. He felt the change in the resisting alloy. The entire wall lost its bitterly held cohesion. It looked the same, but there was no doubt. The flow of energy through his body came easy. He continued to concentrate it for several seconds longer, then he was satisfied. With a snarl of triumph, he leaped into his small craft and manipulated the lever that closed the door behind him.

One of his tentacles embraced the power drive with almost sensuous tenderness. There was a forward surge of his machine as he launched it straight at the thick outer wall. The nose of the craft touched, and the wall dissolved in a glittering shower of dust. He felt tiny jerks of retardation as the weight of the metallic powder that had to be pushed out of the way momentarily slowed the small ship. But it broke through and shot irresistibly off into space.

Seconds went by. Then Coeurl noticed that he had departed from the big vessel at right angles to its course. He was still so close that he could see the jagged hole through which he had escaped. Men in armour stood silhouetted against the brightness behind them. Both they and the ship grew noticeably smaller. Then the men were gone, and there was only the ship with its blaze of a thousand blurring portholes.

Coeurl was turning away from it now, rapidly. He curved a full ninety degrees by his instrument board, and then set the controls for top acceleration. Thus within little more than a minute after his escape, he was heading back in the direction from which the big vessel had been coming all these hours.

Behind him, the gigantic globe shrank rapidly, became too small for individual portholes to be visible. Almost straight ahead, Coeurl saw a tiny, dim ball of light – his own sun, he realized. There, with other coeurls, he could build an interstellar-space ship and travel to stars with inhabited planets. Because it was so important, he felt suddenly frightened. He had turned away from the rear viewing plates. Now he glanced into them again. The globe was still there, a tiny dot of light in the immense blackness of space. Suddenly, it twinkled and was gone.

For a moment, he had the startled impression that, just before it disappeared, it moved. But he could see nothing. He wondered uneasily if they had shut off all their lights and were following him in the darkness. It seemed clear that he would not be safe until he actually landed.

Worried and uncertain, he gave his attention again to the forward viewing plates. Almost immediately, he had a sharp sense of dismay. The dim sun toward which he was heading was not growing larger. *It was visibly smaller*. It became a pin point in the dark distance. It vanished.

Fear swept through Coeurl like a cold wind. For minutes he peered tensely into the space ahead, hoping frantically that his one landmark would become visible again. But only the remote stars glimmered there, unwinking points against a velvet background of unfathomable distance.

But wait! One of the points was growing larger. With every muscle taut, Coeurl watched the point become a dot. It grew into a round ball of light and kept on expanding. Bigger, bigger, it became. Suddenly it shimmered, and there before him, lights glaring from every porthole, was the great globe of the space ship – the very ship which a few minutes before he had watched vanish behind him.

Something happened to Coeurl in that moment. His mind was spinning like a flywheel, faster and faster. It flew apart into a million aching fragments. His eyes almost started from their sockets as, like a maddened animal, he raged in his small quarters. His tentacles clutched at precious instruments and flung them in a fury of frustration. His paws smashed at the very walls of his ship. Finally, in a brief flash of sanity, he knew that he couldn't face the inevitable fire of disintegrators that would now be directed against him from a safe distance.

It was a simple thing to create the violent cell disorganization that freed every droplet of id from his vital organs.

One last snarl of defiance twisted his lips. His tentacles weaved blindly. And then, suddenly weary beyond all his strength to combat, he sank down. Death came quietly after so many, many hours of violence.

Captain Leeth took no chances. When the firing ceased and it was possible to approach what was left of the lifeboat, the searchers found small masses of fused metal, and only here and there remnants of what had been Coeurl's body.

"Poor pussy!" said Morton. "I wonder what he thought when he saw us appear ahead of him, after his own sun disappeared. Understanding nothing of anti-accelerators, he didn't know that we could stop short in space, whereas it would take him more than three hours. He would seem to be heading in the direction of his own planet, but actually he'd be drawing farther and farther away from it. He couldn't possibly have guessed that, when we stopped, he flashed past us, and that then all we had to do was follow him and put on our little act of being his sun until we were close enough to destroy him. The whole cosmos must have seemed topsy-turvy to him."

Grosvenor listened to the account with mixed emotions. The entire incident was rapidly blurring, losing shape, dissolving into darkness. The moment-by-moment details would never again be recalled by an individual exactly as they had occurred. The danger they had been in already seemed remote.

"Never mind the sympathy!" Grosvenor heard Kent say. "We've got a job – to kill every cat on that miserable world."

Korita murmured softly. "That should be simple. They are but primitives. We have merely to settle down, and they will come to us, cunningly expecting to delude us." He half turned to Grosvenor. "I still believe that will be true," he said in a friendly tone, "even if our young friend's 'beast' theory turned out to be correct. What do you think, Mr. Grosvenor?"

"I'd go even a little further," Grosvenor said. "As a historian, you will undoubtedly agree that no known attempt at total extermination has ever proved successful. Don't forget that pussy's attack on us was based on a desperate need for food; the resources of this planet apparently can't support this breed much longer. Pussy's brethren know nothing about us, and therefore are not a menace. So why not just let them die of starvation?"

CHAPTER SEVEN

NEXIALISM is the science of joining in an orderly fashion the knowledge of one field of learning with that of other fields. It provides techniques for speeding up the processes of absorbing knowledge and of using effectively what has been learned. You are cordially invited to attend.

Lecturer, ELLIOTT GROSVENOR
Place, Nexial Department
Time, 1550, 9/7/1*

GROSVENOR hung the notice on the already well-covered bulletin board. Then he stepped back to survey his handiwork. The announcement competed with eight other lectures, three motion pictures, four educational films, nine discussion groups, and several sporting events. In addition, there would be individuals who remained in their quarters to read, the spontaneous gatherings of friends, the half-dozen bars and commissaries, each of which could expect its full quota of customers.

Nevertheless, he was confident his would be read. Unlike the others, it was not just a sheet of paper. It was a gadget about

*The ship operated on what was called Star Time, based on a hundred-minute hour and a twenty-hour day. The week had ten days, with a thirty-day month and a three-hundred-and-sixty-day year. The days were numbered, not named, and the calendar was reckoned from the moment of take-off.

a centimetre in thickness. The print was a silhouette focused on the surface from inside. A paper-thin chromatic wheel, made of light-battery material, turned magnetically and provided the varicoloured light source. The letters changed colour singly and in groups. Because the frequency of the emitted light was subtly, magnetically, altered from moment to moment, the pattern of colour was never repeated.

The notice stood out from its drab surroundings like a neon sign. It would be seen, all right.

Grosvenor headed for the dining salon. As he entered, a man at the door thrust a card into his hand. Grosvenor glanced at it curiously.

KENT FOR DIRECTOR

Mr. Kent is the head of the largest department on our ship. He is noted for his co-operation with other departments. Gregory Kent is a scientist with a heart, who understands the problems of other scientists. Remember, your ship, in addition to its military complement of 180 officers and men, carries 804 scientists headed by an administration, hastily elected by a small minority before the take-off. This situation must be rectified. We are entitled to democratic representation.

ELECTION MEETING, 9/7/1
1500 hours
ELECT KENT DIRECTOR

Grosvenor slipped the card into his pocket and went into the brilliantly lighted room. It seemed to him that tense individuals like Kent seldom considered the long-run effects of their efforts to divide a group of men into hostile camps. Fully fifty per cent of interstellar expeditions in the previous two hundred years had not returned. The reasons could only be deduced from what had happened aboard ships that did come back. The record was of dissension among the members of the expedition, bitter disputes, disagreements as to objectives, and the formation of splinter groups. These latter increased in number almost in direct proportion to the length of the journey.

Elections were a recent innovation in such expeditions. Permission to hold them had been given because men were reluctant to be bound irrevocably to the will of appointed leaders. But a ship was not a nation in miniature. Once on the way, it could not replace casualties. Faced with catastrophe, its human resources were limited.

Frowning over the potentialities, annoyed that the time of the political meeting coincided with his own lecture, Grosvenor headed for his table. The dining room was crowded. He found his companions for the week already eating. There were three of them, junior scientists from different departments.

As he sat down, one of the men said cheerfully, "Well, what defenceless woman's character shall we assassinate today?"

Grosvenor laughed good-naturedly, but he knew that the remark was only partly intended as humour. Conversation among the younger men tended towards a certain sameness. Talk leaned heavily on women and sex. In this all-masculine expedition, the problem of sex had been chemically solved by the inclusion of specific drugs in the general diet. That took away the physical need, but it was emotionally unsatisfying.

No one answered the question. Carl Dennison, a junior chemist, scowled at the speaker, then turned to Grosvenor. "How're you going to vote, Grove?"

"On the secret ballot," said Grosvenor. "Now let's get back to the blonde Allison was telling us about this morning – "

Dennison persisted: "You'll vote for Kent, won't you?"

Grosvenor grinned. "Haven't given it a thought. Election is still a couple of months away. What's wrong with Morton?"

"He's practically a government-appointed man."

"So am I. So are you."

"He's only a mathematician, not a scientist in the true sense of the word."

"That's a new one on me," Grosvenor said. "I've been labouring for years under the delusion that mathematicians were scientists."

"That's just it. Because of the superficial resemblance, it *is* a delusion." Dennison was clearly trying to put over some private conception of his own. He was an earnest, heavy-set individual, and he leaned forward now as if he had already made his point. "Scientists have to stick together. Just imagine, here's an entire shipload of us, and what do they put over us? – a man who deals in abstractions. That's no training for handling practical problems."

"Funny, I thought he was doing rather well in smoothing out the problems of us working men."

"We can smooth out our own problems." Dennison sounded irritated.

Grosvenor had been punching buttons. Now his food began

to slide up from the vertical conveyor at the centre of the table. He sniffed. "Ah, roast sawdust, straight from the chemistry department. It smells delicious. The question is, has the same amount of effort been lavished to make the sawdust from the brushwood of the cat planet as nourishing as the sawdust we brought?" He held up his hand. "Don't answer. I don't wish to be disillusioned about the integrity of Mr. Kent's department, even though I don't like his behaviour. You see, I asked him for some of the co-operation they mention on the card, and he told me to call back in ten years. I guess he forgot about the election. Besides, he's got a nerve scheduling a political meeting on the same night that I'm giving a lecture." He began to eat.

"No lecture is as important as this rally. We're going to discuss matters of policy that will affect everybody on the ship, including you." Dennison's face was flushed, his voice harsh. "Look, Grove, you can't possibly have anything against a man you don't even know very well. Kent is the kind of person who won't forget his friends."

"I'll wager he also has special treatment for those he dislikes," said Grosvenor. He shrugged impatiently. "Carl, to me Kent represents all that is destructive in our present civilization. According to Korita's theory of cycle history, we're in the 'winter – ' stage of our culture. I'm going to ask him to explain that more fully one of these days, but I'll wager Kent's caricature of a democratic campaign is an example of the worst aspects of such a period."

He would have liked to add that this was exactly what he was aboard to prevent, but that, of course, was out of the question. It was just such discord as this that had brought disaster to so many previous expeditions. As a result, unknown to the men, all vessels had become proving grounds for sociological experiments: Nexialists, elections, split command – these and innumerable small changes were being tried out in the hope that man's expansion into space could somehow be made less costly.

There was a sneer on Dennison's face. He said, "Listen to the young philosopher!" He added flatly, "Vote for Kent if you know what's good for you!"

Grosvenor restrained his irritation. "What'll he do – cut off my share of the sawdust? Maybe I'll run for the directorship myself. Get the votes of all men thirty-five and under. After all, we outnumber the oldsters three or four to one. Democracy demands that we have representation on a proportional basis."

Dennison seemed to have recovered himself. He said,

"You're making a grave error, Grosvenor. You'll find out."

The rest of the meal was eaten in silence.

At five minutes before 1550 hours the following evening, Grosvenor began to feel that his lecture notice had drawn a blank. It baffled him. He could understand that Kent might conceivably forbid his followers to attend lectures given by men who had indicated that they would not support him. But even if the chief chemist controlled a majority of the voters, that still left several hundred individuals who had not been influenced. Grosvenor couldn't help remembering what a Nexial-trained government executive had said to him on the eve of departure.

"It won't be easy, this job you've taken aboard the *Beagle*. Nexialism is a tremendous new approach to learning and association. The older men will fight it instinctively. The young men, if they have already been educated by ordinary methods, will automatically be hostile to anything which suggests that their newly acquired techniques are out of date. You yourself have still to use in practice what you learned in theory, although in your case that very transition is part of your training. Just remember that a man who is right often enough gets a hearing in a crisis."

At 1610, Grosvenor visited the bulletin boards in two of the lounges and in the central corridor, and changed the time of his lecture to 1700 hours. At 1700 o'clock he made it 1750 hours, and then still later altered it to 1800 hours. "They'll be coming out," he told himself. "The political meeting can't last forever, and the other lectures are two-hour affairs at most." At five minutes to 1800 hours, he heard the footsteps of two men come slowly along the corridor. There was silence as they paused opposite his open doorway, then a voice said. "This is the place, all right."

They laughed, for no apparent reason. A moment later, two young men entered. Grosvenor hesitated, then nodded friendly greeting. From the first day of the voyage, he had set himself the task of identifying the individuals aboard the ship, their voices, their faces, their names – as much about them as he could discover. With so many men to investigate, the job was not yet completed. But he remembered these two. They were both from the chemistry department.

He watched them warily as they wandered around looking at the display of training devices. They seemed to be secretly amused. They settled finally in two of the chairs, and one of them said with subtly exaggerated politeness, "When does the lecture begin, Mr. Grosvenor?"

Grosvenor looked at his watch. "In about five minutes," he said.

During that interval, eight men came in. It stimulated Grosvenor considerably after his bad start, particularly since one of the men was Donald McCann, head of the geology department. Even the fact that four of his listeners were from the chemistry department did not disturb him.

Pleased, he launched into his lecture on the conditioned reflex, and its development since the days of Pavlov into a cornerstone of the science of Nexialism.

Afterwards, McCann came up and talked to him. He said, "I noticed that part of the technique is the so-called sleep machine, which educates you while you sleep." He chuckled. "I remember one of my old professors pointing out that you could learn all that is known about science in just under a thousand years. You didn't admit that limitation."

Grosvenor was aware of the other's grey eyes watching him with a kindly twinkle. He smiled. "That limitation," he said, "was partly a product of the old method of using the machine without preliminary training. Today, the Nexial Foundation uses hypnosis and psychotherapy to break initial resistance. For instance, when I was tested, I was told that normally for me the sleep machine could only be turned on for five minutes every two hours."

"A very low tolerance," said McCann. "Mine was three minutes every half hour."

"But you accepted that," said Grosvenor pointedly. "Right?"

"What did you do?"

Grosvenor smiled. "*I* didn't do anything. I was conditioned by various methods until I could sleep soundly for eight hours while the machine ran steadily. Several other techniques supplemented the process."

The geologist ignored the final sentence. "Eight solid hours!" he said in astonishment.

"Solid," agreed Grosvenor.

The older man seemed to consider that. "Still," he said finally, "that only reduces the figure by a factor of about three. Even without conditioning, there are many people who can take five minutes out of every quarter hour of a sleep period without waking."

Grosvenor replied slowly, studying the other's face for reaction. "But the information has to be repeated many times." He realized from the staggered expression on McCann's face that the point had been made. He went on quickly: "Surely, sir, you've had the experience of seeing or hearing something – once – and never forgetting it. And yet at other times what seems to be an equally profound impression fades away to a point where you cannot recall it accurately even when it is mentioned. There are reasons for that. The Nexial Foundation found out what they were."

McCann said nothing. His lips were pursed. Over his shoulder, Grosvenor noticed that the four men from the chemistry department were gathered in a group near the corridor door. They were talking together in low tones. He gave them only a glance, and then said to the geologist, "There were times in the beginning when I thought the pressure would be too much for me. You understand, I'm not talking about the sleep machine. In actual quantity of training, that was just about ten per cent of the total."

McCann was shaking his head. "Those figures almost overwhelm me. I suppose you get your largest percentage figure from those little films where each picture stays on but a fraction of a second."

Grosvenor nodded. "We used the tachistoscopic films about three hours a day, but they constituted some forty-five per cent of the training. The secret is speed and repetition."

"An entire science at one sitting!" McCann exclaimed. "That's what you call learning-as-a-whole."

"That's one facet of it. We learned with every sense, through our fingers, our ears, or eyes, and even from smell and taste."

Once more McCann stood frowning. Grosvenor saw that the young chemists were trooping out of the room at last. From the corridor came the sound of low laughter. It seemed to startle McCann out of his brown study. The geologist thrust out his hand and said, "How about coming up to my department one of these days? Perhaps we can work out a method of co-ordinating your integrative knowledge with our field work. We can try it out when we land on another planet."

As Grosvenor walked along the corridor to his own bedroom, he whistled under his breath. He'd won his first victory, and the feeling was pleasant.

CHAPTER EIGHT

THE next morning, as Grosvenor approached his department, he saw with astonishment that the door was open. A bright swath of light cut out from it across the more dimly illuminated corridor. He hurried forward, and stopped short in the doorway.

In his first glance, he saw seven chemist technicians, including two who had attended his lecture. Machinery had been moved into the room. There were a number of large vats, a series of heating units, and an entire system of pipes for supplying chemicals to the vats.

Grosvenor's mind leaped back to the way the chemist technicians had acted at his lecture. He moved through the doorway, tense with the possibilities and sick with the thought of what might have been done to his own equipment. He used this outer room for general purposes. It normally contained some machinery, but it was primarily designed to channel the output from the other rooms for purposes of group instruction. The remaining four rooms contained his special equipment.

Through the open door that led into his film and sound-recording studio, Grosvenor saw that it also had been taken over. The shock of that held him silent. Ignoring the men, he went through the outer room and into each of the four special sections in turn. Three had been occupied by the invading chemists. That included, in addition to the film studio, the laboratory and the toolroom. The fourth section, with its technique devices, and an adjoining storeroom were completely unscathed. Into them had been shoved and piled the movable machinery and furniture from the other rooms. A door led from the fourth section to a smaller corridor. Grosvenor presumed grimly that it was henceforth to be his entrance to the department.

And still he held his anger, weighing the potentialities of the situation. He would be expected to protest to Morton. Somehow, Kent would try to turn that to his own advantage in the election. Grosvenor couldn't see just how it would benefit the chemist in his campaign. But Kent evidently thought it would.

Slowly, Grosvenor returned to the outer room – his auditorium. He noticed for the first time that the vats were food-making machines. Clever. It would look as if the space were being put to good use, something which, it could be argued, had not been true before. The shrewdness of it challenged his own integrity.

There seemed little doubt as to why it had happened. Kent disliked him. In setting himself verbally against Kent's election – a fact which must have been reported – he had intensified that dislike. But the chief chemist's vindictive reaction, if handled in the proper manner, might be used against him.

It seemed to Grosvenor that he must see to it that Kent definitely did not benefit from his invasion.

He walked over to one of the men and said, "Will you pass the word along that I welcome the opportunity to further the education of the staff of the chemistry department, and that I hope no one will object to learning while he works."

He moved off without waiting for a reply. When he glanced back, the man was staring after him. Grosvenor suppressed a smile. He felt quite cheerful as he entered the technique room. Now, at last, he was confronted by a situation in which he could employ some of the training methods he had available.

Because of the way his movable cabinets and other equipment had been jumbled into a comparatively small space, it took him a little time to find the hypnotic gas he wanted. He spent nearly half an hour fitting a baffler to the spout, so that the compressed matter inside wouldn't hiss as it poured out. When that was done, Grosvenor carried the container into the outer room. He unlocked a wall cabinet that had a grated door, placed the container inside, and released the gas. Quickly, he locked the door again.

A faint odour of perfume mingled with the chemical smell from the vat.

Whistling softly, Grosvenor started across the room. He was stopped by the straw boss, one of the men who had attended his lecture the previous night.

"What the hell do you think you're doing."

Grosvenor said mildly, "You'll hardly notice it in a minute. It's part of my educational programme for your staff."

"Who asked you for an educational programme?"

"Why, Mr. Malden," said Grosvenor in simulated astonishment. "What else would you be doing in my department?" He broke off with a laugh. "I'm just kidding you. It's a deodorant. I don't want this place smelled up."

He moved off without waiting for a reply, and then stood to one side watching the men for reactions to the gas. There were fifteen individuals altogether. He could expect five favourable reactions and five partially favourable. There were ways of telling how a person had been affected.

After several minutes of careful observation, Grosvenor walked forward, paused beside one of the men, and said in a low but firm voice, "Come to the washroom in five minutes, and I'll give you something. Now forget about it!"

He retreated to the doorway that connected the outer room with the film studio. As he turned he saw Malden go over and speak to the man. The technician shook his head in evident surprise.

The straw boss's voice held a note of astounded anger. "What do you mean, he didn't speak to you? I saw him."

The technician got angry. "I didn't hear a thing. I ought to know."

If the argument continued, Grosvenor neither heard it nor saw it. From the corner of his eye, he noticed that one of the younger men in the next room was showing signs of sufficient response. He walked over to the man in the same casual way, and spoke the same words that he had to the first subject – with one difference: He made the time fifteen minutes instead of five.

In all, six men responded to the degree Grosvenor considered essential to his plan. Of the remaining nine individuals, three – including Malden – showed a milder reaction. Grosvenor left the latter group alone. At this stage, he needed virtual certainties. Later he could try a different pattern for the others.

Grosvenor was waiting when the first subject of his experiment entered the washroom. He smiled at the man, and said, "Ever seen one of these?" He held out the tiny ear crystal, with its flanges for fastening it inside the ear.

The man accepted the little instrument, looked at it then shook his head in puzzlement. "What is it?" he asked.

Grosvenor commanded, "Turn this way, and I'll fit it into your ear." As the other obeyed without question, Grosvenor went on firmly. "You'll notice, I'm sure, that the part facing outside is flesh coloured. In other words, it can be seen only on close examination. If anyone does notice it, you can say it's a hearing aid."

He completed the fitting and stepped back. "After a minute or so, you won't even know that it's there. You won't feel it."

The technician seemed interested. "I can hardly feel it now. What does it do?"

"It's a radio," Grosvenor explained. He went on slowly, emphasizing each word. "But you will never consciously hear what it says. The words come through, and go directly into your unconscious. You can hear what other people say to you. You can carry on conversations. In fact, you'll just go about your normal business unaware that anything unusual is going on. You'll forget all about it."

"Well, imagine that!" said the technician.

He went out shaking his head. A few minutes later, the second man came in; and then, each in turn, the remaining four who had shown a deep trance response. Grosvenor fitted them all with duplicates of the nearly invisible ear radio.

Humming tunelessly, he brought out another hypnotic gas, put it into a suitable container, and substituted it for the one in the cabinet. This time, the straw boss and four other men responded profoundly. Of the rest, two showed a slight reaction, one – who had previously been slightly affected – seemed to come out of his state completely, and one man gave no sign at all.

Grosvenor decided to be satisfied with eleven out of fifteen deep-trance subjects. Kent was going to be unpleasantly surprised at the number of chemical geniuses that turned up in his department.

Nevertheless, this was far from final victory. That was probably not obtainable except by a somewhat more direct attack on Kent himself.

Swiftly, Grosvenor made a tape recording for an experimental broadcast to the ear radios. He left it running steadily while he wandered among the men and observed how they were reacting. Four individuals seemed to be worried about something. Grosvenor went up to one, who was shaking his head frequently.

"What's the matter?" he asked.

The man laughed unhappily. "I keep hearing a voice. Silly."

"Loud?" It was not exactly the question a solicitous inquirer might normally be expected to ask, but Grosvenor was intent.

"No, it's far away. It keeps going away, and then — "

"It'll fade," said Grosvenor soothingly. "You know how the mind can be overstimulated. I'll wager it's going away right now, just from having someone to talk to you and distract your attention."

The man cocked his head to one side, as if he were listening. He shook his head wonderingly. "It *is* gone." He straightened, and sighed with relief. "Had me worried for a while there."

Of the other three men, two were reassured with comparative ease. But the remaining individual, even with additional suggestion, continued to hear the voice. Grosvenor finally took him aside, and, under the pretence of examining his ear, removed the tiny radio. The man probably needed more training.

Grosvenor talked briefly with the other subjects. Then, satisfied, he returned to the technique room and set up a series of records to play three minutes out of every fifteen. In the outer room again, he glanced around and saw that all was well. He decided that he could safely leave the men to their work. He went out into the corridor and headed for the elevators.

A few minutes later, he entered the mathematics department and asked to see Morton. To his surprise, he was admitted at once.

He found Morton sitting comfortably behind a big desk. The mathematician indicated a chair, and Grosvenor sat down.

It was the first time he had been in Morton's office, and he gazed around curiously. The room was large and had a viewplate occupying one whole wall. At the moment, the plate was focused on space at such an angle that the great wheeled galaxy, of which Sol was but one tiny dust mote, was visible from rim to rim. It was still near enough for innumerable individual stars to be seen, and far enough away from the misty grandeur of it to be at the peak of brilliance.

Also in the field of vision were several of the star clusters which, though outside the galaxy proper, spun with it through space. The sight of them reminded Grosvenor that the *Space Beagle* was at the moment passing through one of the smaller clusters.

The initial greeting being over, he asked, "Any decision yet as to whether we're going to stop at one of the suns of this cluster?"

Morton nodded. "The decision seems to be against. I agree with that. We're heading for another galaxy, and we'll be away from Earth long enough as it is."

The Director leaned forward to pick up a paper from his desk, then sank back in his chair. He said abruptly, "I hear you've been invaded."

Grosvenor smiled wryly. He could imagine the satisfaction

some of the members of the expedition would gain from the incident. He had made the ship's company just aware enough of his presence to cause them to feel uneasy about what Nexialism might be able to do. Such individuals – and many of them were not yet Kent supporters – would be opposed to the Director's interfering in the affair.

Knowing that, he had nevertheless come to find out if Morton understood the necessities of the situation. Tersely, Grosvenor described what had happened. He finished by saying, "Mr. Morton, I want you to order Kent to cease his encroachment." He had no desire for such an order to be issued, but he wanted to see if Morton also realized the danger.

The Director shook his head, and said mildly, "After all, you do have a large space for one man. Why not share with another department?"

The answer was too noncommittal. Grosvenor had no recourse but to press on. He said firmly, "Am I to understand that it is possible for the head of any department aboard this ship to take over space in another department without permission from any authority?"

Morton did not reply immediately. There was a wry smile on his face. He toyed with a pencil as he said, finally, "I have an idea you misunderstand my position aboard the *Beagle*. Before making a decision involving a department head, I must consult with other department heads." He gazed at the ceiling. "Let us suppose that I placed this matter on the agenda, and then it was decided that Kent could have that part of your department he has already taken over. The status, being affirmed, would thereafter be permanent." He finished in a deliberate tone. "It occurred to me that you might not care to have that limitation placed upon you at this stage." His smile broadened.

Grosvenor, his purpose accomplished, smiled back. "I am very happy to have your support in this matter. I can count on you then, not to let Kent place the matter on the agenda?"

If Morton was surprised by the swift reversal of attitude he gave no sign. "The agenda," he said with satisfaction, "is one thing I do have considerable control over. My office prepares it. I present it. The department heads can vote to place Kent's request on the agenda for a subsequent meeting, but not for any that is in progress."

"I gather," said Grosvenor, "that Mr. Kent has already made application to take over four rooms of my department.

Morton nodded. He put down the paper he had been holding and picked up a chronometer. He studied it thoughtfully. "The next meeting takes place in two days. Thereafter, every week unless I postpone them. I think" – he sounded as if he were musing aloud – "I should have no difficulty cancelling the one scheduled for twelve days hence." He put down the chronometer and stood up briskly. "That will give you twenty-two days to defend yourself."

Grosvenor climbed slowly to his feet, He decided not to comment on the time limit. At the moment, it seemed to be far more than adequate, but it might sound egotistical if he said so. Long before the time was up, he would either regain control of his department, or his defeat would be established.

Aloud, he said, "There's another point I've been wanting to bring up. I feel I should be entitled to communicate directly with the other department heads when I am wearing a space suit."

Morton smiled. "I am sure that is merely an oversight. The matter will be rectified."

They shook hands and separated. As he headed back to the Nexial department, it seemed to Grosvenor that, in an extremely indirect manner, Nexialism was gaining ground.

As he entered the outer room, Grosvenor was surprised to see that Siedel was standing off to one side watching the chemists at work. The psychologist saw him and came over, shaking his head.

"Young man," he said, "isn't this a little unethical?"

Grosvenor guessed with a sinking sensation that Siedel had analysed what he had done to the men. He kept that awareness out of his voice as he said quickly, "Absolutely unethical, sir. I feel exactly as you would feel if your department were taken over in flagrant disregard of legal rights."

He thought, Why is he here? Has Kent asked him to investigate?

Siedel stroked his jaw. He was a heavily built man with bright, black eyes. "That isn't what I meant," he said slowly. "But I see that you feel justified."

Grosvenor changed his tactics. "Are you referring to the method of instruction I am using on these men?"

He felt no qualms of conscience. Whatever the reason this man was here, the opportunity had to be turned to his own advantage, if possible. His hope was to set up a conflict in the psychologist's mind, to make him neutral in this fight between Kent and himself.

Siedel said, with a thinly sardonic edge to his words, "I am. At the request of Mr. Kent, I have examined those members of his staff who he thought were acting in an abnormal fashion. It is now my duty to report my diagnosis to Mr. Kent."

"Why?" said Grosvenor. He went on earnestly. "Mr. Siedel, my department has been invaded by a man who dislikes me because I have openly stated that I will not vote for him. Since he acted in defiance of the laws of this ship, I have every right to defend myself as best I can. I beg you, therefore, to remain neutral in this purely private quarrel."

Siedel was frowning. "You don't understand," he said: "I am here as a psychologist. I regard your use of hypnosis without the permission of the subject as completely unethical. I am surprised that you expect me to associate myself with such an act."

Grosvenor said, "I assure you that my code of ethics is just as scrupulous as your own. While I have hypnotized these men without their permission, I have carefully refrained from taking advantage of it to harm or embarrass them in the slightest degree. Under the circumstances, I cannot see that you should feel obliged to take Kent's side."

Siedel frowned. "This is a quarrel between you and Kent – is that right?"

Grosvenor said, "Substantially." He could guess what was coming.

"And yet," said Siedel, "it is not Kent you have hypnotized, but a group of innocent bystanders."

Grosvenor remembered how the four chemist technicians had acted at his lecture. Some of them at least were not quite innocent. He said, "I'm not going to argue with you about that. I could say that, from the beginning of time, the unthinking majority has paid the price for obeying without question the commands of leaders whose motivations they didn't trouble themselves to inquire into. But rather than go into that, I'd like to ask one question."

"Yes?"

"Did you enter the technique room?"

Siedel nodded, but said nothing.

"You saw the records?" Grosvenor persisted.

"Yes."

"You noticed what they dealt with?"

"Information on chemistry."

"That's all I'm giving them," said Grosvenor. "That's all I intend to give them. I regard my department as an educational centre. People who force themselves in here receive an education whether they like it or not."

"I confess," said Siedel, "I don't see how that will help you get rid of them. However, I shall be happy to tell Mr. Kent what you are doing. He shouldn't have any objection to his men learning more chemistry."

Grosvenor did not answer. He had his own opinion as to how much Kent would like having a group of his underlings know, as they shortly would, as much as he did about his own speciality.

He watched gloomily as Siedel disappeared into the corridor. The man would undoubtedly give Kent a full report, which meant a new plan would have to be worked out. Standing there, Grosvenor decided that it was too soon for drastic defence measures. It was hard to be certain that any sustained, positive action would not produce on board the ship the very situation he was supposed to prevent. Despite his own reservations about cyclic history, it was well to remember that civilizations did seem to be born, grow older, and die of old age. Before he did anything more, he'd better have a talk with Korita and find out what pitfalls he might inadvertently be heading towards.

He located the Japanese scientist at Library B, which was on the far side of the ship, on the same floor as the Nexial department. Korita was leaving as he came up, and Grosvenor fell in step beside him. Without preamble, he outlined his problem.

Korita did not reply immediately. They walked the length of the corridor before the tall historian spoke, doubtfully. "My friend," he said, "I'm sure you realize the difficulty of solving specific problems on the basis of generalizations, which is virtually all that the theory of cyclic history has to offer."

"Still," Grosvenor said, "a few analogies might be very useful to me. From what I've read on this subject, I gather we're in the late, or 'winter', period of our own civilization. In other words, right now we are making the mistakes that lead to decay. I have a few ideas about that, but I'd like more."

Korita shrugged. "I'll try to put it briefly." He was silent for a while, then he said, "The outstanding common denominator of the 'winter' periods of civilization is the growing comprehension on the part of millions of individuals of how things work. People become impatient with superstitious or supernatural explanations of what goes on in their minds and bodies, and in the world around them. With the gradual accumulation of knowledge, even the simplest minds for the first time 'see through' and consciously reject the claims of a minority to hereditary superiority. And the grim battle for equality is on."

Korita paused for a moment, then continued. "It is this widespread struggle for personal aggrandisement that constitutes the most significant parallel between all the 'winter' periods in the civilizations of recorded history. For better or worse, the fight usually takes place within the framework of a legal system that tends to protect the entrenched minority. The late-comer to the field, not understanding his motivations, plunges blindly into the battle for power. The result is a veritable mêlée of undisciplined intelligence. In their resentment and lust, men follow leaders as confused as themselves. Repeatedly, the resulting disorder has led by well-defined steps to the final static fellahin state.

"Sooner or later, one group gains the ascendancy. Once in office, the leaders restore 'order' in so savage a blood-letting that the millions are cowed. Swiftly, the power group begins to restrict activities. The licensing systems and other regulative measures necessary to any organized society become tools of suppression and monopoly. It becomes difficult, then impossible, for the individual to engage in new enterprise. And so we progress by swift stages to the familiar caste system of ancient India, and to other, less well-known but equally inflexible societies, such as that of Rome after about A.D. 300. The individual is born into his station of life and cannot rise above it. . . . There, does that brief summary help you?"

Grosvenor said slowly, "As I've already said, I'm trying to solve the problem Mr. Kent has presented me without falling into the egotistical errors of the late-civilization man you have described. I want to know if I can reasonably hope to defend myself against him without aggravating the hostilities that already exist aboard the *Beagle*."

Korita smiled wryly. "It will be a unique victory if you succeed. Historically, on a mass basis, the problem has never been solved. Well, good luck, young man!"

At that moment, it happened.

CHAPTER NINE

THEY had paused at the "glass" room on Grosvenor's floor. It wasn't glass, and it wasn't, by strict definition, a room. It was an alcove of an outer wall corridor, and the "glass" was an enormous curving plate made from a crystallized form of one of the resistance metals. It was so limpidly transparent as to give the illusion that nothing at all was there.

Beyond was the vacuum and darkness of space.

Grosvenor had just noticed absently that the ship was almost through the small star cluster it had been traversing. Only a few of the five thousand-odd suns of the system were still visible. He parted his lips to say, "I'd like to talk with you again, Mr. Korita, when you have time."

He didn't say it. A slightly blurred double image of a woman wearing a feathered hat was taking form in the glass directly in front of him. The image flickered and shimmered. Grosvenor felt an abnormal tensing of the muscles of his eyes. For a moment, his mind went blank. That was followed rapidly by sounds, flashes of light, a sharp sensation of pain. Hypnotic hallucinations! The awareness was like an electric shock.

The recognition saved him. His own conditioning enabled him instantly to reject the mechanical suggestion of the light pattern. He whirled and shouted into the nearest communicator, "Don't look at the images! They're hypnotic. We're being attacked!"

As he turned away, he stumbled over Korita's unconscious body. He stopped and knelt.

"Korita!" he said in a piercing tone, "you *can* hear me?"

"Yes."

"Only *my* instructions influence you. Understand?"

"Yes."

"You're beginning to relax, to forget. Your mind is calm. The effect of the images is fading. Now it's gone. Gone completely. Do you understand? Gone completely."

"I understand."

"They cannot affect you again. In fact, every time you see an image, you're reminded of some pleasant scene from home. Is that clear?"

"Very."

"Now you're beginning to wake up. I'm going to count to three. When I say 'three', you're wide awake. One . . . two . . . three – wake up!"

Korita opened his eyes. "What happened?" he said in a puzzled tone.

Grosvenor explained swiftly, and then said, "But now, quick, come along! The light pattern keeps pulling at my eyes in spite of counter suggestion."

He hurried the bewildered archaeologist along the corridor toward the Nexial department. At the first corner, they came to a human body lying on the floor.

Grosvenor kicked the man, not too lightly. He wanted a shock response. "Do you hear me?" he demanded.

The man stirred, "Yes."

"Then listen. The light images have no further effect on you. Now get up. You're wide awake."

The man climbed to his feet and lunged at him, swinging wildly. Grosvenor ducked, and his assailant staggered past him blindly.

Grosvenor ordered him to halt, but he kept on going without a backward glance. Grosvenor grabbed Korita's arm. "I seem to have got to him too late."

Korita shook his head dazedly. His eyes turned toward the wall, and it was clear from his next words that Grosvenor's suggestion had not taken full effect, or else was already being undermined. "But what are they?" he asked.

"Don't look at them?"

It was incredibly hard not to. Grosvenor had to keep blinking to break the pattern of light flashes that came at his eyes from other images on the walls. At first it seemed to him that the images were everywhere. Then he noticed that the womanish shapes – some oddly double, some single – occupied transparent or translucent wall sections. There were hundreds of such reflecting wall areas, but at least it was a limitation.

They saw more men. The victims lay at uneven intervals along the corridors. Twice they came upon conscious men. One stood in their path with unseeing eyes, and did not move or turn as Grosvenor and Korita hurried by. The other man let out a yell, grabbed his vibrator, and fired it. The tracer beam flashed on the wall beside Grosvenor. And then he had tackled the other and knocked him down. The man – a Kent supporter – glared at him malignantly. "You damned spy!" he said harshly. "We'll get you yet."

Grosvenor didn't pause to discover the reason for the man's astounding behaviour. But he grew tense as he guided Korita to the door of the Nexial department. If one chemist could so quickly be stimulated to open hatred of him, then what about the fifteen who had taken over his rooms?

To his relief, they were all unconscious. Hurriedly, he secured two pairs of dark glasses, one for Korita and one for himself, then turned a barrage of flashing lights against the walls, the ceilings, and the floors. Instantly, the images were eclipsed by the strong light.

Grosvenor headed for his technique room and there broadcast commands intended to free those he had hypnotized. Through the open door, he watched two unconscious bodies for response. After five minutes, there was still no sign that they were paying any attention. He guessed that the hypnotic patterns of the attacker had by-passed, or even taken advantage of, the conditioned state of their minds, nullifying any words he might use. The possibility was that they might awaken spontaneously after a while and turn on him.

With Korita's help, he dragged them into the washroom, and then locked the door. One fact was already evident. This was mechanical-visual hypnosis of such power that he had saved himself only by prompt action. But what had happened was not limited to vision. The image had tried to control him by stimulating his brain through his eyes. He was up to date on most of the work that men had done in that field. And so he knew – though the attackers apparently did not – that control by an alien of a human nervous system was not possible except with an encephalo-adjuster or its equivalent.

He could only guess, from what had almost happened to him, that the other men had been precipitated into deep trance sleeps, or else they were confused by hallucinations and were not responsible for their actions.

His job was to get to the control room and turn on the ship's energy screen. No matter where the attack was coming from – whether from another ship or actually from a planet – that should effectively cut off any carrier beams the enemy might be sending.

With frantic fingers, Grosvenor worked to set up a mobile unit of lights. He needed something that would interfere with the images on his way to the control room. He was making the final connection when he felt an unmistakable sensation – a slight giddy feeling – that passed almost instantly. It was a feeling that usually occurred during a considerable change of course, a result of readjustment of the anti-accelerators.

Had the course actually been changed? It was something he'd have to check – later.

He said to Korita, "I intend to make an experiment. Please remain here."

Grosvenor carried his arrangement of lights to a near-by corridor, and placed it in the rear compartment of a power-driven loading vehicle. Then he climbed on and headed for the elevators.

He guessed that, altogether, ten minutes had gone by since he had first seen the image.

He took the turn into the elevator corridor at twenty-five miles an hour, which was fast for these comparatively narrow spaces. In the alcove opposite the elevators, two men were wrestling each other with a life-and-death concentration. They paid no attention to Grosvenor but swayed and strained and cursed. The sound of their breathing was loud. Their single-minded hatred of each other was not affected by Grosvenor's arrangements of lights. Whatever world of hallucination they were in, it had taken profoundly.

Grosvenor whirled his machine into the nearest elevator and started down. He was beginning to let himself hope that he might find the control room deserted.

The hope died as he came to the main corridor. It swarmed with men. Barricades had been flung up, and there was an unmistakable odour of ozone. Vibrators fumed and fussed. Grosvenor peered cautiously out of the elevator, trying to size up the situation. It was visibly bad. The two approaches to the control room were blocked by scores of overturned loading mules. Behind them crouched men in military uniform. Grosvenor caught a glimpse of Captain Leeth among the defenders and, on the far side, he saw Director Morton behind the barricade of one of the attacking groups.

That clarified the picture. Suppressed hostility had been stimulated by the images. The scientists were fighting the military, whom they had always unconsciously hated. The military, in turn, was suddenly freed to vent its contempt and fury upon the despised scientists.

It was, Grosvenor knew, not a true picture of their feeling for each other. The human mind normally balanced innumerable opposing impulses so that the average individual might live his life span without letting one feeling gain important ascendance over the others. That intricate balance had now been upset. The result threatened disaster to an entire expedition of human beings, and promised victory to an enemy whose purpose could only be conjectured.

Whatever the reason, the way to the control room was blocked. Reluctantly, Grosvenor retreated again to his own department.

Korita met him at the door. "Look!" he said. He motioned to a wall-communicator plate, which was tuned to the finely balanced steering devices in the fore part of the *Space Beagle*. The sending plate there was focused directly along a series of hairline sights. The arrangement looked more intricate than it was. Grosvenor brought his eyes to the sights and saw that the ship was describing a slow curve which, at its climax, would bring it to bear directly on a bright white star. A servo mechanism had been set up to make periodic adjustments that would hold it on its course.

"Could the enemy do that?" Korita asked.

Grosvenor shook his head, more puzzled than alarmed. He shifted the viewer over to the bank of supplementary instruments. Accordingly to the star's spectral type, magnitude, and luminosity, it was just over four light years distant. The ship's speed was up to a light-year every five hours. Since it was still accelerating, that would increase on a calculable curve. He estimated roughly that the vessel would reach the vicinity of the sun in approximately eleven hours.

With a jerky movement, Grosvenor shut off the communicator. He stood there, shocked but not incredulous. Destruction *could* be the purpose of the deluded person who had altered the ship's course. If so, there were just ten hours in which to prevent catastrophe.

Even at that moment, when he had no clear plan, it seemed to Grosvenor that only an attack on the enemy, using hypnotic techniques, would effectively do the job. Meanwhile. . . .

He stood up decisively. It was time for a second attempt to get into the control room.

He needed something that would directly stimulate brain cells. There were several devices that could do that. Most of them were usable for medical purposes only. The exception was the encephalo-adjuster, an instrument that could be used to transmit impulses from one mind to another.

Even with Korita's help, it took Grosvenor several minutes to set up one of his adjusters. Testing it consumed still more time; and, because it was such a delicate machine, he had to fasten it to his loading vehicle with a cushion of springs around it. Altogether, the preparation required thirty-seven minutes.

He had a brief, though rather sharp, argument then with the archaeologist, who wanted to accompany him. In the end, however, Korita agreed to remain behind and guard their base of operations.

Carrying the encephalo-adjuster made it necessary for him to keep down the speed of his vehicle as he headed for the control room. The enforced slowdown irked him, but it also gave him an opportunity to observe the changes that had taken place since the first moment of attack.

He saw only an occasional unconscious body. Grosvenor guessed that most of the men who had fallen into deep trance sleeps had awakened spontaneously. Such awakenings were common hypnotic phenomena. Now they were responding to other stimuli on the same basis. Unfortunately – although it also was to be expected – that seemed to mean that long-suppressed impulses controlled their actions.

And so men who, under normal circumstances, merely disliked each other mildly had, in an instant, had their dislike change to murderous hatred.

The deadly factor was that they would be unaware of the change. For the mind *could* be taught without the individual's knowing it. It could be tangled by bad environmental association, or by the attack that was now being made against a shipload of men. In either case, each person carried on as if his new beliefs were as soundly based as his old ones.

Grosvenor opened the elevator door on the control-room level, and then drew back hastily. A heat projector was pouring flame along the corridor. The metal walls burned with a harsh, sizzling sound. Within his narrow field of vision, three men lay dead. As he waited, there was a thunderous explosion. Instantly, the flames stopped. A blue smoke hazed the air, and there was a sense of suffocating heat. Within seconds, both the haze and the heat were gone. It was obvious that at least the ventilating system was still working.

He peered out cautiously. At first sight, the corridor seemed deserted. Then he saw Morton, half hidden in a protective alcove less than a score of feet away. At almost the same moment, the Director saw him and beckoned him over. Grosvenor hesitated, then realized he had to take the risk. He pushed his vehicle through the elevator doorway and darted across the intervening space. The Director greeted him eagerly as he came up.

"You're just the man I wanted to see," he said, "We've got to get control of the ship away from Captain Leeth before Kent and his group organize their attack."

Morton's gaze was calm and intelligent. He had the look of a man fighting for the right. Nor did it seem to occur to him that an explanation for his statement was required. The Director went on. "We'll need your help particularly against Kent. They're bringing up some chemical stuff I've never seen before. So far, our fans have blown it right back at them, but they're setting up fans of their own. Our big problem is, will we have time to defeat Leeth before Kent can bring his forces to bear?"

Time was also Grosvenor's problem. Unobtrusively, he brought his right hand up to his left wrist and touched the activating relay that controlled the directional-sending plates of the adjuster. He pointed the plates at Morton as he said. "I've got a plan, sir. I think it might be effective against the enemy."

He stopped. Morton was looking down. The Director said, "You've brought along an adjuster, and it's on. What do you expect from that?"

Grosvenor's first tense reaction yielded to a need for a suitable answer. He had hoped that Morton would not be too familiar with adjusters. With that hope blasted, he could still try to use the instrument, though without the initial advantage of surprise. He said in a voice that was taut in spite of himself, "That's it. It's this machine I want to use."

Morton hesitated, then said, "I gather from the thoughts coming into my mind that you're broadcasting – " He stopped. Interest quickened his face. "Say," he said presently, "that's good. If you can put over the notion that we're being attacked by aliens – "

He broke off. His lips pursed. His eyes narrowed with calculation. He said, "Captain Leeth has twice tried to make a deal with me. Now we'll pretend to agree, and you go over with your machine. We'll attack the moment you signal us." He explained with dignity. "You understand, I would not consider dealing with either Kent or Captain Leeth except as a means to victory. You appreciate that, I hope?"

Grosvenor found Captain Leeth in the control room. The commander greeted him with stiff-backed friendliness. "This fight among the scientists," he said earnestly, "has placed the military in an awkward position. We've got to defend the control room and the engine room and so perform our minimum duty to the expedition as a whole." He shook his head gravely. "It's out of the question, of course, that either of them be allowed to win. In the final issue, we of the military are prepared to sacrifice ourselves to prevent the victory of either group."

The explanation startled Grosvenor out of his own purpose. He had been wondering if Captain Leeth was responsible for aiming the ship directly at a sun. Here was at least partial confirmation. The commander's motivation seemed to be that victory for any group but the military was unthinkable. With that beginning, it was probably only a tiny step to the concept that the whole expedition must be sacrificed.

Casually, Grosvenor pointed the directional sender of the adjuster at Captain Leeth.

Brain waves, minute pulsations transmitted from axon to dendrite, from dendrite to axon, always following a previously established path depending on past associations – it was a process that operated endlessly among the ninety million neuron cells of a human brain. Each cell was in its own state of electro-colloidal balance, an intricate interplay of tension and impulse. Only gradually, over the years, had machines been developed that could detect with some degree of accuracy the meaning of the energy flow inside the brain.

The earliest encephalo-adjuster was an indirect descendant of the famous electroencephalograph. But its function was the reverse of that first device. It manufactured artificial brain waves of any desired pattern. Using it, a skilful operator could stimulate any part of the brain, and so cause thoughts, emotions, and dreams, and bring up memories from the individual's past. It was not in itself a controlling instrument. The subject maintained his own ego. However, it could transmit the mind impulses of one person to a second person. Since the impulses varied according to the sender's thoughts, the recipient was stimulated in a highly flexible fashion.

Unaware of the presence of the adjuster, Captain Leeth did not realize that his thoughts were no longer quite his own. He said, "The attack being made on the ship by the images makes the quarrel of the scientists traitorous and unforgivable." He paused, then said thoughtfully, "Here's my plan."

The plan involved heat projectors, muscle-straining acceleration, and partial extermination of both groups of scientists. Captain Leeth failed even to mention the aliens, nor did it seem to occur to him that he was describing his intentions to an emissary of what he regarded as the enemy. He finished by saying, "Where your services will be important, Mr. Grosvenor, is in the science department. As a Nexialist, with a co-ordinative knowledge of many sciences, you can play a decisive role against the other scientists. . . ."

Weary and disheartened, Grosvenor gave up. The chaos was too great for one man to overcome. Everywhere he looked were armed men. Altogether he had seen a score or more dead bodies. At any moment the uneasy truce between Captain Leeth and Director Morton would end in a burst of projector fire. Even now he could hear the roaring of the fans where Morton was holding off Kent's attack.

He sighed as he turned back to the captain. "I'll need some equipment from my own department," he said. "Can you pass me through to the rear elevators? I can be back here in five minutes."

As he guided his machine into the back door of his department a few minutes later, it seemed to Grosvenor that there was no longer any doubt about what he must do. What had seemed a far-fetched idea when he first thought of it was now the only plan he had left.

He must attack the aliens through their myriad images, and with their own hypnotic weapons.

CHAPTER TEN

GROSVENOR was aware of Korita watching him as he made his preparations. The archaeologist came over and looked at the array of electrical instruments he was attaching to the encephalo-adjuster, but he asked no questions. He seemed to be fully recovered from his experience.

Grosvenor kept wiping the perspiration from his face. And yet it was not warm. The room temperature stood at normal. By the time his preliminary work was done, he realized that he had to stop to analyse his anxiety. He just didn't, he decided finally, know enough about the enemy.

It was not sufficient that he had a theory about how they were operating. The great mystery was an enemy who had curiously womanlike bodies and faces, some partly doubled, some single. He needed a reasonable philosophic basis for action. He needed that balance for his plan which only knowledge could give him.

He turned to Korita, and asked, "In terms of cyclic history, what stage of culture could these beings be in?"

The archaeologist sat down in a chair, pursed his lips, and said, "Tell me your plan."

The Japanese grew pale as Grosvenor described it. He said finally, almost irrelevantly, "How is it you were able to save me, and not the others?"

"I got to you right away. The human nervous system learns by repetition. For you, their light pattern hadn't repeated as often as for the others."

"Is there any way we could have avoided this disaster?" he asked grimly.

Grosvenor smiled a wan smile. "Nexial training could have done it, since that includes hypnotic conditioning. There's only one sure protection against hypnosis, and that is to be trained in it in exactly the right way."

He broke off. "Mr. Korita, please answer my question. Cyclic history?"

A thin, wet line of moisture formed on the archaeologist's brow. "My friend," he said, "surely you can't expect a generalization at this stage. What do we know about these beings?"

Grosvenor groaned inwardly. He recognized the need for discussion, but vital time was passing. He said indecisively. "Beings who can use hypnosis over a distance, as these can would probably be able to stimulate each other's minds, and so would have naturally the kind of telepathy that human beings can obtain only through the encephalo-adjuster."

He leaned forward, abruptly excited. "Korita, what effect would the ability to read minds without artificial aids have on a culture?"

The archaeologist was sitting up. "Why of course," he said. "You have the answer. Mind reading would stultify the development of any race, and therefore this one is in the fellahin stage."

His eyes were bright as he stared at the puzzled Grosvenor. "Don't you see? The ability to read another's mind would make you feel that you know about him. On that basis, a system of absolute certainties would develop. How could you doubt when you *know*? Such beings would flash through the early periods of their culture, and arrive at the fellah period in the swiftest possible time."

Alertly, while Grosvenor sat frowning, he described how various civilizations of Earth and galactic history had exhausted themselves, and then stagnated into fellahdom. Fellah people resented newness and change. They were not particularly cruel as a group, but because of their poverty they all too frequently develop an indifference toward the suffering of individuals.

When Korita had finished, Grosvenor said, "Perhaps their resentment of change is responsible for the attack on the ship?"

The archaeologist was cautious. "Perhaps."

There was silence. It seemed to Grosvenor that he had to act as if Korita's total analysis was correct. He had no other hypothesis. With such a theory as a starting point, he could try to obtain verification from one of the images.

A glance at the chronometer tensed him. He had less than seven hours to save the ship.

Hastily, he focused a beam of light through the encephalo-adjuster. With quick movements, he set a screen in front of the light, so that a small area of glass was thrown into shadow except for the intermittent light that played on it from the adjuster.

Instantly, an image appeared. It was one of the partially doubled ones, and because of the encephalo-adjuster, he was able to study it in safety. The first clear look astounded him. It was only vaguely humanoid. And yet it was understandable how his mind had leaped to the woman identification earlier. Its overlapping double face was crowned with a neat bun of golden feathers. But its head, though now unmistakably bird-like, did have a human appearance. There were no feathers on its face, which was covered with a lacework of what seemed to be veins. The human appearance resulted from the way those markings had formed into groups, to give the effect of cheeks and nose.

The second pair of eyes and the second mouth were in each case nearly two inches above the first. They almost made a second head, which was literally growing out of the first. There was also a second pair of shoulders, with a doubled pair of short arms that ended in beautifully delicate, amazingly long hands and fingers – and the overall effect was still feminine. Grosvenor found himself thinking that the arms and fingers of the two bodies would be likely to separate first. The second body would then be able to help support its weight. Parthenogenesis, Grosvenor thought. Reproduction without sex. The growth of a bud from a parent body, and the final separation from the parent into a new individual.

The image in the wall before him showed vestigial wings. Tufts of feathers were visible at the "wrists". It wore a bright blue tunic over an astonishingly straight and superficially humanlike body. If there were other vestiges of a feathery past, they were hidden by the clothing. What was clear was that this bird didn't, and couldn't, fly under its own power.

Korita spoke first, in a helpless tone. "How are you going to let it know you're willing to be hypnotized in exchange for information?"

Grosvenor did not answer in words. He stood up and tentatively drew a picture of the image and of himself on a blackboard. Forty-seven minutes and scores of drawings later the bird image suddenly faded from the wall, and a city scene appeared in its place.

It was not a large community, and his first view of it was from a high vantage point. He had an impression of very tall, very narrow buildings, clustered so close together that all the lower reaches must be lost in gloom for most of each day. Grosvenor wondered, in passing, if that might possibly reflect nocturnal habits in some primeval past. His mind leaped on. He ignored individual buildings in his desire to obtain a whole picture. Above everything else, he wanted to find out the extent of their machine culture, how they communicated, and if this was the city from which the attack on the ship was being launched.

He could see no machines, no aircraft, no cars. Nor was there anything corresponding to the interstellar-communication equipment used by human beings, which, on Earth, required stations spaced over many square miles of land. It seemed likely, therefore, that the origin of the attack was nothing like that.

Even as he made his negative discovery, the view changed. He was no longer on a hill but in a building near the centre of the city. Whatever was taking that perfect colour picture moved forward, and he looked down over the edge. His primary concern was with the whole scene. Yet he found himself wondering how they were showing it to him. The transition from one scene to another had been accomplished in the twinkling of an eye. Less than a minute had passed since his blackboard illustration had finally made known his desire for information.

That thought, like the others, was a flashing one. Even as he had it, he was gazing avidly down the side of the building. The space separating it from the near-by structures seemed no more than ten feet. But now he saw something that had not been visible from the hillside. The buildings were connected on every level by walks only inches wide. Along these moved the pedestrian traffic of the bird city.

Directly below Grosvenor, two individuals strode towards each other along the same narrow walk. They seemed unconcerned by the fact that it was a hundred feet or more to the ground. They passed casually, easily. Each swung his outside leg, wide around the other, caught the walk, bent his inside leg wide out, and then they were by, without having broken pace. There were other people on other levels going through the same intricate manoeuvres in the same nonchalant manner. Watching them, Grosvenor guessed that their bones were thin and hollow, and that they were lightly built.

The scene changed again, and then again. It moved from one section of the street to another. He saw, it seemed to him, every possible variation of the reproductive condition. Some were so far advanced that the legs and arms and most of the body was free. Others were as he had already seen them. In every instance, the parent seemed unaffected by the weight of the new body.

Grosvenor was trying to get a glimpse inside one of the dim interiors of a building when the picture began to fade from the wall. In a moment, the city had disappeared completely. In its place grew the double image. The image fingers pointed at the encephalo-adjuster. Its motion was unmistakable. It had fulfilled its part of the bargain. It was time for him to fulfill his.

It was naive of it to expect that he would do so. The trouble was, he had to. He had no alternative but to carry out his obligation.

CHAPTER ELEVEN

"I AM calm and relaxed," said Grosvenor's recorded voice. "My thoughts are clear. What I see is not necessarily related to what I am looking at. What I hear may be meaningless to the interpretive centres of my brain. But I have seen their city as they think it. Whether what I actually see and hear makes sense or nonsense, I remain calm, relaxed, and at ease. . . ."

Grosvenor listened carefully to the words, and then turned to Korita. "That's it," he said simply.

The time might come, of course, when he would not consciously hear the message. But it would be there. Its patterns would impress ever more firmly on his mind. Still listening, he examined the adjuster for the last time. It was all as he wanted it.

To Korita, he explained, "I'm setting the automatic cutoff for five hours. If you pull this switch" – he indicated a red lever – "you can break me free before then. But only do so in an emergency."

"How do you define emergency?"

"If we're attacked here." Grosvenor hesitated. He would have liked a series of breaks. But what he was about to do was not merely a scientific experiment. It was a life-and-death gamble. Ready for action, he put his hand on the control dial. And there he paused.

For this was the moment. Within a few seconds, the group mind of countless individual bird folk would be in possession of parts of his nervous system. They would undoubtedly try to control him as they were controlling the other men on the ship.

He was fairly positive that he would be up against a group of minds working together. He had seen no machines, not even a wheeled vehicle, that most primitive of mechanical devices. For a short time, he had taken it for granted that they were using television-type cameras. Now he guessed that he had seen the city through the eyes of individuals. With these things, telepathy was a sensory process as sharp as vision itself. The enmassed mind power of millions of bird people could hurdle light-years of distance. They didn't need machines.

He couldn't hope to forsee the result of his attempt to become a part of their collective mind.

Still listening to the recorder, Grosvenor manipulated the dial of the encephalo-adjuster and slightly modified the ryhthm of his own thoughts. It had to be slight. Even if he had wanted to, he could not offer the aliens complete attunement. In those rhythmic pulsations lay every variation of sanity, unsanity, and insanity. He had to restrict his reception to waves that would register "sane" on a psychologist's graph.

The adjuster superimposed them on a beam of light which in turn shone directly on the image. If the individual behind the image was affected by the pattern in the light, it hadn't shown it yet. Grosvenor did not expect overt evidence, and so he was not disappointed. He was convinced that the result would become apparent only in the changes that occurred in the patterns they were directing at him. And that, he was sure, he would have to experience with his own nervous system.

It was hard for him to concentrate on the image, but he persisted. The encephalo-adjuster began to interfere markedly with his vision. And still he stared steadily at the image.

"I am calm and relaxed. My thoughts are clear. . . ."

One instant the words were loud in his ears. The next, they were gone. And in their stead was a roaring sound as of distant thunder.

The noise faded slowly. It became a steady throbbing like the murmur in a large sea shell. Grosvenor was aware of a faint light. It was far away and had the hazy dimness of a lamp seen through thick fog.

"I'm still in control," he assured himself. "I'm getting sense impressions through its nervous system. It's getting impressions through mine."

He could wait. He could sit here and wait until the darkness cleared, until his brain started to make some kind of interpretation of the sense phenomena that were being telegraphed from that other nervous system. He could sit here and –

He stopped. Sit! he thought. Was that what *it* was doing? He poised intent and alert. He heard a distant voice say, "Whether what I actually see and hear makes sense or nonsense, I remain calm. . . ."

His nose began to itch. He thought. They don't have noses; at least I didn't see any. Therefore, it's either my own nose, or a random speculation. He started to reach up to scratch it, and felt a sharp pain in his stomach. He would have doubled up with the hurt of it if he had been able. He couldn't. He couldn't scratch his nose. He couldn't put his hands on his abdomen.

He realized then that the itch and the pain stimuli did not derive from his own body. Nor did they necessarily have any corresponding meaning in the other's nervous system. Two highly developed life forms were sending signals to each other – he hoped that he was sending signals to it also – which neither could interpret. His advantage was that he had expected it. The alien, if it was fellah, and if Korita's theory was valid, hadn't and couldn't. Understanding that, *he* could hope for adjustment. *It* could only become more confused.

The itch went away. The pain in his stomach became a feeling of satiation, as if he had eaten too much. A hot needle stabbed at his spine, digging at each vertebra. Half-way down, the needle turned to ice, and the ice melted and ran in a freezing stream down his back. Something – a hand? a piece of metal? a pair of tongs? – snatched at a bundle of muscles in his arm, and almost tore them out by the roots. His mind shrieked with pain messages. He almost lost consciousness.

Grosvenor was a badly shaken man when that sensation faded into nothingness. These were all illusions. No such things were happening anywhere, not in his body, not in that of the bird being. His brain was receiving a pattern of impulses through his eyes, and was misinterpreting them. In such a relationship, pleasure could become a pain, any stimulus could produce any feeling. He hadn't counted on the misinterpretations being so violent.

He forgot that as his lips were caressed by something soft and squishy. A voice said, "I am loved – " Grosvenor rejected the meaning. No, not "loved." It was, he believed, his own brain again trying to interpret sense phenomena from a nervous system that was experiencing a reaction different from any comparable human emotion. Consciously, he substituted the words. "I am stimulated by – " and then let the feeling run its course. In the end, he still didn't know what it was that he had felt. The stimulation was not unpleasant. His taste buds were titillated by a sense of sweetness. A picture of a flower came into his mind. It was a lovely, red, Earth carnation and thus could have no connection with the flora of the Riim world.

Riim! he thought. His mind poised in tense fascination. Had that come to him across the gulf of space? In some irrational way, the name seemed to fit. Yet no matter what came through, a doubt would remain in his mind. He could not be sure.

The final series of sensations had all been pleasant. Nevertheless, he waited anxiously for the next manifestation. The light remained dim and hazy. Then once more his eyes seemed to water. His feet suddenly itched intensely. The sensation passed, leaving him unaccountably hot and weighed by a suffocating lack of air.

"False!" he told himself. "Nothing like this is happening."

The stimulations ceased. Again there was only the steady throbbing sound, and the all-pervasive blur of light. It began to worry him. It was possible that his method was right and that, given time, he would eventually be able to exercise some control over a member, or a group of members, of the enemy. But time was what he could not spare. Every passing second brought him a colossal distance nearer personal destruction. Out there – here (for an instant he was confused) – in space, one of the biggest and costliest ships ever built by men was devouring the miles at a velocity that had almost no meaning.

He knew which parts of his brain were being stimulated. He could hear a noise only when sensitive areas at the side of the cortex received sensations. The brain surface above the ear, when titillated, produced dreams and old memories. In the same way, every part of the human brain had long ago been mapped. The exact location of stimulation areas differed slightly for each individual, but the general structure, among humans, was always the same.

The normal human eye was a fairly objective mechanism. The lens focused a real image on the retina. To judge by the pictures of their city, as transmitted by the Riim folk, they, also, possessed objectively accurate eyes. If he could co-ordinate his visual centres with their eyes, he would receive dependable pictures.

More minutes went by. He thought, in sudden despair, is it possible that I'm going to sit here the full five hours without ever making a useful contact? For the first time, he questioned his good sense in committing himself so completely to this situation. When he tried to move his hand over the control lever of the encephalo-adjuster, nothing seemed to happen. A number of vagrant sensations came, among them the unmistakable odour of burning rubber.

For the third time, his eyes watered. And then, sharp and clear, a picture came. It flashed off as swiftly as it had flashed on. But to Grosvenor, who had been trained by advanced tachistoscopic techniques, the after-image remained as vivid in his mind as if he had had a leisurely look.

It seemed as if he were in one of the tall, narrow buildings. The interior was dimly lighted by the reflections from the sunlight that came through the open doors. There were no windows. Instead of floors, the residence was fitted with catwalks. A few bird people were sitting on these walks. The walls were lined with doors, indicating the existence of cabinets and storage areas.

The visualization both excited and disturbed him. Suppose he did establish a relationship with this creature whereby he was affected by its nervous system, and it by his. Suppose he reached the point where he could hear with its ears, see with its eyes, and feel to some degree what it felt. These were sensory impressions only.

Could he hope to bridge the gap and induce motor responses in the creature's muscles? Would he be able to force it to walk, turn its head, move its arms, and generally, make it act as his body? The attack on the ship was being made by a group working together, thinking together, feeling together. By gaining control of one member of such a group, could he exercise some control over all?

His momentary vision must have come through the eyes of one individual. What he had experienced so far did not suggest any kind of group contact. He was like a man imprisoned in a dark room, with a hole in the wall in front of him covered with layers of translucent material. Through this filtered a vague light. Occasionally, images penetrated the blur, and he had glimpses of the outside world. He could be fairly certain that the pictures were accurate. But that did not apply to the sounds that came through another hole on a side wall, or the sensations that came to him through still other holes in the ceiling and floor.

Human beings could hear frequencies up to twenty thousand vibrations a second. That was where some races started to hear. Under hypnosis, men could be conditioned to laugh uproariously when they were being tortured, and shriek with pain when tickled. Stimulation that meant pain to one life form could mean nothing at all to another.

Mentally, Grosvenor let the tensions seep out of him. There was nothing for him to do but relax and wait.

He waited.

It occurred to him presently that there might be a connection between his own thoughts and the sensations he received. That picture of the inside of the building – what had he thought just before it came? Principally, he recalled, he had visualized the structure of the eye.

The connection was so obvious that his mind trembled with excitement. There was another thing, also. Until now, he had concentrated on the notion of seeing and feeling with the nervous system of the individual. Yet the realization of his hopes depended on his establishing contact with, and control of, the group of minds that had attacked the ship.

He saw his problem, suddenly, as one that would require

control of his own brain. Certain areas would have to be virtually blacked out, kept at minimum-performance levels. Others must be made extremely sensitive, so that all incoming sensations found it easier to seek expression through them. As a highly-trained auto-hypnotic subject, he could accomplish both objectives by suggestion.

Vision came first, of course. Then muscular control of the individual through whom the group was working against him.

Flashes of coloured light interrupted his concentration. Grosvenor regarded them as evidence of the effectiveness of his suggestions. And he knew that he was on the right track when his vision cleared suddenly, and stayed clear.

The scene was the same. His control still sat on one of the roosts inside one of the tall buildings. Hoping fervently that the vision was not going to fade, Grosvenor began to concentrate on moving the Riim's muscles.

The trouble was that the ultimate explanation of why a movement could occur at all was obscure. His visualization could not possibly include in detail the millions of cell responses involved in the raising of one finger. He thought now in terms of a whole limb. Nothing happened. Shocked but determined, Grosvenor tried symbol hypnosis, using a single cue word to cover the entire complex process.

Slowly, one of the attenuated arms came up. Another cue, and his control stood up cautiously. Then he made it turn its head. The act of looking reminded the bird being that that drawer and that cabinet and that closet were "mine". The memory barely touched the conscious level. The creature knew its own possessions and accepted the fact without concern.

Grosvenor had a hard time fighting down his excitement. With tense patience, he had the bird being get up from a sitting position, raise its arms, lower them, and walk back and forth along the roost. Finally, he made it sit down again.

He must have been keyed up, his brain responsive to the slightest suggestion, because he had barely started to concentrate again when his whole being was flooded by a message that seemed to affect every level of his thought and feeling. More or less automatically, Grosvenor translated the anguished thoughts into familiar verbalisms.

"The cells are calling, calling. The cells are afraid. Oh, the cells know pain! There is darkness in the Riim world. Withdraw from the being – far from Riim. . . . Shadows, darkness, turmoil. . . . The cells must reject him. . . . But they cannot.

They were right to try to be friendly to the being who came out of the great dark, since they did not know he was an enemy.... The night deepens. All cells withdraw. . . . But they cannot. . . ."

Grosvenor thought blankly, Friendly!

It fitted also. He could see how, in a nightmarish fashion, everything that had happened so far could be explained as easily one way as the other. Dismayed, he realized the seriousness of the situation. If the catastrophe that had already occurred aboard the ship were the result of a misguided and ignorant attempt at friendly communication, then what damage might they not be able to do if they were hostile?

His problem was greater than theirs. If he broke his connection with them, they would be free. Now that could mean an attack. By avoiding him they might actually attempt destruction of the *Space Beagle.*

He had no recourse but to continue what he had planned, in the hope that something would happen that he could turn to his favour.

CHAPTER TWELVE

He concentrated first on what seemed the most logical intermediate stage: the transfer of control to another alien. The choice, in the case of these beings, was obvious.

"I am loved!" he told himself, deliberately producing the sensation that had confused him earlier. "I am loved by my parent body, from which I am growing to wholeness. I share my parent's thoughts, but already I see with my own eyes, and know that I am one of the group — "

The transition came suddenly, as Grosvenor had expected it might. He moved the smaller, duplicate fingers. He arched the fragile shoulders. Then he oriented himself again to the parent Riim. The experiment was so completely satisfactory that he felt ready for the bigger jump that would take him into association with the nervous system of a more distant alien.

And that, also, proved to be a matter of stimulating the proper brain centres. Grosvenor came to awareness standing in a wilderness of brush and hill. Directly in front of him was a narrow stream. Beyond it, an orange sun rode low in a dark purple sky that was spotted with fleecy clouds. Grosvenor made his new control turn completely around. He saw that a small roost building nestled among the trees farther along the stream. It was the only habitation in sight. He walked over to it and looked inside. In the dim interior he made out several roosts, one with two birds sitting on it. Both sat with eyes closed.

It was quite possible, he decided, that they were participating in the group assault, on the *Space Beagle*.

From there, by a variation of the stimulus, he transferred his control to an individual on a part of the planet where it was night. The transition this time was even faster. He was in a lightless city, with ghostly buildings and catwalks. Swiftly, Grosvenor moved on to association with other nervous systems. He had no clear idea why the rapport was established with one Riim, and not with another who fitted the same general requirement. It could be that the stimulation affected some individuals slightly faster than it affected others. It was even possible that they were descendants or body relatives of his original parent control. When he had been associated with more than two dozen Riim all over the planet, it seemed to Grosvenor that he had a good over-all impression.

It was a world of brick and stone and wood, and of a neurological community relationship that would probably never be surpassed. And so a race had by-passed the entire machine age of man, with its penetration of the secrets of matter and energy. Now, he felt, he could safely take the next-to-the-last step of his counter attack.

He concentrated on a pattern which would characterize one of the beings who had projected an image to the *Space Beagle*. He had then a sense of a small but noticeable lapse of time. And then. . . .

He was looking forth from one of the images, seeing the ship through an image.

His first concern was with how the battle was progressing. But he had to restrain his will to know, because coming aboard was only part of his necessary pre-conditioning. He wanted to affect a group of perhaps millions of individuals. He had to affect them so powerfully that they would have to withdraw from the *Space Beagle* and have no choice but to stay away from it.

He had proved that he could receive their thoughts and that they could receive his. His association with one nervous system after another would not have been possible unless that were so.

And so now he was ready. He projected his thoughts into the darkness. "You live in a universe; and within you, you form pictures of the universe as it seems to you. And of that universe you know nothing and can know nothing except for the pictures. But the pictures within you of the universe are not the universe. . . . "

How could you influence another's mind? By changing his assumptions. How could you alter another's actions? By changing his basic beliefs, his emotional certainties.

Carefully, Grosvenor went on, "And the pictures within you do not show all about the universe, for there are many things which you cannot know directly, not having senses to know. Within the universe there is an order. And if the order of the pictures within you is not as the order of the universe, then you are deceived. . . . "

In the history of life, few thinking beings had done anything illogical – within their frame of reference. If the frame was falsely based, if the assumptions were untrue to reality, then the individual's automatic logic could lead him to disastrous conclusions.

The assumptions had to be changed. Grosvenor changed them, deliberately, coolly, honestly. His own basic hypothesis behind what he was doing was that the Riim had no defence. There were the first new ideas they had had in countless generations. He did not doubt that the impact would be colossal. This was a fellah civilization, rooted in certainties that had never before been challenged. There was ample historical evidence that a tiny intruder could influence decisively the future of entire fellahin races.

Huge old India had crumbled before a few thousand Englishmen. Similarly, all the fellah peoples of ancient Earth were taken over with ease, and did not revive until the core of their inflexible attitudes was forever shattered by the dawning realization that there was more to life than they had been taught under their rigid systems.

The Riim were peculiarly vulnerable. Their method of communication, unique and wonderful though it was, made it possible to influence them all in a single intensive operation. Over and over Grosvenor repeated his message, adding each time one instruction that had to do with the ship. The instruction was: "Change the pattern you are using against those on the ship, and then withdraw it. Change the pattern, so that they can relax and sleep . . . then withdraw it. . . . Your friendly action caused the ship great harm. We are friendly to you also, but your method of expressing friendship hurt us."

He had only a vague notion as to how long he actually poured his commands into that tremendous neural circuit. He guessed about two hours. Whatever the time involved, it ended as the relay switch on the encephalo-adjuster automatically broke the connection between himself and the image in the wall of his department.

Abruptly, he was aware of the familiar surroundings. He glanced at where the image had been. It was gone. He sent a quick look toward Korita. The archaeologist was crumpled in his chair fast asleep.

Grosvenor sat up jerkily, remembering the instruction he had given – to relax and sleep. This was the result. All over the ship, men would be sleeping.

Pausing only to awaken Korita, Grosvenor headed out into the corridor. As he raced along, he saw that unconscious men lay everywhere but that the walls were bright and clear. Not once on his journey to the control room did he see an image.

Inside the control room, he stepped gingerly over the sleeping form of Captain Leeth, who lay on the floor near the control panel. With a sigh of relief, he threw the switch that energized the outer screen of the ship.

Seconds later, Elliott Grosvenor was in the control chair, altering the course of the *Space Beagle*.

Before leaving the control room, he put a time lock on the steering gear and set it for ten hours. Thus protected against the possiblity that one of the men might wake up in a suicidal mood, he hurried out to the corridor and began to give medical aid to injured men.

His patients were, without exception, unconscious, and so he had to guess at their condition. He played safe. Where laboured respiration indicated shock, he gave blood plasma. He injected specific drugs for pain whenever he saw dangerous-looking wounds, and he applied fast-healing salves for burns and cuts. Seven times – with Korita's help now – he lifted dead men on to loading mules and rushed them to resuscitation chambers. Four revived. Even after that there were thirty-two dead men who, after an examination, Grosvenor did not so much as attempt to revive.

They were still tending the injured when a geology technician near by woke up, yawned lazily – and then groaned in dismay. Grosvenor guessed that a flood of memory had come, but he watched warily as the man climbed to his feet and came over. The technician glanced in puzzlement from Korita to Grosvenor; finally he said: "May I help?"

Soon a dozen men were helping, with a strained concentration and an occasional word that showed awareness of the temporary insanity that had caused such a nightmare of death and destruction.

Grosvenor was not aware that Captain Leeth and Director Morton had arrived until he saw them talking to Korita. Presently, Korita walked off, and the two leaders came over to Grosvenor and invited him to a meeting in the control room. Silently, Morton clapped him on the back. Grosvenor had been wondering if they would remember. Spontaneous amnesia was a common hypnotic phenomenon. Without their own recollections, it would be extremely hard to explain convincingly what had happened.

He was relieved when Captain Leeth said, "Mr. Grosvenor, in looking back over the disaster, Mr. Morton and I were both struck by the attempt you made to make us aware that we were the victims of an outside attack. Mr. Korita has now told us what he saw of your actions. I want you to tell the departmental executives in the control room what exactly took place."

It required over an hour to give an orderly account. When Grosvenor had finished, a man said, "Am I to understand that this was actually an attempt at friendly communications?"

Grosvenor nodded. "I'm afraid it was."

"You mean we can't go over there and bomb hell out of them?" he said harshly.

"It would serve no useful purpose." Grosvenor spoke steadily. "We could drop in on them and make a more direct contact."

Captain Leeth said quickly, "It would take too long. We've got distance to cover." He added in a sour voice, "It seems to be a particularly drab civilization."

Grosvenor hesitated. Before he could speak, Director Morton said quickly, "What have you to say to that, Mr. Grosvenor?"

Grosvenor said, "I assume the commander is referring to the lack of mechanical aids. But living organisms can have satisfactions that do not require machines: food and drink, association with friends and loved ones. I suggest these bird folk find emotional release in the community thinking and in their method of propagation. Time was when man had little more, yet he called it civilization; and there were great men in those days as well as now."

"Still," said physicist von Grossen shrewdly, "you did not hesitate to upset their mode of life."

Grosvenor was cool. "It is unwise for birds – or men – to live too specialized an existence. I broke down their resistance to new ideas, something which I have not yet been able to do aboard this ship."

Several men laughed wryly, and the meeting began to break up. Afterwards, Grosvenor saw Morton speak to Yemens, the only man present from the chemistry department. The chemist – second only to Kent now – frowned, and shook his head several times. Finally, he spoke at some length, and he and Morton shook hands.

Morton came over to Grosvenor, and said in a low tone, "The chemistry department will move its equipment out of your rooms within twenty-four hours, on condition that no further reference is made to the incident, Mr Yemens — "

Grosvenor said quickly, "What does Kent think of this?"

Morton hesitated. "He got a whiff of gas," he said finally, "and will be on his back in bed for several months."

"But," said Grosvenor, "that will take us past the date of the election."

Once more Morton hesitated, then said, "Yes, it will. It means I win the election without opposition, since no one but Kent filed against me."

Grosvenor was silent, thinking of the potentialities. It was good to know that Morton would continue in office. But what about all the discontented men who had supported Kent?

Before he could speak, Morton went on. "I want to ask this as a personal favour, Mr. Grosvenor. I persuaded Mr. Yemens that it would be unwise to continue Kent's attack on you. For the sake of peace, I'd like you to keep silent. Make no attempt to exploit your victory. Admit freely that it was a result of the accident, if you are asked, but do not bring up the matter yourself. Will you promise me?"

Grosvenor promised, then said hesitantly, "I wonder if I could make a suggestion."

"By all means."

"Why not name Kent your alternative?"

Morton studied him with narrowed eyes. He seemed nonplussed. He said finally, "That's a suggestion I wouldn't have expected from you. I'm not, personally, very anxious to boost Kent's morale."

"Not Kent's," said Grosvenor.

This time Morton was silent. In the end, he said slowly, "I suppose it would release tension." But he still seemed reluctant.

Grosvenor said, "Your opinion of Kent himself seems to parallel my own."

Morton laughed grimly. "There are several dozen men aboard whom I would rather see director, but for the sake of peace, I'll follow your suggestion."

They parted, Grosvenor with feelings more mixed than he had indicated. It was an unsatisfactory conclusion to Kent's attack. Grosvenor had the feeling that, in getting the chemistry department out of his rooms, he had won a skirmish and not a battle. Nevertheless, from his own point of view, it was the best solution to what might have been a bitterly fought engagement.

CHAPTER THIRTEEN

IXTL sprawled unmoving in the boundless night. Time paced slowly toward the eternity, and space was fathomlessly black. Across the immensity, vague patches of light gleamed coldly at him. Each, he knew, was a galaxy of blazing stars, shrunk by incredible distance to shining swirls of mist. Life was out there, spawning on the myriad planets that wheeled endlessly around their parent suns. In the same way, life had once crawled out of the primaeval mud of ancient Glor, before a cosmic explosion destroyed his own mighty race and flung his body out into the intergalactic deeps.

He lived; that was his personal catastrophe. Having survived the cataclysm, his almost unkillable body maintained itself in a gradually weakening state on the light energy that permeated all space and time. His brain pulsed on and on in the same old, old cycle of thought – thinking: one chance in decillions that he would ever again find himself in a galactic system. And then an even more infinitesimal chance that he fall on a planet and find a precious guul.

A billion billion times that thought had pounded to its unvarying conclusion. It was a part of him now. It was like an endless picture unrolling before his mind's eye. Together with those remote wisps of shiningness out there in that gulf of blackness, it made up the world in which he had his existence. He had almost forgotten the far-flung field of sensitivity his body maintained. In past ages that field had been truly vast, but now that his powers were waning, no signals came to him beyond the range of a few light-years.

He expected nothing, and so the first stimulus from the ship scarcely more than touched him. Energy, hardness – matter! The vague sense perception fumbled into his dulled brain. It brought a living pain, like a disused muscle briefly, agonizingly forced into action.

The pain went away. The thought faded. His brain slid back into its sleep of ages. He lived again in the old world of hopelessness and shining light splotches in a black space. The very idea of energy and matter became a dream that receded. A remote corner of his mind, somehow more alert, watched it go, watched the shadows of forgetfulness reach out with their enveloping folds of mist, striving to engulf the dim consciousness that had flashed into such an anguish of ephemeral existence.

And then once more, stronger, sharper, the message flashed from a remote frontier of his field. His elongated body convulsed in senseless movement. His four arms lashed out, his four legs jackknifed with blind, unreasoning strength. That was his muscular reaction.

His dazed, staring eyes refocused. His stultified vision was galvanized into life. The part of his nervous system that controlled the field took its first unbalancing action. In a flash of tremendous effort, he withdrew it from the billions of cubic miles from which no signals had come, and concentrated its forces in an attempt to pinpoint the area of greatest stimulation.

Even as he fought to locate it, it moved a vast distance. For the first time, then, he thought of it as a ship flying from one galaxy to another. He had a moment of awful fear that it would move beyond where he could sense it, and that he would lose contact forever before he could do anything.

He let the field spread out slightly, and felt the shock of impact as once more he received the unmistakable excitation of alien matter and energy. This time he clung to it. What had been his field became a beam of all the energy his weakened body could concentrate.

Along the tightly held beam, he drew tremendous bolts of

power from the ship. There was more energy – by many millions of times – than he could handle. He had to deflect it from himself, had to discharge it into the darkness and the distance. But, like some monstrous leech, he reached out four, five, ten light years, and drained the great ship of its drive power.

After countless aeons of eking out his existence on fragile darts of light energy, he did not even dare to try to handle the colossal power. The vastness of space absorbed the flow as if it had never been. What he did let himself receive shocked the life back into his body. With a savage intensity, he realized the extent of the opportunity. Frantically, he adjusted his atomic structure and drove himself along the beam.

In the far distance, the ship – its drive off but its momentum carrying it forward – coasted past him and began to draw farther away. It receded an entire light-year, then two, and then three. In a black despair, Ixtl realized it was going to escape in spite of all his efforts. And then. . . .

The ship stopped. In mid-flight. One instant, it was coasting along at a velocity of many light-years a day. The next, it was poised in space, all its forward momentum inhibited and transformed. It was still a tremendous distance away, but it was no longer receding.

Ixtl could guess what had happened. Those aboard the vessel had become aware of his interference and were deliberately stopping to find out what had happened, and what had caused it. Their method of instantaneous deceleration suggested a very advanced science, though he could not decide just what technique of anti-acceleration they had used. There were several possibilities. He himself intended to stop by converting his gross velocity into electronic action within his body. Very little energy would be lost in the process. The electrons in each atom would speed up slightly – so slightly – and thus the microscopic speed would be transformed to movement on the microscopic level.

It was on that level that he suddenly sensed the ship was near.

A number of things happened then, following each other too swiftly for thought. The ship put up an impenetrable energy screen. The concentration of so much energy set off the automatic relays he had established in his body. That stopped him a fraction of a microsecond before he had intended to. In terms of distance, that came to just over thirty miles.

He could see the ship as a point of light in the blackness ahead. Its screen was still up, which meant, in all probability, that those inside could not detect him, and that he could no longer hope to get to the ship itself. He assumed that delicate instruments aboard had sensed his approach, identified him as a projectile, and raised the screen as a defence.

Ixtl flashed to within yards of the almost invisible barrier. And there, separated from the realization of his hopes, he gazed hungrily at the ship. It was less than fifty yards away, a round, dark-bodied metal monster, studded with row on row of glaring lights, like diamonds. The space ship floated in the velvet-black darkness, glowing like an immense jewel, quiescent but alive, enormously, vitally alive. It brought nostalgic and vivid suggestion of a thousand far-flung planets and of an indomitable, boisterous life that had reached for the stars, and grasped them. And – in spite of present frustration – it brought hope.

Till this instant there had been so many physical things to do that he had only dimly comprehended what it might mean to him if he could get aboard. His mind, grooved through the uncounted ages to ultimate despair, soared up insanely. His legs and arms glistened like tongues of living fire as they writhed and twisted in the light that blazed from the portholes. His mouth, a gash in his caricature of a human head, slavered a white frost that floated away in little frozen globules. His hope grew so big that the thought of it kept dissolving in his mind, and his vision blurred. Through the blur, he saw a thick vein of light form a circular bulge in the metallic surface of the ship. The bulge became a huge door that rotated open and tilted to one side. A flood of brilliance spilled out of the opening.

There was a pause, and then a dozen two-legged beings came into view. They wore almost transparent armour, and they dragged, or guided, great floating machines. Swiftly, the machines were concentrated around a small area on the ship's surface. From a distance, the flames that poured forth seemed small, but their dazzling brightness indicated either enormous heat or else a titanic concentration of other radiation. What was obviously repair work proceeded at an alarming rate.

Frantically, Ixtl probed the screen that barred him from the ship, looking for weak spots. He found none. The force was too complex, its coverage too wide, for anything that he could muster against it. He had sensed that at a distance. Now he faced the reality of it.

The work – Ixtl saw they had removed a thick section of the outer wall and replaced it with new material – was finished almost as quickly as it had begun. The incandescent glare of the welders died spluttering into darkness. Machines were unclamped, floated toward the opening, down into it, and out of sight. The two-legged beings scrambled after them. The large, curved plain of metal was suddenly as deserted and lifeless as space itself.

The shock of that nearly unseated Ixtl's reason. He couldn't let them escape him now, when the whole universe was in his grasp – a few short yards away. His arms reached out, as if he would hold the ship by his need alone. His body ached with a slow, rhythmical hurt. His mind spun toward a black, bottomless pit of despair, but poised just before the final plunge.

The great door was slowing in its swift rotation. A solitary being squeezed through the ring of light and ran to the area that had been repaired. He picked up something and started back towards the open air lock. He was still some distance from it when he saw Ixtl.

He stopped as if he had been struck. Stopped, that is, in a physically unbalanced fashion. In the glow from the portholes, his face was plainly visible through his transparent space suit. His eyes were wide, his mouth open. He seemed to catch himself. His lips began to move rapidly. A minute later, the door was rotating again, outward. It swung open, and a group of the beings came out and looked at Ixtl. A discussion must have followed, for their lips moved at uneven intervals, first one individual's, then another's.

Presently, a large metal-barred cage was floated up out of the air lock. There were two men sitting on it, and they seemed to be steering it under its own power. Ixtl guessed that he was to be captured.

Curiously, he had no sense of lift. It was as if a drug was affecting him, dragging him down into an abyss of fatigue. Appalled, he tried to fight the enveloping stupor. He would need all his alertness if his race, which had attained the very threshold of ultimate knowledge, was to live again.

CHAPTER FOURTEEN

"How in the name of all the hells can anything live in intergalactic space?"

The voice, strained and unrecognizable, came through the

communicator of Grosvenor's space suit as he stood with the others near the air lock. It seemed to him that the question made the little group of men crowd closer together. For him, the proximity of the others was not quite enough. He was too aware of the impalpable yet inconceivable night that coiled about them, pressing down to the very blazing portholes.

Almost for the first time since the voyage had begun, the immensity of the darkness struck home to Grosvenor. He had looked at it so often from inside the ship that he had become indifferent. But now he was suddenly aware that man's farthest stellar frontiers were but a pin point in this blackness that reached billions of light-years in every direction.

The voice of Director Morton broke through the scared silence. "Calling Gunlie Lester inside the ship. . . . Gunlie Lester. . . ."

There was a pause; then, "Yes, Director?"

Grosvenor recognized the voice of the head of the astronomy department.

"Gunlie," Morton went on, "here's something for your astro-mathematical brain. Will you please give us the ratio of chance that blew out the drivers of the *Beagle* at the exact point in space where that thing was floating? Take a few hours to work it out."

The words brought the whole scene into even sharper focus. It was typical of mathematician Morton that he let another man have the limelight in a field in which he himself was a master.

The astronomer laughed, then said in an earnest tone, "I don't have to do any figuring. One would need a new system of notation to express the chance arithmetically. What you've got out there can't happen, mathematically speaking. Here we are, a shipload of human beings, stopping for repairs, halfway between two galaxies – the first time we've ever sent an expedition outside our own island universe. Here we are, I say, a tiny point intersecting with pre-arrangement, exactly the path of another tinier point. It's impossible, unless space is saturated with such creatures."

It seemed to Grosvenor that there was a more likely explanation. The two events could conceivably be in the simple relationship of cause and effect. A huge hole had been burned in the engine-room wall. Torrents of energy had poured out into space. Now they had stopped to repair the damage. He parted his lips to say as much, and then closed them. There was another factor, the factor of the forces and probabilities involved in *that* assumption. Just how much power would be needed to drain the output of a pile of a few minutes? Briefly, he considered the formula applicable, and shook his head slightly. The figures that came through were so enormous that the hypothesis he had intended to offer seemed automatically ruled out. A thousand coeurls amongst them couldn't have handled energy in such quantities, which suggested that machines, not individuals, were involved.

Someone was saying, "We ought to turn a mobile unit on anything that looks like that."

The shudder in his voice stirred a like emotion in Grosvenor. The reaction must have run along the communicators, because, when Director Morton spoke, his tone indicated he was trying to throw off the chill of the other man's words. Morton said, "A regular blood-red devil spewed out of a nightmare, ugly as sin – and possibly as harmless as our beautiful pussy a few months ago was deadly. Smith, what do you think?"

The gangling biologist was coldly logical. "This thing, as far as I can make it out from here, has arms and legs, a development of purely planetary evolution. If it is intelligent, it will begin to react to the changing environment the moment it is inside the cage. It may be a venerable old sage, meditating in the silence of space where there are no distractions. Or it may be a young murderer, condemned to exile, consumed with desire to get back home and resume life in his own civilization."

"I wish Korita had come out with us," said Pennons, the chief engineer, in his quiet, practical fashion. "His analysis of pussy on the cat planet gave us an idea of what we had to face and—"

"Korita speaking, Mr. Pennons." As usual, the Japanese archaeologist's voice came over the communicators with meticulous clarity. "Like many of the others, I have been listening to what is happening, and I must admit I am impressed by the image I can see of this creature on the vision plate before me. But I'm afraid analysis on the basis of cyclic history would be dangerous at this factless stage. In the case of pussy, we had the barren, almost foodless planet on which he lived, and the architectural realities of the crumbled city. But here we have a being living in space a quarter of a million light-years from the nearest planet, existing apparently without food, and without means of spatial locomotion. I suggest the following: Keep the screen up, except for an opening for the cage to be taken out. When you have your creature actually in the cage, study him – every action, every reaction. Take pictures of his internal organs working in the vacuum of space. Find out everything about him, so that we shall know what we are bringing aboard. Let us avoid killing, or being killed. The greatest precautions are in order."

"And that," said Morton, "is sense."

He began to issue orders. More machines were brought up from inside the ship. They were set up on a smooth, curving expanse of the outer surface, except for a massive fluorite camera. That was attached to the mobile cage.

Grosvenor listened uneasily while the Director gave final instructions to the men guiding the cage. "Open the door as wide as possible," Morton was saying, "and drop it over him. Don't let his hands grab the bars."

Grosvenor thought, It's now or never. If I have any objections, I've got to offer them.

There seemed nothing to say. He could outline his vague doubts. He could carry Gunlie Lester's comment to its logical conclusion and say that what had happened could not be an accident. He might even suggest that a shipload of the red, devil-like beings was probably waiting in the distance for their fellow to be picked up.

But the fact was that all the precautions against such eventualities had been taken. If there were a ship, then by opening the protective screen only enough to admit the cage, they were offering a minimum target. The outer skin might be seared, the men on it killed. But the vessel itself would surely be safe.

The enemy would find that his action had served no useful purpose. He would find arrayed against him a formidable armed and armoured vessel, manned by members of a race that could pursue a battle to a remorseless conclusion.

Grosvenor reached that point in his speculation, and decided to make no comment. He would hold his doubts in reserve.

Morton was speaking again. "Any final remarks from anyone?"

"Yes." The new voice belonged to von Grossen. "I'm in favour of making a thorough examination of this thing. To me, thorough means a week, a month."

"You mean," said Morton, "we sit here in space while our technical experts study the monster?"

"Of course," said the physicist.

Morton was silent for several seconds, then he said slowly, "I'll have to put that up to the others, von Grossen. This is an exploratory expedition. We are equipped to take back specimens by the thousand. As scientists, all is grist for our mill. Everything must be investigated. Yet I feel sure that the objection will be made that if we sit out in space an entire month for each specimen we plan to take aboard, this journey will take five hundred years instead of five or ten. I do not offer that as a personal objection. Obviously, every specimen must be examined and dealt with on its own merits."

"My point," said von Grossen, "is let's think it over."

Morton asked, "Any other objections?" When none was made, he finished quietly, "All right boys, go out and get him!"

CHAPTER FIFTEEN

IXTL waited. His thoughts kept breaking up into kaleidoscopic memories of all the things he had ever known or thought. He had a vision of his home planet, long ago destroyed. The picture brought pride, and a gathering contempt for these two-legged beings who actually expected to capture him.

He could remember a time when his race could control the movement of entire sun systems through space. That was before they dispensed with space travel as such and moved on to a quieter existence, building beauty from natural forces in an ecstasy of prolonged creative production.

He watched as the cage was unerringly driven towards him. It passed successfully through an opening in the screen, which closed instantly behind it. The transition was smoothly made. Even had he wanted to, he could not have taken advantage of the opening in the screen during the brief moment it existed. He had no desire to do so. He must be careful not to make a single hostile move until he was inside the ship. Slowly the metal-barred construction floated towards him. Its two operators were wary and alert. One held a weapon of some kind. Ixtl sensed that it discharged an atomic missile. It made him respectful, but he also recognized its limitations. It could be used against him out here, but they would not dare to employ such a violent energy within the confines of the ship.

More sharply, more clearly, that focused his purpose. Get aboard the ship! Get inside!

Even as the determination struck deeper, the gaping mouth of the cage closed over him. The metal door snapped noiselessly shut behind him. Ixtl reached for the nearest bar, caught it, and held on grimly. He clung there, dizzy from reaction. For he was safe! His mind expanded with the force of that reality. There was a physical as well as a mental effect. Free electrons discharged in swarms from the chaos of spinning atom systems inside his body, and frantically sought union with other systems. He was safe after quadrillions of years of despair. Safe on a material body. No matter what else happened, control of the energy source of this power-driven cage forever freed him from his past inability to direct his movements. He would never again be subject to the pull and equally feeble counter-pull of remote galaxies. Henceforth, he could travel in any direction he desired. And that much he had gained from the cage alone.

As he clung to the bars, his prison started to move toward the surface of the ship. The protective screen parted as they came to it, and closed behind them. Close up, the men looked puny. Their need of space suits proved their inability to adapt themselves to environments radically different from their own, which meant that they were physically on a low plane of evolution. It would be unwise, however, to under-estimate their scientific achievements. Here were keen brains, capable of creating and using mighty machines. And they had now brought up a number of these machines, evidently with the purpose of studying him. That would reveal his purpose, identify the precious objects concealed within his breast, and expose at least a few of his life processes. He could not allow such an examination to be made.

He saw that several of the beings carried not one but two weapons. The instruments were attached to holsters, which were fitted in with the hand-arm mechanisms of each space suit. One of the weapons was the atomic-missile type with which he had already been threatened. The other had a sparkling, translucent handle. He analysed it as a vibration gun. The men on the cage were also armed with the latter type of weapon.

As the cage settled into the hastily arranged laboratory, a camera was pushed towards the narrow opening between two of the bars. That was Ixtl's cue. With effortless ease, he jerked himself to the ceiling of the cage. His vision intensified, and became sensitive to very short frequencies. Instantly, he could see the power source of the vibrator as a bright spot well within his reach.

One arm, with its eight wirelike fingers, lashed out with indescribable swiftness at the metal, *through* it; and then he had the vibrator from the holster of one of the men on the cage.

He did not attempt to readjust its atomic structure as he had adjusted his arm. It was important that they should not be able to guess who had fired the weapon. Straining to maintain his awkward position, he aimed the weapon at the camera and at the group of men behind it. He pressed the trigger.

In one continuous movement, Ixtl released the vibrator, withdrew his hand, and, by the act, pushed himself to the floor. His immediate fear was gone. The purely molecular energy had resonated through the camera and had affected to some extent most of the equipment in the makeshift laboratory. The sensitive film would be useless; meters would have to be reset, gauges examined, and each machine tested. Possibly the entire lot of paraphernalia would have to be replaced. And best of all, by its very nature, what had happened would have to be regarded as an accident.

Grosvenor heard curses in his communicator, and he guessed, with relief, that the others were fighting, as he was, the stinging vibration that had been only partly stopped by the material of their space suits. His eyes adjusted slowly. Presently, he could see again the curved metal on which he stood, and beyond that the brief, barren crest of the ship, and the limitless miles of space – dark, fathomless, unthinkable gulfs. He saw, too, a blur among the shadows, the metal cage.

"I'm sorry, Director," one of the men on the cage apologized. "The vibrator must have fallen out of my belt and discharged."

Grosvenor said quickly, "Director, that explanation is unlikely in view of the virtual absence of gravity."

Morton said, "That's a good point, Grosvenor. Did anybody see anything significant?"

"Maybe I knocked against it, sir, without noticing," volunteered the man whose weapon had caused the turmoil.

There was a spluttering from Smith. The biologist muttered something that sounded like "The erysipelatous, strabismic, steatopygean . . . " Grosvenor didn't catch the rest, but he guessed that it was a biologist's private curse. Slowly, Smith straightened. "Just a minute," he mumbled, "and I'll try to remember what I saw. I was right here in the line of fire – ah, there, my body has stopped throbbing." His voice became sharp as he went on. "I can't swear to this, but just before that vibrator shocked me, the creature moved. I have an idea he jumped to the ceiling. I admit it was too black to see more than a blur, but. . . . " He left the sentence unfinished.

Morton said, "Crane, turn the cage light on, and let's see what we've got here.

With the others, Grosvenor faced about as a blaze of light showered down upon Ixtl crouching at the bottom of the cage. And then he stood silent, shocked in spite of himself. The almost red metallic sheen of the creature's cylindrical body, the eyes like coals of fire, the wirelike fingers and toes, and the over-all scarlet hideousness of it startled him.

Through the communicator, Siedel said breathlessly, "He's probably very handsome – to himself!"

The halfhearted attempt at humour broke the spell of horror. A man said stiffly, "If life is evolution, and nothing evolves except for use, how can a creature living in space have highly developed legs and arms? Its insides should be interesting. But now – the camera's useless. That vibration would have the effect of distorting the lens, and of course the film has been ruined. Shall I have another sent up?"

"No-o-o!" Morton sounded doubtful, but he continued in a firmer tone, "We've been wasting a lot of time; and after all, we can recreate vacuum of space conditions inside the ship's laboratories. and be travelling at top acceleration while we're doing it."

"Am I to understand that you are going to ignore my suggestion?" It was von Grossen, the physicist. He went on. "You will recall that I recommended at least a week's study of this creature before any decision is made about taking him aboard."

Morton hesitated, then said, "Any other objections?" He sounded concerned.

Grosvenor said, "I don't think we should jump from the extreme of precaution to no precaution at all."

Morton said quietly, "Anybody else?" When no one replied, he added, "Smith?"

Smith said, "Obviously, we're going to take him aboard sooner or later. We mustn't forget that a creature existing in space is the most extraordinary thing we've run across. Even pussy, who was equally at home with oxygen and chlorine, needed warmth of a kind, and would have found the cold and lack of pressure in space deadly. If, as we suspect, this creature's natural habitat is not space, then we must find out why and how he came to be where he is."

Morton was frowning. "I can see we'll have to vote on this. We could enclose the cage in metal that will take an outer screen. Would that satisfy you, von Grossen?"

Von Grossen said, "Now we are talking sensibly. But we shall have more arguments before the energy screen is taken down."

Morton laughed. "Once we're on our way again, you and the others can discuss the pro and con of that from now till the end of the voyage." He broke off. "Any other objections? Grosvenor?"

Grosvenor shook his head. "The screen sounds effective to me, sir."

Morton said, "All those against, speak up." When no one spoke, he directed a command to the men on the cage. "Move that thing over here, so we can start preparing it for energization."

Ixtl felt the faint throb in the metal as the motors started. He saw the bars move. Then he grew conscious of a sharp, pleasant tingling sensation. It was a physical activity inside his body, and while it was in progress it hampered the working of his mind. When he could think again, the cage floor was rising above him – and he was lying on the hard surface of the space ship's outer shell.

With a snarl, he scrambled to his feet as he realized the truth. He had forgotten to readjust the atoms in his body after firing the vibrator. And now he had passed through the metal floor of the cage.

"Good heavens!" Morton's bass exclamation almost deafened Grosvenor.

A scarlet streak of elongated body, Ixtl darted across the shadowy reach of the impenetrable metal of the ship's outer wall to the air lock. He jerked himself down into its dazzling depths. His adjusted body dissolved through the two inner doors. And then he was at one end of a long, gleaming corridor, safe – for the moment. And one fact stood out.

In the imminent struggle for control of the ship, he would have one important advantage, aside from his individual superiority. His opponents did not yet know the deadliness of his purpose.

CHAPTER SIXTEEN

IT was twenty minutes later. Grosvenor sat in one of the auditorium seats in the control room and watched Morton and Captain Leeth consulting together in low tones on one of the tiers leading up to the main section of the instrument board.

The room was packed with men. With the exception of guards left in key centres, everybody had been ordered to attend. The military crew and its officers, the heads of science departments and their staffs, the administrative branches, and the various technical men who had no departments – all were either in the room or congregated in the adjoining corridors.

A bell clanged. The babble of conversation began to fade. The bell clanged again. All conversation ceased. Captain Leeth came forward.

"Gentlemen," he said, "These problems keep arising, do they not? I am beginning to feel that we military men have not properly appreciated scientists in the past. I thought they lived out their lives in laboratories, far from danger. But it's beginning to dawn on me that scientists can find trouble where it never existed before."

He hesitated briefly, then went on in the same dryly humorous tone. "Director Morton and I have agreed that this is not a problem for military forces alone. So long as the creature is at large, every man must be his own policeman. Go armed, go in pairs or groups – the more the better."

Once more he surveyed his audience, and his manner was grimmer when he continued. "It would be foolish for you to believe that this situation will not involve danger or death for some among us. It may be me. It may be you. Nerve yourself for it. Accept the possibility. But if it is your destiny to make contact with this immensely dangerous creature, defend yourself to the death. Try to take him with you. Do not suffer, or die, in vain.

"And now" – he turned to Morton – "the Director will guide a discussion regarding the utilization against our enemy of the very considerable scientific knowledge which is aboard this ship. Mr. Morton."

Morton walked slowly forward. His large and powerful body

was dwarfed by the gigantic instrument board behind him, but nevertheless he looked imposing. The Director's grey eyes flicked questioningly along the line of faces, pausing at none, apparently simply assessing the collective mood of the men. He began by praising Captain Leeth's attitude, and then he said, "I have examined my own recollections of what happened, and I think I can say honestly that no one – not even myself – is to blame for the creature's being aboard. It had been decided, you may remember, to bring him aboard in the confines of a force field. That precaution satisfied our most precise critics, and it was unfortunate that it was not taken in time. The being actually came into the ship under his own power by a method which could not be foreseen." He stopped. His keen gaze once more swept the room. "Or did anybody have something stronger than a premonition? Please hold up your hand if you did."

Grosvenor craned his neck, but no hands were raised. He settled back in his seat, and was a little startled to see that Morton's grey eyes were fixed on him. "Mr. Grosvenor," said Morton, "did the science of Nexialism enable you to predict that this creature could dissolve his body through a wall?"

In a clear voice, Grosvenor said, "It did not."

"Thank you," said Morton.

He seemed satisfied, for he did not ask anyone else. Grosvenor had already guessed that the Director was trying to justify his own position. It was a sad commentary on the ship's politics that he should have felt it necessary. But what particularly interested Grosvenor was that he had appealed to Nexialism as a sort of final authority.

Morton was speaking again. "Siedel," he said, "give us a psychologically sound picture of what has happened."

The chief pyschologist said, "In setting about to capture this creature, we must first of all straighten our minds about him. He has arms and legs, yet floats in space and remains alive. He allows himself to be caught in a cage, but knows all the time that the cage cannot hold him. Then he slips through the bottom of the cage, which is very silly of him if he does not want us to know that he can do it. There is a reason why intelligent beings make mistakes, a fundamental reason that should make it easy for us to do some shrewd guessing as to where he came from, and, of course, to analyse why he is here. Smith, dissect his biological make-up!"

Smith stood up, lank and grim. "We've already discussed

the obvious planetary origin of his hands and feet. The ability to live in space, if evolutionary at all, is certainly a remarkable attribute. I suggest that here is a member of a race that has solved the final secrets of biology; and if I knew how we should even begin to start looking for a creature that can escape from us through the nearest wall, my advice would be: Hunt him down, and kill him on sight."

"Ah..." Kellie, the sociologist, said. He was a bald-headed man, fortyish, with large, intelligent eyes. "Ah – any being who could fit himself to live in a vacuum would be lord of the universe. His kind would dwell on every planet, clutter up every galaxy. Swarms of him would be floating in space. Yet we know for a fact that his race does not infest our galactic area. A paradox that is worthy of investigation."

"I don't quite understand what you mean, Kellie," said Morton.

"Simply – ah – that a race which has solved the ultimate secrets of biology must be ages in advance of man. It would be highly sympodial, that is, capable of adaptation to any environment. According to the law of vital dynamics, it would expand to the farthest frontier of the universe just as man is trying to do."

"It is a contradiction," acknowledged Morton, "and would seem to prove that the creature is not a superior being. Korita, what is this thing's history?"

The Japanese scientist shrugged, but he stood up and said, "I'm afraid I can be of only slight assistance on present evidence. You know the prevailing theory: that life proceeds upward – whatever we mean by upward – by a series of cycles. Each cycle begins with the peasant, who is rooted to his bit of soil. The peasant comes to market; and slowly the market place transforms into a town, with ever less 'inward' connection to the earth. Then we have cities and nations, finally the soulless world cities and a devastating struggle for power, a series of frightful wars which sweep men to fellahdom, and so to primitiveness, and on to a new peasanthood. The question is: Is this creature in the peasant part of his particular cycle, or in the big-city, megalopolitan era? Or where?"

He stopped: It seemed to Grosvenor that some very sharp pictures had been presented. Civilizations did appear to operate in cycles. Each period of the cycle must in a very rough fashion have its own psychological background. There were many possible explanations for the phenomenon, of which the old Spenglerian notion of cycles was only one. It was even possible that Korita could foresee the alien's actions on the basis of the cyclic theory. He had proved in the past that the system was workable and had considerable predictability. At the moment, it had the advantages that it was the only historical approach with techniques that could be applied to a given situation.

Morton's voice broke the silence. "Korita, in view of our limited knowledge of this creature, what basic traits should we look for, supposing him to be in the big-city stage of his culture?"

"He would be a virtually invincible intellect, formidable to the ultimate possible degree. At his own game, he would make no errors of any kind, and he would be defeatable only through circumstances beyond his control. The best example" – Korita was suave – "is the highly trained human being of our own era."

"But he has already made an error!" von Grossen said in a silken tone. "He very foolishly fell through the bottom of the cage. Is that the kind of thing a peasant would do?"

Morton asked, "Suppose he was in the peasant stage?"

"Then," Korita replied, "his basic impulses would be much simpler. There would first of all be the desire to reproduce, to have a son, to know that his blood was being carried on. Assuming great fundamental intelligence, this impulse might, in a superior being, take the form of a fanatic drive toward race survival."

He finished quietly, "And that's all I will say, on available evidence." He sat down.

Morton stood stiffly on the tier of the instrument board and looked over his audience of experts. His gaze paused at Grosvenor. He said, "Recently, I have personally come to feel that the science of Nexialism may have a new approach to offer to the solution of problems. Since it is the whole-istic approach of life, carried to the nth degree, it may help us to a quick decision at a time when a quick decision is important. Grosvenor, please give us your views on this alien being."

Grosvenor stood up briskly. He said, "I can give you a conclusion based on my observations. I could go into a little theory of my own as to how we made contact with this creature – the way the pile was drained of energy, with the result that we had to repair the outer wall of the engine room – and there were a number of significant time intervals – but rather than develop on such backgrounds I'd like to tell you in the next few minutes how we should kill—"

There was an interruption. Half a dozen men were pushing their way through the group that crowded the doorway. Grosvenor paused, and glanced questioningly at Morton. The Director had turned and was watching Captain Leeth. The captain moved towards the new arrivals, and Grosvenor saw that Pennons, chief engineer of the ship, was one of them.

Captain Leeth said, "Finished, Mr. Pennons?"

The chief engineer nodded. "Yes, sir." He added in a warning tone, "It is essential that every man be dressed in a rubberite suit and wear rubberite gloves and shoes."

Captain Leeth explained. "We've energized the walls around the bedrooms. There may be some delay in catching this creature, and we are taking no chances of being murdered in our beds. We – " He broke off, asking sharply, "What is it, Mr. Pennons?"

Pennons was staring at a small instrument in his hand. He said slowly, "Are we all here, Captain?"

"Yes, except for the guards in the engine and machine rooms."

"Then . . . then something's caught in the walls of force. Quick, we must surround it!"

CHAPTER SEVENTEEN

To Ixtl, returning to the upper floors from exploring the lower ones, the shock was devastating, the surprise complete. One moment he was thinking complacently of the metal sections in the hold of the ship, where he would secrete his guuls. The next moment he was caught in the full sparkling, furious centre of an energy screen.

His mind went black with agony. Clouds of electrons broke free inside him. They flashed from system to system, seeking union, only to be violently repelled by atom systems fighting stubbornly to remain stable. During those long, fateful seconds, the wonderfully balanced flexibility of his structure nearly collapsed. What saved him was that even this dangerous eventuality had been anticipated by the collective genius of his race.

In forcing artificial evolution upon his body – and their own – they had taken into account the possibility of a chance encounter with violent radiation. Like lightning, his body adjusted and readjusted, each new-built structure carrying the intolerable load for a fraction of a microsecond. And then he had jerked back from the wall, and was safe.

He concentrated his mind on the immediate potentialities. The defensive wall of force would have an alarm system connected to it. That meant the men would be bearing down on all the adjacent corridors in an organized attempt to corner him. Ixtl's eyes were glowing pools of fire as he realized the opportunity. They would be scattered, and he would be able to catch one of them, investigate him for his guul properties, and use him for his first guul.

There was no time to waste. He darted into the nearest unenergized wall, a tall, gaudy, ungraceful shape. Without pausing, he sped through room after room, keeping roughly parallel to a main corridor. His sensitive eyes followed the blurred figures of the men as they raced by. One, two, three, four, five in this corridor. The fifth man was some distance behind the others. Comparatively, it was a slight advantage, but it was all Ixtl needed.

Like a wraith he glided through the wall just ahead of the last man and pounced forth in an irresistible charge. He was a rearing, frightful monstrosity with glaring eyes and ghastly mouth. He reached out with his four fire-coloured arms, and with his immense strength clutched the human being. The man squirmed and jerked in one contorted effort; and then he was overwhelmed, and flung to the floor.

He lay on his back, and Ixtl saw that his mouth opened and shut in an uneven series of movement. Every time it opened, Ixtl felt a sharp tingling in his feet. The sensation was not hard to identify. It was the vibrations of a call for help. With a snarl, Ixtl pounced forward. With one great hand he smashed at the man's mouth. The man's body sagged. But he was still alive and conscious as Ixtl plunged two hands into him.

The action seemed to petrify the man. He ceased to struggle. With widened eyes, he watched as the long, thin arms vanished under his shirt and stirred around in his chest. Then, horrified, he stared at the blood-red, cylindrical body that loomed over him.

The inside of the man's body seemed to be solid flesh. And Ixtl's need was for an open space, or one that could be pressed open, so long as the pressing did not kill his victim. For his purposes, he needed living flesh.

Hurry, hurry! His feet registered the vibrations of approaching footsteps. They came from one direction only, but they came swiftly. In his anxiety, Ixtl made the mistake of actually speeding up his investigation. He hardened his searching fingers momentarily into a state of semi-solidity. In that moment, he touched the heart. The man heaved convulsively, shuddered, and slumped into death.

An instant later, Ixtl's probing fingers discovered the stomach and intestines. He drew back in a violence of self-criticism. Here was what he wanted; and he had rendered it useless. He straightened slowly, his anger and dismay fading. For he had not anticipated that these intelligent beings could die so easily. It changed and simplified everything. They were at his mercy, not he at theirs. No need for him to be more than casually cautious in dealing with them.

Two men with drawn vibrators whipped around the nearest corner and slid to a halt at the sight of the apparition that snarled at them across the dead body of their companion. Then, as they came out of the momentary paralysis, Ixtl stepped into the nearest wall. One instant he was a blur of scarlet in that brightly lighted corridor, the next he was gone as if he had never been. He felt the transmitted vibration from the weapons as the energy tore futilely at the walls behind him.

His plan was quite clear now. He would capture half a dozen men and make guuls of them. Then he could kill all the others, since they would not be necessary to him. That done, he could proceed on to the galaxy towards which the ship was evidently heading and there take control of the first inhabited planet. After that, domination of the entire reachable universe would be a matter of a short time only.

Grosvenor stood in front of a wall communicator with several other men, and watched the image of the group that had gathered around the dead technician. He would have liked to be on the scene, but it would have taken him several minutes to get there. During that time he would be out of touch. He preferred to watch, and see and hear everything.

Director Morton stood nearest the sending plate, less than three feet from where Dr. Eggert was bending over the dead man. He looked tense. His jaw was clenched. When he spoke, his voice was little more than a whisper. Yet the words cut across the silence like a whiplash.

"Well, Doctor?"

Dr. Eggert rose up from his kneeling position beside the body and turned to Morton. The action brought him to face the sending plate. Grosvenor saw that he was frowning.

"Heart failure," he said.

"Heart failure?"

"All right, all right." The doctor put up his hands as if to defend himself. "I know his teeth look as if they've been smashed back into his brain. And, having examined him many times, I know his heart was perfect. Nevertheless, heart failure is what it looks like to me."

"I can believe it," a man said sourly. "When I came around that corner and saw that beast, I nearly had heart failure myself."

"We're wasting time." Grosvenor recognized the voice of von Grossen before he saw the physicist standing between two men on the other side of Morton. The scientist continued. "We can beat this fellow, but not by talking about him and feeling sick every time he makes a move. If I'm next on his list of victims, I want to know that the best damned bunch of scientists in the system are not crying over my fate but instead are putting their brains to the job of avenging my death."

"You're right." That was Smith. "The trouble with us is we've been feeling inferior. He's been on the ship less than an hour, but I can see clearly that some of us are going to get killed. I accept my chance. But let's get organized for combat."

Morton said slowly, "Mr. Pennons, here's a problem. We've got about two square miles of floor space in our thirty levels. How long will it take to energize every inch of it?"

Grosvenor could not see the chief engineer. He was not within range of the plate's curving lens. But the expression on the officer's face must have been something to witness. His voice, when he responded to Morton, sounded aghast. He said, "I could sweep the ship, and probably wreck it completely within an hour. I won't go into details. But uncontrolled energization would kill every living thing aboard."

Morton's back was partly to the communicating plate that was transmitting the images and voices of those who stood beside the body of the man who had been killed by Ixtl. He said questioningly, "You could feed more energy to those walls, couldn't you, Mr. Pennons?"

"No-o!" The ship's engineer sounded reluctant. "The walls couldn't stand it. They'd melt."

"*The walls couldn't stand it!*" a man gasped. "Sir, do you realize what you're making this creature out to be?"

Grosvenor saw that there was consternation in the faces of the men whose images were being transmitted. Korita's voice cut across the pregnant silence. He said, "Director, I am watching you on a communicator in the control room. To the suggestion that we are dealing with a super-being. I want to say this: Let us not forget that he did blunder into the wall of force, and that he recoiled in dismay without penetrating into the sleeping quarters. I use the word 'blunder' deliberately. His action proves once again that he does make mistakes."

Morton said, "That takes me back to what you said earlier about the psychological characteristics to be expected at the various cyclic stages. Let us suppose he's a peasant of his cycle."

Korita's reply was crisp for one who usually spoke with such care. "The inability to understand the full power of organization. He will think, in all likelihood, that in order to gain control of the ship he need only fight the men who are in it. Instinctively, he would tend to discount the fact that we are part of a great galactic civilization. The mind of the true peasant is very individualistic, almost anarchic. His desire to reproduce himself is a form of egoism, to have his own blood, particularly, carried on. This creature – if he is in the peasant stage of his development – will very possibly want to have numbers of beings similar to himself to help him with his fight. He likes company, but he doesn't want interference. Any organized society can dominate a peasant community, because its members never form anything more than a loose union against outsiders."

"A loose union of those fire-eaters ought to be enough!" a technician commented acidly. "I . . . aaa-a-a. . . . "

His words tailed into a yell. His lower jaw sagged open. His eyes, plainly visible to Grosvenor, took on a goggly stare. All the men who could be seen in the plate retreated several feet.

Full into the centre of the viewing plate stepped Ixtl.

CHAPTER EIGHTEEN

He stood there, forbidding spectre from a scarlet hell. His eyes were bright and alert, though he was no longer alarmed. He had sized up these human beings, and he knew, contemptuously, that he could plunge into the nearest wall before any of them could loose a vibrator on him.

He had come for his first guul. By snatching that guul from the centre of the group, he would to some extent demoralize everybody aboard. Grosvenor felt a wave of unreality sweep over him as he watched the scene. Only a few of the men were within the field of the plate. Von Grossen and two technicians stood nearest Ixtl. Morton was just behind von Grossen, and part of the head and body of Smith could be seen near one of the technicians. As a group, they looked like insignificant opponents of the tall, thick, cylindrical monstrosity that towered above them.

It was Morton who broke the silence. Deliberately, he held his hand away from the translucent handle of his vibrator, and said in a steady voice, "Don't try to draw on him. He can move like a flash. And he wouldn't be here if he thought we could blast him. Besides, we can't risk failure. This may be our only chance."

He continued swiftly, in an urgent tone. "All emergency crews listening in on this get above and below and around this corridor. Bring up the heaviest portables, even some of the semi-portables, and burn the walls down. Cut a clear path around this area, and have your beams sweep that space at narrow focus. Move!"

"Good idea, Director!" Captain Leeth's face appeared for a moment on Grosvenor's communicator, superseding the image of Ixtl and the others. "We'll be there if you can hold that hellhound three minutes." His face withdrew as swiftly as it had come.

Grosvenor deserted his own viewing plate. He had been acutely aware that he was too far from the scene for the kind of precise observation on which a Nexialist was supposed to base his actions. He was not part of any emergency crew, and so his purpose was to join Morton and the other men in the danger area.

As he ran, he passed other communicators, and realized that Korita was giving advice from a distance. "Morton, take this chance, but do not count on success. Notice that he has appeared once again before we have been able to prepare against him. It doesn't matter whether he is pressing us intentionally or accidentally. The result, whatever his motivation, is that we are on the run, scurrying this way and that, futilely. So far, we have not clarified our thoughts."

Grosvenor had been in an elevator, going down. Now he flung open the door and raced out. "I am convinced," Korita's voice continued from the next corridor communicator, "that the vast resources of this ship can defeat any creature – I mean, of course, any single creature – that has ever existed. . . . " If Korita said anything after that Grosvenor didn't hear it. He had rounded the corner. And there, ahead, were the men and beyond them Ixtl. He saw that von Grossen had finished sketching something in his notebook. As Grosvenor watched with misgivings, von Grossen stepped forward and held the sheet out to Ixtl. The creature hesitated, then accepted it. He took one glance at it, and stepped back with a snarl that split his face.

Morton yelled, "What the devil have you done?"

Von Grossen was grinning tensely. "I've just shown him how we can defeat him," he said softly. "I — "

His words were cut off. Grosvenor, still in the rear, saw the entire incident merely as a spectator. All the others in the group were involved in the crisis.

Morton must have realized what was about to happen. He stepped forward, as if instinctively trying to interpose his big body in front of von Grossen. A hand with long, wirelike fingers knocked the Director against the men behind him. He fell, unbalancing those nearest him. He recovered himself, clawed for his vibrator, and then froze with it in his hand.

As through a distorted glass, Grosvenor saw that the thing was holding von Grossen in two fire-coloured arms. The two-hundred-and-twenty-pound physicist squirmed and twisted, vainly. The thin, hard muscles held him as if they were so many manacles. What prevented Grosvenor from discharging his own vibrator was the impossibility of hitting the creature without also hitting von Grossen. Since the vibrator could not kill a human being but could render him unconscious, the conflict inside him was: Should he activate the weapon, or try in a desperate bid to get information from von Grossen? He chose the latter.

He called to the physicist in an urgent voice, "Von Grossen, what did you show him? How can we defeat him?"

Von Grossen heard, because he turned his head. That was all he had time for. At that moment, a mad thing happened. The creature took a running dive and vanished into the wall, still holding the physicist. For an instant, it seemed to Grosvenor that his vision had played a trick on him. But there were only the hard smooth, gleaming wall and eleven staring, perspiring men, seven of them with drawn weapons, which they fingered helplessly.

"We're lost!" a man whispered. "If he can adjust our atomic structures and take us with him through solid matter, we can't fight him."

Grosvenor saw that Morton was irritated by the remark. It was the irritation of a man who is trying to maintain his balance under trying circumstances. The Director said angrily, "While we're living, we can fight him!" He strode to the nearest communicator, and asked, "Captain Leeth, what's the situation?"

There was a delay, then the commander's head and shoulders came into focus on the plate. "Nothing," he said succinctly. "Lieutenant Clay thinks he saw a flash of scarlet disappearing through a floor, going down. We can, for the time being, narrow our search down to the lower half of the ship. As for the rest, we were just lining up our units when it happened. You didn't give us enough time."

Morton said grimly: "We didn't have anything to say about it."

It seemed to the listening Grosvenor that the statement was not strictly true. Von Grossen had hastened his own capture by showing the creature a diagram of how he could be defeated. It was a typically egotistical human action, with little survival value. More than that, it pointed up his own argument against the specialist who acted unilaterally and was incapable of co-operating intelligently with other scientists. Behind what von Grossen had done was an attitude centuries old. That attitude had been good enough during the early days of scientific research. But it had a limited value now that every development required knowledge and co-ordination of many sciences.

Standing there, Grosvenor questioned that von Grossen had actually evolved a technique for defeating Ixtl. He questioned that a successful technique would be limited to the field of a single specialist. Any picture von Grossen had drawn for the creature would probably have been limited to what a physicist would know.

His private thought ended as Morton said, "What I'd like is some theory as to what was drawn on the sheet of paper von Grossen showed the creature."

Grosvenor waited for someone else to reply. When no one did he said, "I think I have one, Director."

Morton hesitated the barest moment, then said, "Go ahead."

Grosvenor began, "The only way one could gain the attention of an alien would be to show him a universally recognized symbol. Since von Grossen is a physicist, the symbol he would have used suggests itself."

He paused deliberately and looked around him. He felt as if he were being melodramatic, but it was unavoidable. In spite of Morton's friendliness, and the Riim incident, he was not recognized as an authority aboard this ship, and so it would be better if the answer would occur spontaneously at this point to several people.

Morton broke the silence. "Come, come, young man. Don't keep us in suspense."

"An atom," said Grosvenor.

The faces around him looked blank. "But that doesn't mean anything," said Smith. "Why should he show him an atom?"

Grosvenor said, "Not just any atom, of course. I'll wager that von Grossen drew for the creature a structural representation of the eccentric atom of the metal that makes up the outer shell of the *Beagle*."

Morton said, "You've got it!"

"Just a minute." Captain Leeth spoke from the communicator plate. "I confess I'm no physicist, but I'd like to know just what it is that he's got."

Morton explained. "Grosvenor means that only two parts of the ship are composed of that incredibly tough material, the outer shell and the engine room. If you had been with us when we first captured the creature, you would have noticed that when it slipped through the floor of the cage it was stopped short by the hard metal of the outer shell of the ship. It seems clear that it cannot pass through such metal. The fact that it had to run for the air lock in order to get inside is further proof. The wonder is that we didn't all of us think of that right away."

Captain Leeth said, "If Mr. von Grossen was showing the creature the nature of our defences, couldn't it be that he depicted the energy screens we put up in the walls? Isn't that just as possible as the atom theory?"

Morton turned and glanced questioningly at Grosvenor. The Nexialist said, "The creature had already experienced the energy screen at that time and had survived it. Von Grossen clearly believed he had something new. Besides the only way you can show a field of force on paper is with an equation involving arbitrary symbols."

Captain Leeth said, "This is very welcoming reasoning. We have at least one place aboard where we are safe – the engine room – and possibly somewhat lesser protection from the wall screens of our sleeping quarters. I can see why Mr. von Grossen would feel that gave us an advantage. All personnel on this ship will hereafter concentrate only in those areas, except by special permission or command." He turned to the nearest communicator, repeated the order, and then said, "Heads of departments be prepared to answer questions relating to their specialities. Necessary duties will probably be assigned to suitably trained individuals. Mr. Grosvenor, consider yourself in this latter category. Dr. Eggert, issue anti-sleep pills where required. No one can go to bed until this beast is dead."

"Good work, Captain!" Morton said warmly.

Captain Leeth nodded, and disappeared from the communicator plate.

In the corridor, a technician said hesitantly, "What about von Grossen?"

Morton said harshly, "The only way we can help von Grossen is by destroying his captor!"

CHAPTER NINETEEN

In that vast room of vast machines, the men seemed like dwarfs in a hall of giants. Grosvenor blinked involuntarily at each burst of unearthly blue light that sparkled and coruscated upon the great, glistening sweep of ceiling. And there was a sound that rasped his nerves as much as the light affected his eyes. It was imprisoned in the air itself. A hum of terrifying power, a vague rumble like thunder from the horizon, a quivering reverberation of an inconceivable flow of energy.

The drive was on. The ship was accelerating, going ever

deeper and faster through the gulf of blackness that separated the spiral galaxy, of which Earth was one tiny, spinning atom, from another galaxy of almost equal size. That was the background to the decisive struggle that was now taking place. The largest, most ambitious exploratory expedition that had ever set out from the solar system was in the gravest danger of its existence.

Grosvenor believed that firmly. This was no Coeurl, whose overstimulated body had survived the murderous wars of the dead race that had performed biological experiments upon the animals of the cat planet. Nor could the danger from the Riim folk be compared. After their first misguided effort at communication, he had controlled every subsequent action in what he had thought of as the struggle between one man and a race.

The scarlet monster was clearly and unmistakably in a class by himself.

Captain Leeth climbed up a metal stairway that led to a small balcony. A moment later Morton joined him and stood looking down at the assembled men. He held a sheaf of notes in his hand, divided by one interposed finger into two piles. The two men studied the notes, then Morton said, "This is the first breathing spell we've had since the creature came aboard less than – incredible as it may seem – less than two hours ago. Captain Leeth and I have been reading the recommendations given us by heads of departments. These recommendations we have roughly divided into two categories. One category, being of a theoretical nature, we will leave till later. The other category, which concerns itself with mechanical plans for cornering our enemy, naturally takes precedence. To begin with, I am sure that we are all anxious to know that plans are afoot to locate and rescue Mr. von Grossen. Mr. Zeller, tell the rest of the men what you have in mind."

Zeller came forward, a brisk young man in his late thirties. He had succeeded to the headship of the metallurgy department after Breckenridge was killed by Coeurl. He said, "The discovery that the creature cannot penetrate the group of alloys we call resistance metals automatically gave us a clue as to the type of material we would use in building a space suit. My assistant is already working at the suit, and it should be ready in about three hours. For the search, naturally, we'll use a fluorite camera. If anybody has any suggestions. . . ."

A man said, "Why not make several suits?"

Zeller shook his head. "We have only a very limited amount of material. We could make more, but only by transmutation, which takes time." He added. "Besides, ours has always been a small department. We'll be fortunate to get one suit completed in the time I have set."

There were no more questions. Zeller disappeared into the machine shop adjoining the engine room.

Director Morton raised his hand. When the men had settled again to silence, he said, "For myself, I feel better knowing that, once the suit is built, the creature will have to keep moving von Grossen in order to prevent us from discovering the body."

"How do you know he's alive?" someone asked.

"Because the damned thing could have taken the body of the man he killed, but he didn't. He wants us alive. Smith's notes have given us a possible clue to his purpose, but they are in category two, and will be discussed later."

He paused, then went on, "Among the plans put forward for actually destroying the creature, I have here one offered by two technicians of the physics department, and one by Elliott Grosvenor. Captain Leeth and I have discussed these plans with chief engineer Pennons and other experts, and we have decided that Mr. Grosvenor's idea is too dangerous to human beings, and so will be held as a last resort. We will begin immediately on the other plan unless important objections to it are raised. Several additional suggestions were made, and these have been incorporated. While it is customary to let individuals expound their own ideas, I think time will be saved if I briefly outline the plan as it has been finally approved by the experts.

"The two physicists" – Morton glanced down at the papers in his hand – "Lomas and Hindley, admit that their plan depends on the creature's permitting us to make the necessary energy connections. That appears probable on the basis of Mr. Korita's theory of cyclic history, to the effect that a 'peasant' is so concerned with his own blood purposes that he tends to ignore the potentialities of organized opposition. On this basis, under the modified plan of Lomas and Hindley, we are going to energize the seventh and ninth levels – only the floor and not the walls. Our hope is this. Until now, the creature has made no organized attempt to kill us. Mr. Korita says that, being a peasant, the thing has not yet realized that he must destroy us or we will destroy him. Sooner or later, however, even a peasant will realize that killing us should come first, before anything else. If he doesn't interfere with our work, then we'll trap him on the eighth level, between the two energized floors. There, under circumstances where he won't be able to get down or up, we'll search him out with our projectors. As Mr. Grosvenor will realize, this plan is considerably less risky than his own, and therefore should take precedence."

Grosvenor swallowed hard, hesitated, and then said grimly, "If it's the amount of risk we're considering, why don't we just crowd together here in the engine room and wait for him to develop a method of coming in after us?" He went on earnestly, "Please don't think I'm trying to push my own ideas. But personally" – he hesitated, then took the plunge – "I consider the plan you outlined as worthless."

Morton looked genuinely startled. Then he frowned. "Isn't that rather a sharp judgment?"

Grosvenor said, "I understand the plan as described by you was not the one originally put forward, but a modified version of it. What was taken out?"

"The two physicists," said the Director, "recommended energizing four levels – seven, eight, nine, and ten."

For the third time Grosvenor hesitated. He had no desire to be over critical. At any moment, if he persisted, they would simply cease asking his opinion. He said finally, "That's better."

From behind Morton, Captain Leeth interrupted. "Mr. Pennons, tell the group why it would be inadvisable to energize more than two floors."

The chief engineer stepped forward. He said with a frown, "The principal reason is that it would take an extra three hours, and we are all agreed that time is of the essence. If time were not a factor, it would be much better to energize the entire ship under a controlled system, walls as well as floors. That way, he couldn't escape us. But it would require about fifty hours. As I stated previously, uncontrolled energization would be suicide. There's another factor involved that we discussed purely as human beings. The reason the creature will seek us out will be that he wants more men, so that when he starts down, he'll have one of us with him. We want that man, whoever he is, to have a chance for life." His voice grew harsh. "During the three hours it will take us to put the modified plan into effect, we'll be helpless against him except for high-powered mobile vibrators and heat projectors. We dare not use anything heavier inside the ship, and those will have to be used with care since they can kill human beings. Naturally, each man is expected to defend himself with his own vibrator." He stepped back. "Let's get going!"

Captain Leeth said unhappily, "Not so fast. I want to hear more of Mr. Grosvenor's objections."

Grosvenor said, "If we had time, it might be interesting to see how this creature reacts to such energized walls."

A man said irritably, "I don't get the argument. Why, if this creature ever gets caught between two energized levels, that's the end of him. We know he can't get through."

"We don't know anything of the kind," Grosvenor said firmly. "All we know is that he got into a wall of force, and that he escaped. We assume he didn't like it. In fact, it seems clear that he definitely could not remain in such an energy field for any length of time. It is our misfortune, however, that we cannot use a full force screen against him. The walls, as Mr. Pennons pointed out, would melt. My point is, *he escaped from what we've got.*"

Captain Leeth looked disconcerted. "Gentlemen," he said, "why was this point not brought out at the discussion? It is certainly a valid objection."

Morton said, "I was in favour of inviting Grosvenor to the discussion, but I was voted down on the basis of a long-standing custom, whereby the man whose plan is under consideration is not present. For the same reason, the two physicists were not invited."

Siedel cleared his throat. "I don't think," he said, "that Mr. Grosvenor realizes what he has just done to us. We have all been assured that the ship's energy screen is one of man's greatest scientific achievements. This has given me personally a sense of well being and security. Now he tells us this being can penetrate it."

Grosvenor said, "I didn't say the ship's screen was vulnerable, Mr. Siedel. In fact, there is reason to believe the enemy could not and cannot get through it. The reason is that he waited beyond it till we brought him inside it. The floor energization, now being discussed, is a considerably weaker version."

"Still," said the psychologist, "don't you think the experts unconsciously assumed a similarity between the two forms? The rationale would be: If this energization is ineffective, then we are lost. Therefore, it must be effective."

Captain Leeth broke in wearily. "I'm afraid that Mr. Siedel

has accurately analysed our weakness. I recall now having such a thought."

From the centre of the room, Smith said, "Perhaps we'd better hear Mr. Grosvenor's alternative plan."

Captain Leeth glanced at Morton, who hesitated, then said, "He suggested that we divide ourselves into as many groups as there are atomic projectors aboard — "

That was as far as he got. A physics technician said in a shocked voice, "Atomic energy – inside a ship!"

The uproar that began lasted for more than a minute. When it died away, Morton went on as if there had been no interruption.

"We have forty-one such projectors at the moment. If we accepted Mr. Grosvenor's plan, each one would be manned by a nucleus of military personnel, with the rest of us spread out as bait within sight of one of the projectors. Those manning the projector would be under orders to activate it even if one or more of us is in the line of fire."

Morton shook his head slightly, and went on. "It is possibly the most effective suggestion that has been put forward. However, the ruthlessness of it shocked us all. The idea of firing at one's own people, while not new, strikes much deeper than Mr. Grosvenor – I think – realizes. In fairness, though, I must add that there was one other factor that decided the scientists against it. Captain Leeth stipulated that those who acted as bait must be unarmed. To most of us, that was carrying the thing too far. Every man should be entitled to defend himself." The Director shrugged. "Since there was an alternative plan, we voted for it. I am now personally in favour of Mr. Grosvenor's idea, but I still object to Captain Leeth's stipulation."

At the first mention of the commander's suggestion Grosvenor had swung around and stared at the officer. Captain Leeth looked back steadily, almost grimly. After a moment, Grosvenor said aloud in a deliberate tone, "I think you ought to take the risk, Captain."

The commander acknowledged the words with a slight, formal bow. "Very well," he said, "I withdraw my stipulation."

Grosvenor saw that Morton was puzzled by the brief interchange. The Director glanced at him, then at the captain, then back again to Grosvenor. Then a startled look flashed into his heavy-set face. He came down the narrow metal steps and over to Grosvenor. He said in a low tone, "To think that I never realized what he was getting at. He obviously believes that in a crisis. . . ." He stopped, and turned to stare up at Captain Leeth.

Grosvenor said placatingly, "I think he now realizes he made a mistake in bringing up the matter."

Morton nodded, and said reluctantly, "I suppose, when you come right down to it, he's right. The impulse to survive, being basic, could supersede all subsequent conditionings. Still" – he frowned – "we'd better not mention it. I think the scientists would feel insulted, and there's enough bad feeling aboard."

He turned and faced the group. "Gentlemen," he said resonantly, "it seems clear that Mr. Grosvenor has made a case for his plan. All in favour of it, raise their hands."

To Grosvenor's intense disappointment, only about half a hundred hands came up, Morton hesitated, then said, "All against, raise theirs."

This time just over a dozen hands were raised.

Morton pointed at a man in the front line. "You didn't put yours up either time. What seems to be the trouble?"

The man shrugged. "I'm neutral. I don't know whether I'm for it or against it. I don't know enough."

"And you?" Morton indicated another individual.

The man said, "What about secondary radiation?"

Captain Leeth answered that. "We'll block it off. We'll seal the entire area." He broke off. "Director," he said, "I don't understand why this delay. The vote was fifty-nine to fourteen in favour of the Grosvenor plan. While my jurisdiction over scientists is limited even during a crisis, I regard that as a decisive vote."

Morton seemed taken back. "But," he protested, "nearly eight hundred men abstained."

Captain Leeth's tone was formal. "That was their privilege. It is expected that grown men know their own minds. The whole idea of democracy is based on that supposition. Accordingly, I order that we act at once."

Morton hesitated, then said slowly, "Well, gentlemen, I am compelled to agree. I think we'd better get about our business. It'll take time to set up the atomic projectors, so let's start energizing levels seven and nine while we're waiting. As I see it, we might as well combine the two plans, and abandon one or the other depending on the developing situation."

"Now that," said a man, with evident relief, "makes sense."

The suggestion seemed to make sense to a lot of the men. Resentful faces relaxed. Somebody cheered, and presently the great human mass was flowing out of the huge chamber. Grosvenor turned to Morton.

"That was a stroke of genius," he said. "I was too set against such limited energization to have thought of such a compromise."

Morton acknowledged the compliment gravely. "I was holding it in reserve," he said. "In dealing with human beings, I've noticed there is usually not only a problem to be solved but the matter of tension among those who have to solve it." He shrugged. "During danger, hard work. During hard work, relaxation in every practicable form."

He held out his hand. "Well, good luck, young man. Hope you come through safely."

As they shook hands, Grosvenor said, "How long will it take to roll out the atomic cannon?"

"About an hour, perhaps a little longer. Meanwhile, we'll have the big vibrators to protect us. . . . "

The reappearance of the men brought Ixtl up to the seventh level with a rush. For many minutes, he was an abnormal shape that flitted through the wilderness of walls and floors. Twice he was seen, and projectors flashed at him. They were vibrators as different from the hand weapons he had faced so far as life from death. They shattered the walls through which he jumped to escape them. Once, the beam touched one of his feet. The hot shock from the molecular violence of the vibration made him stumble. The foot came back to normal in less than a second, but he had his picture of the limitations of his body against these powerful mobile units.

And still he was not alarmed. Speed, cunning, careful timing and placing of any appearance he made – such precautions would offset the effectiveness of the new weapons. The important thing was: What were the men doing? Obviously when they had shut themselves up in the engine room, they had conceived a plan, and they were carrying it out with determination. With glittering, unwinking eyes, Ixtl watched the plan take form.

In every corridor, men slaved over furnaces, squat things of dead-black metal. From a hole in the top of each furnace, a white glare spewed up, blazing forth furiously. Ixtl could see that the men were half blinded by the white dazzle of the fire. They wore space armour, but the ordinarily transparent glassite of which it was made was electrically darkened. Yet no light-metal armour could ward off the full effect of that glare. Out of the furnaces rolled long, dully glowing strips of material. As each strip emerged, it was snatched by machine tools, skilfully machined to exact measurements, and slapped on to the metal floors. Not an inch of floor, Ixtl noted, escaped being enclosed by the strips. And the moment the hot metal was down, massive refrigerators hugged close to it and drew its heat.

His mind refused at first to accept the result of his observations. His brain persisted in searching for deeper purposes, for a cunning of vast and not easily discernible scope. Presently, he decided that this was all there was. The men were attempting to energize two floors under a system of controls. Later, when they realized that their limited trap was not effective, they would probably try other methods. Just when their defensive system would be dangerous to him, Ixtl wasn't certain. The important thing was that as soon as he did regard it as dangerous, it would be a simple matter to follow the men about and tear loose their energization connections.

Contemptuously, Ixtl dismissed the problem from his mind. The men were only playing into his hands, making it easier for him to get the guuls he still needed. He selected his next victim carefully. He had discovered in the man he had unintentionally killed that the stomach and intestinal tract were suitable for his purposes. Automatically, the men with the largest stomachs were on his list.

He made his preliminary survey, and then launched himself. Before a single projector could be turned towards him, he was gone with the writhing, struggling body. It was simple to adjust his atomic structure the moment he was through a ceiling, and so break his fall to the floor beneath. Swiftly, he let himself dissolve through that floor also, and down to the level below. Into the vast hold of the ship, he half fell, half lowered himself. He could have gone faster, but he had to be careful not to damage the human body.

The hold was familiar territory now to the sure-footed tread of his long-toed feet. He had explored the place briefly but thoroughly after he first boarded the ship. And, in handling von Grossen, he had learned the pattern he needed now. Unerringly, he headed across the dim-lit interior toward the far wall. Great packing cases were piled up to the ceiling. He went through them or around them, as it suited him, and presently found himself in a great pipe. The inside was big enough for him to stand up in. It was part of the miles long system of air conditioning.

His hiding place would have been dark by ordinary light. But to his infra-red-sensitive vision, a vague twilight glow suffused the pipe. He saw the body of von Grossen, and laid his new victim beside it. Carefully, then, he inserted one of his wiry hands into his own breast, removed a precious egg, and deposited it into the stomach of the human being.

The man was still struggling, but Ixtl waited for what he knew must happen. Slowly, the body began to stiffen. The muscles grew progressively rigid. In panic, the man squirmed and jerked as he evidently recognized that paralysis was creeping over him. Remorselessly, Ixtl held him down until the chemical action was completed. In the end, the man lay motionless, every muscle rigid. His eyes were open and staring. There was sweat on his face.

Within hours, the eggs would be hatching inside each man's stomach. Swiftly, the tiny replicas of himself would eat themselves to full size. Satisfied, Ixtl started up out of the hold. He needed more hatching places for his eggs, more guuls.

By the time he had put a third captive through the process, the men were working on the ninth level. Waves of heat rolled along the corridor. It was an inferno wind. Even the refrigeration unit in each space suit was hard put to it to handle the superheated air. Men sweated inside their suits. Sick from the heat, stunned by the glare, they laboured almost by instinct.

Beside Grosvenor, a man said suddenly, harshly, "Here they come now!"

Grosvenor turned in the direction indicated, and stiffened in spite of himself. The machine that was rolling towards them under its own power was not big. It was a globular mass with an outer shell of wolfram carbide, and had a nozzle that protruded from the globe. The strictly functional structure was mounted on a universal bearing, which, in its turn, rested on a base of four rubber wheels.

All around Grosvenor, men had ceased work. Their faces pale, they stared at the metal monstrosity. Abruptly, one of them came over to Grosvenor and said angrily, "Damn you, Grove, you're responsible for this. If I'm due to get irradiated by one of those things, I'd like to punch you one in the nose first."

"I'll be right here," said Grosvenor in a steady voice. "If you get killed, so will I."

That seemed to take some of the anger out of the other. But there was still violence in his manner and tone, as he said, "What the hell of nonsense is this? Surely there must be better plans than to make bait out of human beings."

Grosvenor said, "There is another thing we can do."

"What's that?"

"Commit suicide!" said Grosvenor. And he meant it.

The man glared at him, then turned away muttering something about stupid jokes and moronic jokesters. Grosvenor smiled mirthlessly and went back to work. Almost immediately, he saw that the men had lost their zest for the job. An electric tension leaped from one individual to another. The slightest untoward action on the part of one person brought the others tautly erect.

They were bait. All over the various levels, men would be reacting to the death fear. No one could be immune, for the will to survive was built-in in the nervous system. Highly trained military men like Captain Leeth could put on an impassive front, but the tension would be there just under the surface. Similarly, people like Elliott Grosvenor could be grim but determined, convinced of the soundness of a course of action and prepared to take their chance.

"Attention, all personnel!"

Grosvenor jumped with the rest as that voice came out of the nearest communicator. It took a long moment before he recognized it as belonging to the commander of the ship.

Captain Leeth continued. "All projectors are now in position to levels seven, eight, and nine. You will be glad to know that I have been discussing the dangers involved with my officers. We make the following recommendations: If you see the creature, don't wait, don't look around! Throw yourself instantly to the floor. All weapon crews – right now – adjust your nozzles to fire at 50: 1½. That gives you all a clearance of one and a half feet. This will not protect you from secondary radiation, but I think we can honestly say that if you hit the floor in time, Dr. Eggert and his staff in the engine room will save your life.

"In conclusion" – Captain Leeth seemed more at ease, now that his main message had been delivered – "let me assure all ranks that there are no shirkers aboard. With the exception of the doctors and three invalid patients, every individual is in as great danger as you. My officers and I are divided among the various groups. Director Morton is down on the seventh level. Mr. Grosvenor – whose plan this is – is on level nine, and so on. Good luck, gentlemen!"

There was a moment's silence. Then the leader of the gun crew near Grosvenor called in a friendly voice, "Hey, you fellows! We've made the adjustments. You'll be safe if you can hit the deck in nothing flat."

Grosvenor called, "Thanks, friend."

Just for a moment, then, the tension eased. A mathematical-biology technician said, "Grove, butter him up some more with soft talk."

"I always did love the military," said another man. In a hoarse aside, he said loud enough for the gun crew to hear, "That ought to hold 'em off for that extra second I need."

Grosvenor scarcely heard. Bait, he was thinking again. And no group would know when the moment of danger came for some other group. At the instant of "guncrit" – a modified form of critical mass, in which a small pile developed enormous energy without exploding – a tracer light would leap out of the muzzle. Along it and around it would pour the hard, silent invisible radiation.

When it was all over, the survivors would notify Captain Leeth on his private band. In due course, the commander would inform the other groups.

"*Mr. Grosvenor!*"

Instinctively, as the sharp voice sounded, Grosvenor dived for the floor. He struck painfully, but came up almost immediately as he recognized Captain Leeth's voice.

Other men were climbing ruefully to their feet. One man muttered, "Dammit, that wasn't fair."

Grosvenor reached the communicator. He kept his gaze warily on the corridor ahead of him, as he said, "Yes, Captain?"

"Will you come down to level seven at once? Central corridor. Approach from nine o'clock."

"Yes, sir."

Grosvenor went with a sense of dread. There had been a tone in the captain's voice. Something was wrong.

He found a nightmare. As he approached, he saw that one of the atomic cannon was lying on its side. Beside it, dead, burned beyond recognition, lay what had been three of the four military crew men of the projector. On the floor beside them unconscious but still twitching and squirming, all too evidently from a vibrator discharge, was the fourth crew man.

On the far side of the cannon, twenty men lay unconscious or dead, among them Director Morton.

Stretcher-bearers, wearing protective clothing, were dashing in, picking up a victim, and then racing off with him on a loading mule.

The rescue work had clearly been going on for several minutes, so there were probably more unconscious men already being tended in the engine room by Dr. Eggert and his staff.

Grosvenor stopped at a barrier that had been hastily erected at a turn in the corridor. Captain Leeth was there. The commander was pale but calm. In a few minutes, Grosvenor had the story.

Ixtl had appeared. A young technician – Captain Leeth did not name him – forgot in panic that safety lay on the floor. As the muzzle of the cannon came up inexorably, the hysterical youngster fired his vibrator at the crew, stunning them all. Apparently, they had hesitated slightly when they saw the technician in their line of fire. The next instant, each crew man was unknowingly contributing his bit to the disaster. Three of them fell against the cannon, and, instinctively clinging to it, swung it over on its side. It rolled away from them, dragging the fourth man along.

The trouble was he had hold of the activator, and for what must have been nearly a second he pressed it.

His three companions were in the direct line of fire. They died instantly. The cannon finished rolling over on its side, spraying one wall.

Morton and his group, though never in the direct line of fire, were caught by the secondary radiation. It was too soon to tell how badly they were injured, but at a conservative estimate they would all be in bed for a year. A few would die.

"We were a little slow," Captain Leeth confessed. "This apparently happened a few seconds after I finished talking, but it was nearly a minute before somebody who heard the crash of the cannon toppling grew curious and glanced around this corner." He sighed wearily. "At the very worst, I never expected anything as bad as an entire group being wiped out."

Grosvenor was silent. This was why, of course, Captain Leeth had wanted the scientists unarmed. In a crisis, a man protected himself. He couldn't help it. Like an animal he fought blindly for his life.

He tried not to think of Morton, who had realized that the scientists would resist being disarmed and who had thought up the *modus operandi* that would make the use of atomic energy acceptable to all. He said steadily, "Why did you call me?"

"My feeling is that this failure affects your plan. What do you think?"

Grosvenor nodded reluctantly. "The surprise element is gone," he said. "He must have come up without suspecting what was waiting for him. Now, he'll be careful."

He could picture the scarlet monster poking his head through a wall, surveying a corridor – then boldly coming out beside one of the cannon and snatching one of the crew men. The only adequate precaution would be to set up a second projector to cover the first one. But that was out of the question – there were only forty-one available for the whole ship.

Grosvenor shook his head. Then he said, "Did he get another man?"

"No."

Once more Grosvenor was silent. Like the others, he could only guess at the creature's reason for wanting living men. One of those guesses was based on Korita's theory that the being was in a peasant stage and intent on reproducing himself. That suggested a bloodcurdling possibility, and a pressure of need on the part of the creature that would drive him after more human victims.

Captain Leeth said, "As I see it, he'll be up again. My idea is that we leave the cannon where they are for the time being and finish energizing three levels. Seven is completed, nine is almost ready, and so we might as well go on to eight. This will give us three floors altogether. As far as the possible effectiveness of such a plan goes, we should consider that the creature has now captured three men in addition to von Grossen. In each case, he was seen to take them in what we call a downward direction. I suggest that, as soon as we have energized all three levels, we go to the ninth floor and wait for him. When he captures one of us, we wait momentarily; and then Mr. Pennons will throw the switch that sets up the force field in the floors. The creature will strike the eighth level, and find it energized. If he tries to go through, he will find that seven is also energized. If he comes up, he finds nine in the same deadly state. Either way, we force him to make contact with two energized floors." The commander paused, looked thoughtfully at Grosvenor, and then said, "I know you considered that contact with only one level would not kill him. You were not so positive about two." He stopped, and waited questioningly.

Grosvenor said, after a moment of hesitation, "I'll buy that. Actually, we can only guess how it will affect him. Maybe we'll all be pleasantly surprised."

He didn't believe that. But there was another factor in this developing situation: the convictions and hopes that men had. Only an actual event would change the minds of some people. When their ideas were altered by reality, then – and then only – they would be emotionally ready for more drastic solutions.

It seemed to Grosvenor that he was learning slowly but surely how to influence men. It was not enough to have information and knowledge, not enough to be right. Men had to be persuaded and convinced. Sometimes that might take more time than could safely be spared. Sometimes it couldn't be done at all. And so civilizations crumbled, battles were lost, and ships destroyed because the man or group with the saving ideas would not go through the long-drawn-out ritual of convincing others.

If he could help it, that was not going to happen here.

He said, "We can keep the atomic projectors in place till we finish energizing the floors. Then we'll have to move them. Energization would bring guncrit even without the nozzle being open. They'd blow up."

As deliberately as that he withdrew the Grosvenor plan from the battle against the enemy.

CHAPTER TWENTY

IXTL came up twice during the hour and three quarters that was needed to do level eight. He had six eggs left, and he intended to use all except two of them. His only annoyance was that each guul took more time. The defence against him seemed more alert, and the presence of atomic cannon made it necessary for him to go after the men who actually manned the projectors.

Even with that limitation rigidly observed, each escape turned out to be an achievement in timing. Nevertheless, he was not worried. These things had to be done. In due course, he would attend to the men.

When the eighth level was completed, the cannon withdrawn, and everyone on the ninth level, Grosvenor heard Captain Leeth say curtly, "Mr. Pennons, are you ready to use power?"

"Yes, sir." The engineer's voice was a dry rasp on the communicators. He finished even more harshly. "Five men gone, and one to go. We've been lucky, but there is at least one more to go."

"Do you hear that, gentlemen? One to go. One of us will be bait whether he likes it or not." It was a familiar voice, but one that had long been silent. The speaker went on gravely. "This is Gregory Kent. And I'm sorry to have to say that I am speaking to you from the safety of the engine room. Dr. Eggert tells me it'll be another week before I'm off the invalid list. The reason I am speaking to you now is that Captain Leeth has turned Director Morton's papers over to me, and so I'd like Kellie to elaborate on the note of his that I have here. It will clear up something very important. It will give us a sharper picture of what we're facing. We might as well all know the worst."

"Ah. . . . " The cracked voice of the sociologist sounded on the communicators. "Here's my reasoning. When we discovered the creature, it was floating a quarter of a million light-years from the nearest star system, apparently without means of spatial locomotion. Picture that appalling distance, and then ask yourself how long it would require, relatively, for an object to move it by chance alone. Lester gave me my figures, so I would like him to tell you what he told me."

"Lester speaking!" The voice of the astronomer sounded surprisingly brisk. "Most of you know the prevailing theory of the beginnings of the present universe. There is evidence to believe that it came into being as a result of the break-up of an earlier universe several million million years ago. It is believed today that a few million million years hence, our universe will complete its cycle, and blow up in a cataclysmic explosion. The nature of such an explosion can only be surmised."

He went on, "As for Kellie's question, I can only offer a picture to you. Let us suppose that the scarlet being was blown out into space when the great explosion occurred. He would find himself heading out into intergalactic space, with no means of changing his course. Under such circumstances, he could float along forever without coming nearer to a star than a quarter of a million light-years. That is what you wanted, Kellie?"

"Ah, yes. Most of you will recall my mentioning before that it was a paradox that a pure sympodial development, such as this creature is, did not populate the entire universe. The answer to that is, logically, if his race *should* have controlled the universe, then it *did* control it. We can see now, however, that they ruled a previous universe, not our present one. Naturally, the creature now intends that his kind shall also dominate our universe. This at least is a plausible theory, if no more."

Kent said in a placating tone, "I'm sure that all the scientists aboard realize that we are speculating by necessity on matters about which little evidence is as yet available. I think it is a good thing for us to believe that we are confronted with a survivor of the supreme race of a universe. There may be others like him in the same predicament. We can only hope that no other ship ever comes near one. Biologically, this race could be billions of years ahead of us. Thinking thus, we can feel justified in demanding the utmost contribution in effort and personal sacrifice from every person aboard — "

The shrill scream of a man interrupted him. "Got me! . . . Quick! . . . ripping me out of my suit – " The words ended in a gurgle.

Grosvenor said tensely, "That was Dack, chief assistant in the geology department." He spoke the identification without thinking. His recognition of voices was now as quick and automatic as that.

Another voice sounded shrilly on the communicators. "He's going down. I saw him go down!"

"The power," said a third, calmer voice, "is on." That was Pennons.

Grosvenor found himself staring curiously at his feet. Sparkling, brilliant, beautiful blue fire shimmered there. Little tendrils of the pretty flame reared up hungrily a few inches from his rubberite suit, as if baffled by some invisible force protecting the suit. Now there was no sound. With almost blank mind, he gazed along a corridor that was alive with the unearthly blue fire. Just for a moment, he had the illusion that he was looking not out at it but down into the depths of the ship.

With a rush, his mind came back into focus. And with fascinated eyes he watched the blue ferocity of the energization that was struggling to break through his protected suit.

Pennons spoke again, this time in a whisper. "If the plan worked, we've now got that devil on the eighth or seventh levels."

Captain Leeth commanded efficiently, "All men whose last names begin with the letter 'A' to 'L', follow me to the seventh group level! Group 'M' to 'Z', follow Mr. Pennons to the eighth level! All projector crews remain at their posts! Camera teams carry on as ordered!"

The men ahead of Grosvenor stopped short at the second corner from the elevators on the seventh level. Grosvenor was among those who went forward and stood staring down at the human body that sprawled on the floor. It was seemingly held to the metal by brilliant fingers of blue fire. Captain Leeth broke the silence.

"Pull him loose!"

Two men stepped gingerly forward and touched the body. The blue flame leaped at them, as if trying to fight them off. The men jerked, and the unholy bonds yielded. They carried the body up in an elevator to the unenergized tenth level. Grosvenor followed with the others, and stood silently by as the body was laid on the floor. The lifeless thing continued to kick for several minutes, discharging torrents of energy, then gradually took on the quietness of death.

"I'm waiting for reports!" Captain Leeth spoke stiffly.

Pennons said after a second's silence, "The men are spread out over the three levels, according to plan. They're taking continuous pictures with fluorite cameras. If he's anywhere around, he'll be seen. It will take at least thirty more minutes."

Finally the report came. "Nothing!" Pennons's tone reflected his dismay. "Commander, he must have got through safely."

Somewhere a voice sounded plaintively on the momentarily open circuit of the communicators, "Now what are we going to do?"

It seemed to Grosvenor that the words probably expressed the doubt and anxiety of every person on the *Space Beagle*.

CHAPTER TWENTY-ONE

THE silence grew long. The great men of the ship, who were ordinarily so articulate, seemed to have lost their voices. Grosvenor shrank a little from the purpose, the new plan, in his own mind. And then, slowly, he faced up to the reality that now confronted the expedition. But still he waited. For it was not up to him to speak first.

It was chief chemist Kent who finally broke the spell. "It would appear," he said, "that our enemy can pass through energized walls as easily as through unenergized ones. We can continue to assume that he does not care for the experience, but that his recuperation is so swift that what he feels in one floor has no effect on him by the time he falls through the air to the next one."

Captain Leeth said, "I should like to hear from Mr. Zeller. Where are you now, sir?"

"Zeller speaking!" The brisk voice of the metallurgist sounded on the communicators. "I've finished the resistance suit, Captain. And I've started my search at the bottom of the ship."

"How long would it take to build resistance suits for everybody on the ship?"

Zeller's reply was slow in coming. "We'd have to set up a production unit," he said finally. "First we'd have to make the tools to make the tools that would make such suits in quantity from any metal. Simultaneously, we would start one of the hot piles to the task of making resistance metal. As you probably know, it comes out radioactive with a half life of five hours, which is a long time. My guess is that the first suit would roll off the assembly line in about two hundred hours from now."

To Grosvenor, it sounded like a conservative estimate. The difficulty of machining resistance metal could hardly be overstated. Captain Leeth seemed to have been struck into silence by the metallurgist's words. It was Smith who spoke.

"Then that's out!" The biologist sounded uncertain. "And since the complete energization would also take too long, we've shot our bolt. We've got nothing else."

The usually lazy voice of Gourlay, the communications expert, snapped, "I don't see why those ways are out. We're still alive. I suggest we get to work, and do as much as we can as soon as we can."

"What makes you think," Smith asked coldly, "that the creature is not capable of smashing down resistance metal? As a superior being, his knowledge of physics probably transcends our own. He might find it comparatively simple to construct a beam that could destroy anything we have. Don't forget, pussy could pulverize resistance metal. And heaven knows there are plenty of tools available in the various laboratories."

Gourlay said scornfully, "Are you suggesting that we give up?"

"No!" The biologist was angry. "I want us to use common sense. Let's not just work blindly towards an unrealizable goal."

Korita's voice sounded on the communicators, and ended the verbal duel. "I am inclined to agree with Smith. I say further that we are now dealing with a being who must shortly realize that he cannot allow us time for anything important. For that and other reasons, I believe the creature would interfere if we attempted to prepare the ship for complete controlled energization."

Captain Leeth remained silent. From the engine room, Kent's voice came again. "What do you think he will do when he begins to understand that it's dangerous to let us continue organizing against him?"

"He'll start to kill. I can't think of any method by which we can stop him, short of retreating into the engine room. And I believe, with Smith, that he will be able to come in there after us, given time."

"Have you any suggestions?" That was Captain Leeth, Korita hesitated. "Frankly, no. I would say we mustn't forget we are dealing with a creature who seems to be in the peasant stage of his particular cycle. To a peasant, his land and his son – or, to use a higher level of abstraction – his property and his blood are sacred. He fights blindly against encroachment. Like a plant, he attaches himself to a piece of property, and there he sinks his roots and nourishes his blood."

Korita hesitated, then said, "That is the generalized picture, gentlemen. At the moment, I have no idea how it should be applied."

Captain Leeth said, "I seriously can't see how it can help us. Will each department head consult on his private band with his lower-echelon executives? Report in five minutes if any-body has come up with a worth-while idea?"

Grosvenor, who had no assistants in his department, said, "I wonder if I could ask Mr. Korita a few questions while the departmental discussions are in progress."

Captain Leeth shook his head. "If no one else objects, you have my permission."

There were no objections, so Grosvenor said, "Mr. Korita, are you available?"

"Who is this?"

"Grosvenor."

"Oh, yes, Mr. Grosvenor. I recognize your voice now. Proceed."

"You mentioned that the peasant clings with an almost senseless tenacity to his plot of land. If this creature is in the peasant stage of one of his civilizations, could he imagine our feeling differently about our property?"

"I'm sure he could not."

"He would make his plans in the full conviction that we cannot escape him, since we are cornered aboard this ship?"

"It is a fairly safe assumption on his part. We cannot abandon the ship and survive."

Grosvenor persisted, "But we are in a cycle where any particular property means little to us? We are not blindly attached to it?"

"I still don't think I understand what you mean." Korita sounded puzzled.

"I am," said Grosvenor steadily, "pursuing your notion to its logical conclusion in this situation."

Captain Leeth interrupted. "Mr. Grosvenor, I think I am beginning to get the direction of your reasoning. Are you about to offer another plan?"

"Yes." In spite of himself, his voice trembled slightly.

Captain Leeth sounded taut. "Mr. Grosvenor," he said, "if I'm anticipating you correctly, your solution shows courage and imagination. I want you to explain it to the others in –" he hesitated, and glanced at his watch – "as soon as the five minutes are up."

After a very brief silence, Korita spoke again. "Mr. Grosvenor," he said, "your reasoning is sound. We can make such a sacrifice without suffering a spiritual collapse. It is the only solution."

A minute later, Grosvenor gave his analysis to the entire membership of the expeditionary force. When he finished, it was Smith who said in a tone that was scarcely more than a loud whisper, "Grosvenor, you've got it! It means sacrificing von Grossen and the others. It means individual sacrifice for every one of us. But you're right. Property is not sacred to us. As for von Grossen and the four with him" – his voice grew stern and hard – "I haven't had a chance to tell you about the notes I gave Morton. He didn't tell you because I suggested a possible parallel with a certain species of wasp back home on

Earth. The thought is so horrible that I think quick death will come as a release to those men."

"The wasp!" a man gasped. "You're right, Smith. The sooner they're dead the better!"

It was Captain Leeth who gave the command. "To the engine room!" he said. "We—"

A swift, excited voice clamouring into the communicators interrupted him. A long second went by before Grosvenor recognized it as belonging to Zeller, the metallurgist.

"Captain – quick! Send men and projectors down to the hold! I've found them in the air-conditioning pipe. The creature's here, and I'm holding him off with my vibrator. It's not doing him much damage, so – hurry!"

Captain Leeth snapped orders with machine-gun speed as the men swarmed toward the elevators. "All scientists and their staff proceed to the air locks. Military personnel take the freight elevators and follow me!" He went on, "We probably won't be able to corner him or kill him in the hold. But, gentlemen" – his voice became grave and determined – "we're going to get rid of this monster, and we're going to do so at any cost. We can no longer consider ourselves."

Ixtl retreated reluctantly as the man carried off his guuls. The first shrinking fear of defeat closed over his mind like the night that brooded beyond the enclosing walls of the ship. His impulse was to dash into their midst and smash them. But those ugly, glittering weapons held back the desperate urge. He retreated with a sense of disaster. He had lost the initiative. The men would discover his eggs now, and, in destroying them, would destroy his immediate chances of being reinforced by other ixtls.

His brain spun into a tightening web of purpose. From this moment, he must kill, and kill only. He was astounded that he had thought first of reproduction, with everything else secondary. Already he had wasted valuable time. To kill he must have a weapon that would smash everything. After a moment's thought, he headed for the nearest laboratory. He felt a burning urgency, unlike anything he had ever known.

As he worked, tall body and intent face bent over the gleaming metal of the mechanism, his sensitive feet grew aware of a difference in the symphony of vibrations that throbbed indiscordant melody through the ship. He paused and straightened. Then he realized what it was. The drive engines were silent. The monster ship of space had halted in its headlong acceleration and was lying quiescent in the black deeps. An indefinable sense of alarm came to Ixtl. His long, black, wirelike fingers became flashing things as he made delicate connections deftly and frantically.

Suddenly, he paused again. Stronger than before came the sensation that something was wrong, dangerously wrong. The muscles of his feet grew taut with straining. And then he knew what it was. He could no longer feel the vibrations of the men. *They had left the ship!*

Ixtl whirled from his almost completed weapon and plunged through the nearest wall. He knew his doom with a certainty that found hope only in the blackness of space.

Through deserted corridors he fled, slavering hate, a scarlet monster from ancient, ancient Glor. The gleaming walls seemed to mock him. The whole world of the great ship, which had promised so much, was now only the place where a hell of energy would break loose at any moment. With relief, he saw an air lock ahead. He flashed through the first section, the second, the third – and then he was out in space. He anticipated that the men would be watching for him to appear, so he set up a violent repulsion between his body and the ship. He had a sensation of increasing lightness as his body darted from the side of the ship out into that black night.

Behind him, the porthole lights were snuffed out and were replaced by an unearthly blue glow. The blue first flashed out from every inch of the ship's immense outer skin. The blue glow faded slowly, almost reluctantly. Long before it died away completely, the potent energy screen came on, blocking him forever from access to the ship. Some of the porthole lights came on again, flickered weakly and then slowly began to brighten. As mighty engines recovered from the devastating flare of energy, the lights already shining grew stronger, others began to flash on.

Ixtl, who had withdrawn several miles, drove himself nearer. He was careful. Now that he was out in space, they could use atomic cannon on him and destroy him without danger to themselves. He approached to within half a mile of the screen, and there, uneasy, stopped. He saw the first of the lifeboats dart out of the darkness inside the screen into an opening that yawned in the side of the big vessel. Other dark craft followed, whipping down in swift arcs, their shapes blurred against the background of space. They were vaguely visible in the light that glowed steadily again from the lighted portholes.

The opening shut, and without warning the ship vanished. One instant it was there, a vast sphere of dark metal. The next, he was staring through the space where it had been at a spiral-shaped bright splotch, a galaxy that floated beyond a gulf of a million light-years.

Time dragged drearily towards eternity. Ixtl sprawled unmoving and hopeless in the boundless night. He couldn't help thinking of the young ixtls, who now would never be born, and of the universe that was lost because of his mistakes.

Grosvenor watched the skilful fingers of the surgeon as the electrified knife cut into the fourth man's stomach. The last egg was deposited in the bottom of the tall resistance-metal vat. The eggs were round, greyish objects, one of them slightly cracked.

Several men stood by with drawn heat blasters as the crack widened. An ugly, round, scarlet head with tiny, beady eyes and a tiny slit of a mouth poked out. The head twisted on its short neck and the eyes glittered up at them with hard ferocity. With a swiftness that almost took them by surprise, the creature reared up and tried to climb out of the vat. The smooth walls defeated it. It slid back and dissolved in the flame that was poured down upon it.

Smith, licking his lips, said, "Suppose he'd got away and dissolved into the nearest wall!"

No one answered that. Grosvenor saw that the men were staring into the vat. The eggs melted reluctantly under the heat from the blasters, but finally burned with a golden light.

"Ah," said Dr. Eggert; and attention turned to him and to the body of von Grossen, over which he was bending. "His muscles are beginning to relax, and his eyes are open and alive. I imagine he knows what's going on. It was a form of paralysis induced by the egg, and fading now that the egg is no longer present. Nothing fundamentally wrong. They'll be all right shortly. What about the monster?"

Captain Leeth replied, "The men in two lifeboats claim to have seen a flash of red emerge from the main lock just as we swept the ship with uncontrolled energization. It must have been our deadly friend, because we haven't found his body. However, Pennons is going around with the camera staff taking pictures with fluorite cameras, and we'll know for certain in a few hours. Here he is now. Well, Mr. Pennons?"

The engineer strode in briskly and placed a misshapen thing of metal on one of the tables. "Nothing definite to report yet

– but I found this in the main physics laboratory. What do you make of it?"

Grosvenor was pushed forward by department heads who drew in around the table for a closer look. He frowned down at the fragile-looking object with its intricate network of wires. There were three distinct tubes that might have been muzzles running into and through three small, round balls that shone with a queer, silvery light. The light penetrated the table, making it as transparent as glassite. And, strangest of all, the balls absorbed heat like a thermal sponge. Grosvenor reached out towards the nearest ball, and felt his hands stiffen as the heat was drawn from them. He drew back quickly.

Pennons nodded. And Smith carried on the thought. "It would appear that the creature was working on it when he suspected that something was amiss. He must have realized the truth, for he left the ship. That seems to discount your theory, Korita. You said that, as a true peasant, he couldn't even imagine what we were going to do."

The Japanese archaeologist smiled faintly through the fatigue that paled his face. "Mr. Smith," he said politely, "there is no question but that this one did imagine it. The probable answer is that the peasant category amounted to an analogy. The red monster was, by all odds, the most superior peasant we have yet encountered."

Pennons groaned. "I wish we had a few peasant limitations. Do you know that it will take us three months at least to get this ship properly repaired after those three minutes of uncontrolled energization? For a time I was afraid that. . . ." His voice trailed off doubtfully.

Captain Leeth said with a grim smile, "I'll finish that sentence for you, Mr. Pennons. You were afraid the ship would be completely destroyed. I think that most of us realized the risk we were taking when we adopted Mr. Grosvenor's final plan. We knew that our lifeboats could be given only partial anti-acceleration. So we'd have been stranded here a quarter of a million light-years from home."

A man said, "I wonder whether, if the scarlet beast had actually taken over this ship, it would have gotten away with its obvious intent to take over the galaxy. After all, man is pretty well established in it – and pretty stubborn, too."

Smith shook his head. "It dominated once, and it could dominate again. You assume far too readily that man is a paragon of justice, forgetting, apparently, that he has a long and savage history. He has killed other animals not only for meat but for pleasure; he has enslaved his neighbours, murdered his opponents, and obtained the most unholy sadistical joy from the agony of others. It is not impossible that we shall, in the course of our travels, meet other intelligent creatures far more worthy than man to rule the universe."

"By heaven!" said a man, "no dangerous-looking creature should even be allowed aboard this ship again. My nerves are all shot; and I'm not so good a man as I was when I first came aboard the *Beagle*."

"You speak for us all!" came the voice of Acting Director Kent over the communicator.

CHAPTER TWENTY-TWO

SOMEBODY whispered in Grosvenor's ear, so softly that he could not catch the words. The whisper was followed by a trilling sound, as gentle as the whisper and equally meaningless.

Involuntarily, Grosvenor looked around.

He was in the film room of his own department, and there was nobody in sight. He walked uncertainly to the door that led to the auditorium door. But no one was there either.

He came back to his workbench, frowning, wondering if someone had pointed an encephalo-adjuster at him. It was the only comparison he could think of, for he had seemed to hear a sound.

After a moment, that explanation struck him as improbable. Adjusters were effective at short ranges only. More important, his department was shielded against most vibrations. Besides, he was only too familiar with the mental process involved in the illusion he had experienced. That made it impossible for him to dismiss the incident.

As a precaution, he explored all five of his rooms and examined the adjusters in his technique room. They were as they ought to be, properly stored away. In silence, Grosvenor returned to the film room and resumed his study of the hypnotic light-pattern variations, which he had developed from the images that the Riim had used against the ship.

Terror struck his mind like a blow. Grosvenor cringed. And

then there was the whisper again, as soft as before, yet somehow angry now, and unthinkably hostile.

Amazed, Grosvenor straightened. It *must* be an encephalo-adjuster. Somebody was stimulating his mind from a distance with a machine so powerful that the protective shield of his room was penetrated.

With a frown, he considered who it might be, and finally called up the psychology department as the most likely offender. Siedel answered personally, and Grosvenor started to explain what had happened. He was cut off.

"I was just about to contact you," said Siedel. "I thought you might be responsible."

"You mean everybody's affected?" Grosvenor spoke slowly, trying to imagine the implications.

"I'm surprised you got any of it at all in that specially constructed department of yours," said Siedel. "I've been receiving complaints for more than twenty minutes, and some of my instruments were affected several minutes before that."

"Which instruments?"

"Brain-wave detector, nerve-impulse register, and the more sensitive electrical detectors." He broke off. "Kent is going to call a meeting in the control room. I'll see you there."

Grosvenor did not let him go so quickly. "Has there been any discussion as yet?" he asked.

"We-e-l-ll, we're all making an assumption."

"What's that?" he asked quickly.

"We're about to enter the great galaxy M-33. We're assuming this comes from there."

Grosvenor laughed grimly. "It's a reasonable hypothesis. I'll think about it, and see you in a few minutes."

"Be prepared for a shock when you first go out into the corridor. The pressure out here is continuous. Sounds, light flashes, dreams, emotional turmoil – we're really getting a dose of stimulation."

Grosvenor nodded, and broke the connection. By the time he had put away his films, Kent's announcement of the meeting was coming over the communicator. A minute later, as he opened his outer door, he realized what Siedel had meant.

He paused as the barrage excitations instantly began to affect his brain. Then, uneasily, he headed for the control room.

He sat presently with the others; and the night whispered, the immense night of space that pressed against the hurtling ship. Capricious and deadly, it beckoned and it warned. It trilled with frenzied delight, then hissed with savage frustration. It muttered in fear and growled in hunger. It died, revelling in agony, and burgeoned again into ecstatic life. Yet always and insidiously it threatened.

"This is an opinion," said somebody behind Grosvenor. "The ship ought to go home."

Grosvenor, unable to identify the voice, glanced around to see who had spoken. Whoever it was said nothing more. Facing forward again, Grosvenor saw that Acting Director Kent had not turned from the eyepiece of the telescope through which he was peering. Either he considered the remark had been unworthy of reply, or else he hadn't heard it. Nor did anyone comment.

As the silence continued, Grosvenor manipulated the communicator arm of his chair, and presently he was seeing a slightly burred image of what Kent and Lester were gazing at directly through the telescope. Slowly, then, he forgot the spectators and concentrated on the night scene shown by the plate. They were near the outer environs of an entire galactic system; yet the nearest stars were still so far away that the telescope could barely resolve the myriad needle points of brilliance that made up the spiral nebula, M-33, in Andromeda, their destination.

Grosvenor glanced up just as Lester turned from the telescope. The astronomer said, "What is happening seems incredible. Vibrations we can actually sense, spilling out from a galaxy of billions of suns." He paused, then said, "Director, it seems to me this is not a problem for an astronomer."

Kent released his own eyepiece and said, "Anything that embraces an entire galaxy comes under the category of astronomical phenomena. Or would you care to name the science that is involved?"

Lester hesitated, then replied slowly. "The scale of magnitude is fantastic. I don't think we should assume galactic scope yet. This barrage may be coming on a beam which is concentrated on our ship."

Kent turned toward the men who sat in tiers of cushioned seats facing the broad and colourful control panel. He said, "Has anyone a suggestion or a thought?"

Grosvenor glanced around, hoping that the unidentified man who had spoken earlier would explain himself. But whoever it was remained silent.

Undeniably, the men no longer felt so free to speak up as they had under the leadership of Morton. One way or another, Kent had made it rather plain that he deemed the opinions of those other than department heads impertinent. It was also evident that he personally declined to regard Nexialism as a legitimate department. For several months, he and Grosvenor had been polite to each other on a basis of minimum contact. During that time, the Acting Director had, by way of consolidating his position, introduced several motions in the council giving his office more authority in certain activities, the ostensible reason being to avoid duplication of effort.

The importance to this ship's morale of encouraging individual initiative, even at the cost of some efficiency, was a point that could have been demonstrated only to another Nexialist, Grosvenor felt sure. He had not bothered to protest. And so a few more slight restrictions had been imposed on the already dangerously regimented and confined shipload of human beings.

From the rear of the control room, Smith was the first to answer Kent's request for suggestions. The angular and bony biologist said dryly, "I notice Mr. Grosvenor is twisting about in his chair. Can it be that he is politely waiting for the older men to have their say? Mr. Grosvenor what's on your mind?"

Grosvenor waited until the faint wave of laughter – in which Kent did not join in – had died away. Then he said, "A few minutes ago, someone suggested that we turn around and go home. I'd like whoever did so to give his reasons."

There was no reply. Grosvenor saw that Kent was frowning. It did seem strange that there was anyone aboard unwilling to acknowledge an opinion, however briefly held, however quickly discarded. Other men were glancing about in astonishment.

It was the sad-faced Smith who said finally, "When was that statement uttered? I don't recall hearing it."

"Nor I!" echoed half a dozen voices.

Kent's eyes were gleaming. It seemed to Grosvenor that he moved into the discussion like a man anticipating personal victory. He said, "Let me get this straight. There was such a statement, or there wasn't. Who else heard it? Raise hands."

Not a single hand went up. Kent's voice was subtly malicious as he said, "Mr. Grosvenor, what exactly did you hear?"

Grosvenor said slowly, "As I remember them, the words were: 'This is an opinion. The ship should go home.' " He paused. When there was no comment, he went on. "It seems clear that the words themselves came as the result of stimulation of the auditory centres of my brain. Something out there feels strongly that it wants us to go home, and I sensed it." He shrugged. "I do not, of course, offer this as a positive analysis."

Kent said stiffly, "The rest of us, Mr. Grosvenor, are still trying to understand why you should have heard this request, and no one else."

Once again Grosvenor ignored the tone in which the words were spoken, as he replied earnestly, "I've been considering that for the past few seconds. I can't help but remember that during the Riim incident my brain was subjected to sustained stimulation. It is possible that I am now more sensitive to such communication." It struck him that his special sensitivity could also explain why he had been able to receive the whisper in his shielded rooms.

Grosvenor was not surprised at Kent's slight frown. The chemist had shown that he preferred not to think about the bird people and what they had done to the minds of the members of the expedition. Now Kent said acidly, "I had the privilege of listening to a transcription of your account of the episode. If I recall correctly, you stated that the reason for your victory was that these Riim beings did not realize that it was difficult for a member of one race to control the nervous system of a member of an alien life form. How then do you explain that whatever is out there" – he waved in the direction the ship was heading – "reached into your mind and stimulated with pinpoint accuracy those areas in your brain that produced exactly the warning words you have just repeated to us?"

It seemed to Grosvenor that Kent's tone, his choice of words, and his attitude of satisfaction all seemed unpleasantly personal. Grosvenor said pointedly, "Director, whoever stimulated my brain could be aware of the problem presented by an alien nervous system. We don't have to assume that it can speak our language. Besides, its solution of the problem was a partial one, because I'm the only person who responded to the stimulation. My feeling is that we should not at the moment discuss how I received it, but why, and what are we going to do about it."

Chief geologist McCann cleared his throat and said, "Grosvenor is right. I think, gentlemen, we had better face the fact that we have entered somebody else's stamping ground. And it's *some* somebody!"

The Acting Director bit his lip, seemed about to speak, then hesitated. In the end, he said, "I think we should be careful about letting ourselves believe that we have evidence enough to draw a conclusion. But I do feel that we should act as if we are confronted by an intelligence larger than man – larger than life as we know it."

There was silence in the control room. Grosvenor noticed that men were unconsciously bracing themselves. Their lips tightened and their eyes narrowed. He saw that others also had observed the reaction.

Kellie, the sociologist, said softly, "I am glad – ah – to see that no one shows any sign of wanting to turn back. That is all to the good. As servants of our government and our race, it is our duty to investigate the potentialities of a new galaxy, particularly now that its dominating life form knows *we* exist. Please note that I am adopting Director Kent's suggestion and talking as if we actually are dealing with a sentient being. Its ability to stimulate more or less directly the mind of even one person aboard indicates that it has definitely observed us and therefore knows a great deal about us. We cannot permit that type of knowledge to be one-sided."

Kent was at ease again, as he said, "Mr. Kellie, what do you think of the environment we're heading into?"

The balding sociologist adjusted his pince-nez. "That – ah – is a large one, Director. But this whispering could be the equivalent of criss-crossing radio waves that blanket our own galaxy. They – ah – may be simply the outward signs, like coming out of a wilderness into an area of cultivation."

Kellie paused. When no one commented, he went on. "Remember, man also has left his imperishable imprint on his own galaxy. In the process of rejuvenating dead suns, he has lighted fires in the form of novae that will be seen a dozen galaxies away. Planets have been led from their orbits. Dead worlds have come alive with verdure. Oceans now swirl where deserts lay lifeless under suns hotter than Sol. And even our presence here in this great ship is an emanation of man's power, reaching out farther than these whispers around us have ever been able to go."

Gourlay, of the communications department, said, "Man's imprints are scarcely permanent in the cosmic sense. I don't see how you can speak of them in the same breath with this. These pulsations are live. They're thought forms so strong, so all-pervading, that the whole of space whispers at us. This is no tentacled pussy, no scarlet monstrosity, no fellah race confined to one system. It could be an inconceivable totality of minds speaking to each other across the miles and the years of their space time. This is the civilization of the second galaxy; and if a spokesman for it has now warned us—" Gourlay broke off with a gasp, and flung up an arm as if to defend himself.

He was not the only one who did just that. All over the room, men crouched or slumped in their seats – as Director Kent, in a single spasmodic movement, snatched his vibrator and fired it at his audience. It was not until Grosvenor had instinctively ducked that he saw that the tracer beam from the weapon pointed over his head, and not at it.

Behind him, there was a thunderous howl of agony, and then a crash that shook the floor.

Grosvenor whirled with the others, and stared with a sense of unreality at the thirty-foot armoured beast that lay squirming on the floor a dozen feet behind the last row of seats. The next instant, a red-eyed replica of the first beast materialized in mid-air and landed with a thud ten feet away. A third devil-faced monster appeared, slid off the second, rolled over and over – and got up, roaring.

Seconds later, there were a dozen of the things.

Grosvenor drew his own vibrator and discharged it. The bestial roaring redoubled in intensity. Metal-hard scales scraped metal wall and metal floors. Steely claws rattled, and heavy feet stamped.

All around Grosvenor now, men were firing their vibrators. And still more beasts materialized. Grosvenor turned and scrambled over two rows of seats, then leaped to the lowest platform of the instrument board. The Acting Director ceased firing as Grosvenor climbed up to his level, and yelled angrily, "Where the hell do you think you're going, you yellow dog?"

His vibrator swung around – and Grosvenor knocked him down, mercilessly kicking the weapon out of his hand. He was furious, but said nothing. As he leaped to the next platform, he saw Kent crawling after the vibrator. There was no doubt in Grosvenor's mind that the chemist would fire at him. It was with a gasp of relief that he reached the switch that activated the great multiple-energy screen of the ship, pulled it all the way over, and flung himself to the floor – just in time. The tracer beam of Kent's vibrator impinged on the metal of the control panel where Grosvenor's head had been. Then the beam snapped off. Kent climbed to his feet and shouted above the uproar, "I didn't realize what you were trying to do."

As an apology, it left Grosvenor cold. The Acting Director had evidently believed that he could justify his murderous action on the grounds that Grosvenor was running from the battle. Grosvenor brushed by the chemist, too angry to talk. For months he had tolerated Kent, but now he felt that the man's behaviour proved him unfit to be director. In the critical weeks ahead, his personal tensions might act as a trigger mechanism that could destroy the ship.

As Grosvenor came down to the lowest platform, he again added the energy from his vibrator to that of the other men's. From the corner of his eye, he saw that three men were wrestling a heat projector into position. By the time the projector's intolerable flame poured forth, the beasts were unconscious from the molecular energy, and it was not difficult to kill them.

The danger past, Grosvenor had time to realize that these monstrous things had been transported alive across light-centuries. It was like a dream, too fantastic to have happened at all.

But the odour of burning flesh was real enough. And so was the bluish-grey beast blood that slimed the floor. The final evidence was the dozen or so armoured and scaly carcasses that were sprawled about the room.

CHAPTER TWENTY-THREE

WHEN Grosvenor saw Kent again a few minutes later, the Acting Director was coolly and efficiently giving orders into a communicator. Cranes floated in and began to remove bodies. Communicators buzzed with a criss-cross of messages. Swiftly, the whole picture clarified.

The creatures had been precipitated only into the control room. The ship's radar registered no material object such as an enemy ship. The distance to the nearest star in any direction was a thousand light-years. All over the room, sweating men cursed as those scanty facts penetrated.

"Ten light-centuries!" Selenski, the chief pilot, said. "Why, we can't even transmit messages that far without relays."

Captain Leeth came hurrying in. He talked briefly to several scientists, then called a council of war. The commander began the discussion.

"I need hardly emphasize the hazard confronting us. We are one ship against what seems to be a hostile galactic civilization. For the moment we are safe behind our energy screen. The nature of the menace requires us to set ourselves limited, though not too limited, objectives. We must discover why we are being warned away. We must ascertain the nature of the danger and measure the intelligence behind it. I see our chief biologist is still examining our late adversaries. Mr. Smith, what kind of beasts are they?"

Smith turned from the monster he had been studying. He said slowly, "Earth could have produced something like their type during the dinosaur age. Judging by the minute size of what appears to be the brainpan, the intelligence must have been extremely low."

Kent said, "Mr. Gourlay tells me the beasts could have been precipitated through hyperspace. Perhaps we could ask him to develop on that."

Captain Leeth said, "Mr. Gourlay, you have the floor."

The communications expert said in his familiar drawl, "It's only a theory, and fairly recent at that, but it likens the universe to an expanded balloon. When you prick the skin, the balloon instantly starts to deflate, and simultaneously begins to repair the break. Now, oddly enough, when an object penetrates the outer skin of the balloon, it does not necessarily come back to the same point in space. Presumably, if one knew some method of controlling the phenomenon, he might use it as a form of teleportation. If all this sounds fanciful, remember that what has actually happened seems equally so."

Kent said acidly, "It's hard to believe that anyone is that much smarter than we are. There must be simple solutions to the problems of hyperspace, which human scientists have missed. Maybe we'll learn something." He paused, then said, "Korita, you've been singularly silent. How about telling us what we're up against?"

The archaeologist stood up and spread his hands in a gesture of bewilderment. "I can't even offer a guess. We shall have to learn somewhat more about the motivation behind the attack before we can make comparisons on the basis of cyclic history. For example, if the purpose was to seize the ship, then to assail us as they did was a mistake. If the intent was merely to scare us, the attack was a howling success."

There was a flurry of laughter as Korita sat down. But Grosvenor noticed that the expression on Captain Leeth's face remained solemn and thoughtful.

"As to motivation," the captain said slowly, "one unpleasant possibility has occurred to me that we should be prepared to face. It fits the evidence to date. It is this: Supposing this potent intelligence, or whatever it is, would like to know where we came from?"

He paused, and from the way feet shifted and men stirred in their seats, it was clear that his words had struck a responsive chord. The officer went on. "Let's look at it from – his – point of view. Here is a ship approaching. In the general direction from which it is coming, within ten million light-years, are a considerable number of galaxies, star clusters, and nebulae. Which is us?"

There was silence in the room. The commander turned to Kent. "Director, if it's all right with you, I suggest we examine some of the planetary systems of this galaxy."

Kent said, "I have no objection. But now, unless someone else. . . ."

Grosvenor raised his hand.

Kent continued, "I declare the meeting – "

Grosvenor stood up, and said loudly, "Mr. Kent!"

" – adjourned!" said Kent.

The men remained sitting. Kent hesitated, and then said lamely, "I beg your pardon, Mr. Grosvenor, you have the floor."

Grosvenor said firmly, "It is hard to believe that this being will be capable of refined interpretation of our symbols, but I think we should destroy our star maps."

"I was about to suggest the same thing," said von Grossen excitedly. "Continue, Grosvenor."

There was a chorus of approval, Grosvenor went on. "We are taking action in the belief that our main screen can protect us. Actually, we have no choice but to carry on as if that were true. But when we finally land, we might be advised to have available some large encephalo-adjusters. We could use them to create confusing brain waves, and so prevent any further mind reading."

Once more, the audience made enough noise to show that they favoured the suggestion.

Kent said in a flat voice, "Anything else, Mr. Grosvenor?"

"A general comment only," said Grosvenor. "The department heads might make a survey of material they control with a view to destroying any that might endanger our race if the *Beagle* were captured."

He sat down amid a chilling silence.

As time went on, it seemed clear that the inimical intelligence was deliberately refraining from further action, or else that the screen was doing an effective job. No further incident occurred.

Lonely and remote were the suns at this distant rim of the galaxy. The first sun grew big out of space, a ball of light and heat that burned furiously into the great night. Lester and his staff located five planets close enough to the parent body to be worth investigating. One of the five – all were visited – was habitable, a world of mists and jungles and giant beasts. The ship left it after flying low over an inland sea and across a great continent of marsh growth. There was no evidence of civilization of any kind, much less the stupendous one whose existence they had reason to suspect.

The *Space Beagle* sped three hundred light-years, and came to a small sun with two planets crowding up close to its cherry-red warmth. One of the two planets was habitable, and it also was a world of mists and jungles and saurianlike beasts. They left it, unexplored, after darting down low over a marshy sea and a land choked with riotous growth.

There were more stars now. They pinpointed the blackness of the next hundred and fifty light-years. A large blue-white sun, with a retinue of at least twenty planets, attracted Kent's eye; and the swift ship flashed towards it. The seven planets nearest the sun were burning hells, without hope of supporting life. The ship spiralled past three close-together planets that were habitable, and then sped off to interstellar vastness without investigating the others.

Behind them, three steamy jungle planets whirled in their orbits around the hot sun that had spawned them. And, on board, Kent called a meeting of the heads of departments and their chief assistants.

He began the discussion without preamble. He said, "Personally, I don't think the evidence is very significant as yet. But Lester has urgently requested me to call you." He shrugged. "Perhaps we'll learn something."

He paused, and Grosvenor, watching him, was puzzled by a faint aura of satisfaction that radiated from the little man. He thought, What is he up to? It seemed odd that the Acting Director had taken the trouble to disclaim in advance all credit for any good results that might come from the meeting.

Kent was speaking again, and his tone was friendly. "Gunlie, will you come up here and explain yourself?"

The astronomer climbed to the lower platform. He was a man as tall and thin as Smith. He had eyes of royal blue set in an expressionless face. But there was a hint of emotion in his voice as he spoke.

"Gentlemen, the three habitable planets of that last system were identical triplets, and it was an artificially induced state. I don't know how many of you are familiar with the current theory regarding the formation of planetary systems. Those of you who are not will perhaps take my word for it that the distribution in mass in the system we have just visited is dynamically impossible. I can say definitely that two of the three habitable planets of that sun were moved into their present position. In my opinion we should go back and investigate. Somebody seems to be deliberately creating primeval planets; for what reason I don't pretend to guess."

He stopped and glared belligerently at Kent. The chemist came forward, a faint smile on his face. He said, "Gunlie came to me and asked me to order that we return to one of those jungle planets. In view of his feeling on the matter, I now call for a discussion, and a vote."

So that was it. Grosvenor sighed, not exactly with admiration for Kent, but at least with appreciation. The Acting Director had made no attempt to build up a case for his opposition. It was quite possible that he did not really oppose the astronomer's plan. But by calling a meeting when his own views would be overruled, he was proving that he regarded himself as subject to democratic procedure. It was an adroit if somewhat demagogic means of maintaining the good will of his supporters.

Actually, there were valid objections to Lester's request. It was hard to believe that Kent knew of them, for that would mean he was deliberately ignoring possible danger for the ship. He decided to give Kent the benefit of the doubt, and waited patiently while several scientists asked the astronomer questions of minor importance. When those had been answered, when it seemed clear that the discussion was over except for himself, Grosvenor stood up and said, "I should like to argue in favour of Mr. Kent's viewpoint in this matter."

Kent replied coldly, "Really, Mr. Grosvenor, the attitude of the group seems to be indicated by the briefness of the discussion so far, and taking up any more time — "

At that point, he stopped. The real meaning of Grosvenor's words must finally have penetrated. A thunderstruck expression came into his face. He made an uncertain gesture toward the others, as if appealing for help. When no one spoke, he dropped his arm to his side and muttered, "Mr. Grosvenor, you have the floor."

Grosvenor said firmly, "Mr. Kent is right: It is too soon. So far we have visited three planetary systems. It should be not less than thirty, taken at random. This is the minimum number, with respect to the order of magnitude of our search, that could have any conclusive significance. I shall be glad to turn over my mathematics to the mathematics department for corroboration. Moreover, in landing we would have to come out from inside our protective energy screen. We would have to be prepared to resist a surprise attack by an intelligence that can use the instantaneous medium of hyperspace to deliver his forces. I have a mental picture of a billion tons of matter projected down upon us as we sit helpless on some planet. Gentlemen, as I see it, there is a good month or two of detailed preparation ahead of us. During that time, naturally, we should visit as many suns as we can. If their habitable planets also are exclusively – or even predominantly – the primeval type, then we shall have a sound basis for Mr. Lester's idea that it is an artificial state." Grosvenor paused, then finished. "Mr. Kent, have I expressed what you had in mind?"

Kent had full control of himself again. "Almost precisely, Mr. Grosvenor." He glanced about him. "Unless there are any further comments, I move that we vote on Gunlie's proposal."

The astronomer stood up. "I withdraw it," he said, "I confess I hadn't considered some of the points against an early landing." He sat down.

Kent hesitated, then said, "If someone cares to take up Gunlie's proposal. . . . " When, after several seconds, no one had spoken, Kent continued confidently. "I want each department head to prepare for me a detailed account of what he can contribute to the success of the landing we must eventually make. That's all, gentlemen."

In the corridor outside the control room, Grosvenor felt a hand on his arm. He turned and recognized McCann, the chief geologist. McCann said, "We've been so busy doing repair work this last few months that I haven't had a chance to invite you to come to my department. I anticipate that when we finally make a landing, the equipment of the geology department will be used for purposes for which it was not precisely intended. A Nexialist could come in very handy."

Grosvenor considered that, then nodded his acceptance. "I'll be there tomorrow morning. I want to prepare my recommendations for the Acting Director."

McCann looked at him quickly, hesitated, and then said, "You don't think he'll be interested, do you?"

So others had noticed Kent's dislike of him. Grosvenor said slowly, "Yes, because he won't have to give individual credit."

McCann nodded, "Well, good luck to you, my boy."

He was turning away when Grosvenor stopped him. Grosvenor said, "What, in your opinion, is the basis for Kent's popularity as a leader?"

McCann hesitated, and seemed to be deliberating. Finally he said, "He's human. He has likes and dislikes. He gets excited about things. He has a bad temper. He makes mistakes, and tries to pretend that he didn't. He's desperately anxious to be director. When the ship gets back to Earth, the publicity will flow around the executive officer. There's something of Kent in all of us. He's – well – he's a human being."

"I notice," said Grosvenor, "you didn't say anything about his qualifications for the job."

"It's not a vital position, generally speaking. He can get advice from experts on anything he wants to know." McCann pursed his lips. "It's hard to put Kent's appeal into words, but I think that scientists are constantly on the defensive about their alleged unfeeling intellectualism. So they like to have someone fronting for them who is emotional but whose scientific qualifications cannot be questioned."

Grosvenor shook his head. "I disagree with you about the director's job not being vital. It all depends on the individual as to how he exercises the very considerable authority involved."

McCann studied him shrewdly. He said finally, "Strictly logical men like you have always had a hard time understanding the mass appeal of the Kents. They haven't much chance against his type, politically."

Grosvenor smiled grimly. "It's not their devotion to the scientific method that defeats the technologists. It's their integrity. The average trained man often understands the tactics that are used against him better than the person who uses them, but he cannot bring himself to retaliate in kind without feeling tarnished."

McCann frowned. "That's too pat. Do you mean you have no such qualms?"

Grosvenor was silent.

McCann persisted. "Suppose you decided that Kent ought to be ousted, what would you do?"

"At the moment my thoughts are quite constitutional," Grosvenor said carefully.

Grosvenor was surprised to see that there was relief in McCann's expression. The older man gripped his arm in a friendly gesture. "I'm glad to hear your intentions are legal," he said earnestly. "Ever since that lecture you gave, I've realized what hasn't yet dawned on anyone else – that you are potentially the most dangerous man on this ship. The integrated knowledge you have in your mind, applied with determination and purpose, could be more disastrous than any outside attack."

After a moment of astonishment, Grosvenor shook his head. "That is an overstatement," he said. "One man is too easy to kill."

"I notice," said McCann, "you don't deny possessing the knowledge."

Grosvenor held out his hand in farewell. "Thanks for your high opinion of me. Although considerably exaggerated, it's psychologically uplifting."

CHAPTER TWENTY-FOUR

The thirty-first star they visited was Sol-size, Sol-type. Of its three planets, one followed an orbit of eighty million miles. Like all the other habitable worlds they had seen, it was a steaming jungle and primeval sea.

The *Space Beagle* settled through its gaseous envelope of air and water vapour, and began to fly along at a low level, a great alien ball of metal in a fantastic land.

In the geology laboratory, Grosvenor watched a bank of instruments that metred the nature of the terrain below. It was a complex job which demanded the closest attention, since much of the interpretation of the data called for the associative processes of a highly trained mind. The constant stream of reflexions of the ultrasonic and short-wave signals being sent out had to be channelled into the proper computing devices at precisely the right time for comparative analysis. To the standard techniques with which McCann was familiar, Grosvenor had added certain refinements in accordance with Nexial principles, and an amazingly complete picture of the planet's outer crust was being tabulated.

For an hour Grosvenor sat there, deeply involved in his educated guesswork. The facts emerging varied widely in detail, but consideration of molecular structure, arrangement and distribution of the different elements indicated a certain geologic sameness: mud, sandstone, clay, granite, organic debris – probably coal deposits – silicates in the form of sand overlying rock, water —

Several needles on the dials before him swung over sharply and held steady. Their reaction showed indirectly the presence of metallic iron in large quantities with traces of carbon, molybdenum —

Steel! Grosvenor snatched at a lever which precipitated a series of events. A bell started to ring. McCann came running. The ship stopped. A few feet from Grosvenor, McCann began to talk to Acting Director Kent.

"Yes, Director," he was saying, "steel, not just iron ore." He did not mention Grosvenor by name, but went on, "We set our instruments at a hundred feet maximum. This could be a city buried – or hidden – in a jungle mud."

Kent said matter-of-factly, "We'll know in a few days."

Cautiously, the ship was kept well above the surface, and the necessary equipment was lowered through a temporary gap in its energy screen. Giant shovels, cranes, mobile conveyors were set up, along with supplementary devices. So carefully had everything been rehearsed that thirty minutes after the ship started to disgorge material it was again heading out into space.

The entire excavating job was done by remote control. Trained men watched the scene in communicator plates and operated the machines on the ground. In four days, the highly integrated mass of implements had dug a hole two hundred and fifty feet deep by four hundred feet wide and eight hundred feet long. What was exposed then was not so much a city as the incredible rubble of what had been a city.

The buildings looked as if they had crumpled under the weight of a burden too great for them to carry. The street level was at the full two-hundred-and-fifty-foot depth, and there they began to turn up bones. Cease-digging orders were given, and several lifeboats made their way down through the muggy atmosphere. Grosvenor went along with McCann, and presently he was standing with several other scientists beside what was left of one of the skeletons.

"Rather badly crushed," said Smith. "But I think I can piece it together."

His trained fingers arranged bones into a rough design. "Four-legged," he said. He brought a fluoroscopic device to bear on one of the limbs. He said presently, "This one seems to have been dead about twenty-five years."

Grosvenor turned away. The shattered relics that lay around might hold the secret of the fundamental physical character of a vanished race. But it was unlikely that the skeletons held any clue to the identity of the unimaginably merciless beings who had murdered them. These were the pitiful victims, not the arrogant and deadly destroyers.

He made his way gingerly to where McCann was examining soil dug up from the street itself. The geologist said, "I think we'll be justified in taking a stratigraphical survey from here on down several hundred feet."

At his word, a drill crew sprang into action. During the next hour, as the machine tore its way through rock and clay, Grosvenor was kept busy. A steady trickle of soil samplings passed under his eyes. Occasionally, he put a bit of rock or earth through a chemical-breakdown process. By the time the lifeboats headed back to the parent ship, McCann was in a position to give a fairly accurate generalized report to Kent. Grosvenor stayed out of the receptive field of the communicator plate while McCann gave the report.

"Director, you will recall that I was particularly asked to check if this could be an artificial jungle plant. It seems to be. The strata below the mud appears to be that of an older, less primitive planet. It is hard to believe that a layer of jungle could have been skimmed from some distant planet and super-imposed on this one, but the evidence points in that direction."

Kent said, "What about the city itself? How was it destroyed?"

"We have made a few of the calculations, and we can say cautiously that the enormous weight of rock and soil and water could have done all the damage we saw."

"Have you found any evidence to indicate how long ago this catastrophe took place?"

"We have a little geomorphological data. In several places we examined, the new surface has formed depressions in the old one, indicating that the extra weight is forcing down weaker areas below. By identifying the type of land fault that would sag under such circumstances, we have some figures that we intend to feed into a computing machine. A competent mathematician" – he meant Grosvenor – "has roughly estimated that the pressure of the weight was first applied not more than a hundred years ago. Since geology deals in events that require thousands and millions of years to mature, all the machine can do is to check the manual calculation. It cannot give us a closer estimate."

There was a pause, and then Kent said formally, "Thank you. I feel that you and your staff have done a good job. One more question: In your investigation, did you find anything that might be a clue to the nature of the intelligence that could bring about such a cataclysmic destruction?"

"Speaking only for myself, without having consulted with my assistants – no!"

It was, Grosvenor reflected, just as well that McCann had so carefully limited his denial. For the geologist, the investigation of this planet was the beginning of the search for the enemy. For himself, it had proved to be the final link in a chain of discovery and reasoning that had started when they first began to hear the strange murmurings in space.

He knew the identity of the most monstrous alien intelligence conceivable. He could guess its terrible purpose. He had carefully analysed what must be done.

His problem was no longer: What is the danger? He had reached the stage where he needed, above all, to put over his solution without compromise. Unfortunately, men who had knowledge of only one or two sciences might not be able, or even willing, to comprehend the potentialities of the deadliest danger that had ever confronted all the life of the entire intergalactic universe. The solution itself might become the centre of a violent controversy.

Accordingly Grosvenor saw the problem as both political and scientific. He analysed, with a sharp awareness of the possible nature of the forthcoming struggle, that his tactics must be carefully thought out and carried through with the utmost determination.

It was too soon to decide how far he would have to go. But it seemed to him that he dared not place any limitation upon his actions. He would do what was necessary.

CHAPTER TWENTY-FIVE

WHEN he was ready to act, Grosvenor wrote a letter to Kent:

Acting Director
Administrative Offices
Expeditionary Ship *Space Beagle*
DEAR MR. KENT:

I have an important communication to make to all heads of departments. The communication relates to the alien intelligence of this galaxy, about the nature of which I have accumulated evidence adequate for action on the largest scale.

Would you please call a special meeting, so that I may present my suggested solution?

He signed it, "Sincerely yours, Elliott Grosvenor," and wondered if Kent would notice that he was offering a solution, but not supporting evidence. While he waited for a reply, he quietly moved the rest of his personal belongings from his cabin to the Nexial department. It was the last act in a defence plan that included the possibility of a siege.

The answer arrived the following morning.

DEAR MR. GROSVENOR:

I have communicated to Mr. Kent the gist of your memo of yesterday afternoon. He suggests that you make a report on the enclosed form, A – 16 – 4, and expressed surprise that you had not done so as a matter of course.

We are in receipt of other evidence and theory on this

matter. Yours will be given careful consideration along with the rest.

Will you please submit the form, properly filled out, as soon as possible.

Yours truly
JOHN FOHRAN
For Mr. Kent.

Grosvenor read the letter grimly. He did not doubt that Kent had made sharp remarks to the secretary about the only Nexialist on the ship. Even as it was, Kent had probably restrained his language. The turmoil, the reservoir of hatred that was in the man, was still suppressed. If Korita was right, it would come out in a crisis. This was the "winter" period of man's present civilization, and entire cultures had been torn to pieces by the vaulting egotism of individuals.

Although he had not intended to offer factual information, Grosvenor decided to fill in the form the secretary had sent him. However, he only listed the evidence. He did not interpret it, nor did he offer his solution. Under the heading, "Recommendations," he wrote, "The conclusion will be instantly obvious to any qualified person."

The titanic fact was that every item of evidence he had presented was known to one or another of the spacious science departments aboard the *Space Beagle.* The accumulated data had probably been on Kent's desk for weeks.

Grosvenor delivered the form in person. He didn't expect a prompt reply, but he remained in his department. He even had his meals sent up. Two twenty-hour periods went by, and then a note arrived from Kent.

DEAR MR. GROSVENOR

In glancing over Form A – 16 – 4, which you have submitted for consideration of the council, I notice that you have failed to specify your recommendations. Since we have received other recommendations on this matter, and intend to combine the best features of each in to comprehensive plan, we would appreciate receiving from you a detailed recommendation.

Will you please give this your prompt attention?

It was signed, "Gregory Kent, Acting Director". Grosvenor took Kent's personal signature to the letter to mean that he had scored a direct hit, and that the main action was about to begin.

He doctored himself with drugs that would produce symptoms indistinguishable from influenza. While he waited for his body to react, he wrote another note to Kent, this time to the effect that he was too sick to prepare the recommendations – "which are necessarily long, since they would have to include a considerable body of interpretive reasoning based on the known facts of many sciences. Still, it might be wise to start immediately on the preliminary propaganda in order to accustom the members of the expedition to the notion of spending an extra five years in space."

As soon as he had slipped the letter into the mail chute, he called Dr. Eggert's office. His timing, as it turned out, was sharper than he had anticipated. In ten minutes Dr. Eggert came in and put down his bag.

As he straightened, footsteps sounded in the corridor. A moment later, Kent and two husky chemistry technicians entered.

Dr. Eggert glanced round casually, and nodded cheerfully as he recognized the chemist chief. "Hello, Greg," he said in his deep voice. Having acknowledged the other's presence, he gave his full attention to Grosvenor. "Well," he said finally, "looks like we've got a bug here, my friend. It's amazing. No matter how much protection we give on these landings, some virus or bacteria break through occasionally. I'll have you taken down to the isolation ward."

"I'd rather stay up here."

Dr. Eggert frowned, then shrugged. "In your case, it's feasible." He packed his instruments. "I'll have an attendant up right away to look after you. We don't take any chances with strange bugs."

There was a grunt from Kent. Grosvenor who had glanced occasionally at the Acting Director with simulated puzzlement, looked up questioningly. Kent said in an annoyed tone, "What seems to be the trouble, Doctor?"

"Can't tell yet. We'll see what the lab tests bring out." He frowned. "I've taken samples from almost every part of him. So far, the symptoms are fever and some evidence of fluid in the lungs." He shook his head. "I'm afraid I can't let you talk to him now, Greg. This may be serious."

Kent said brusquely, "We'll have to take the risk. Mr. Grosvenor is in possession of valuable information and" – he spoke deliberately – "I feel sure he is still strong enough to give it."

Dr. Eggert looked at Grosvenor. "How do you feel?" he asked.

"I can still talk," Grosvenor said weakly. His face felt hot. His eyes ached. But one of the two reasons why he had made himself sick was the hope that it would impel Kent to come up, as he now had.

The other reason was that he didn't want to attend in person any meeting of scientists Kent might call. Here in this department and here alone he could defend himself from hasty actions the others might decide to take against him.

The doctor glanced at his watch. "Tell you what," he said to Kent, and more indirectly to Grosvenor, "I'm sending up an attendant. The conversation has to be over by the time he gets here. All right?"

Kent said with false heartiness, "Fine!"

Grosvenor nodded.

From the door, Dr. Eggert said, "Mr. Fander will be up in about twenty minutes."

When he had gone, Kent came slowly to the edge of the bed and looked down at Grosvenor. He stood like that for a long moment, and then said in a deceptively mild voice, "I don't understand what you're trying to do. Why are you not giving us the information you have?"

Grosvenor said, "Mr. Kent, are you really surprised?"

Once more there was silence. Grosvenor had the distinct impression of a very angry man restraining himself with difficulty. Finally, Kent said in a low, tense voice, "I am the Director of this expedition. I demand that you make your recommendations at once."

Grosvenor shook his head, slowly. He suddenly felt hot and heavy. He said, "I don't know just what to say to that. You're a pretty predictable man, Mr. Kent. You see, I expected you to handle my letters the way you did. I expected you to come up here with" – he glanced at the other two men – "a couple of hatchetmen. Under the circumstances, I think I'm justified in insisting on a meeting of the heads, so that I can personally present my recommendations."

If he had had time, he would have jerked up his arm then to defend himself. Too late, he saw that Kent was more furious than he had suspected.

"Pretty smart, eh!" the chemist said savagely. His hand came up. He struck Grosvenor in the face with his palm. He spoke again through clenched teeth. "So you're sick, are you? People sick with strange diseases sometimes go out of their heads, and they sometimes have to be severely handled because they insanely attack their dearest friends."

Grosvenor stared at him blurrily. He put his hand up to his face. And, because he was feverish and genuinely weak, he had trouble slipping the antidote into his mouth. He pretended to be holding his cheek where Kent had struck him. He swallowed the new drug, and then said shakily, "All right, I'm insane. Now what?"

If Kent was surprised by the reaction, his words did not show it. He asked curtly, "What do you really want?"

Grosvenor had to fight a moment of nausea. When that was past, he replied, "I want you to start propaganda to the effect that, in your judgment, what has been discovered about the enemy intelligence will require the members of this ship to adjust themselves to staying in space five years longer than was anticipated. That's all for now. When you've done that, I'll tell you what you want to know."

He was beginning to feel better. The antidote was working. The fever was down. And he meant exactly what he had said. His plan was not inflexible. At any stage, Kent or, later on, the group could accept his proposals, and that would end his series of stratagems.

Twice, now, Kent parted his lips as if he intended to speak. Each time, he closed them again. Finally, he said in a choked voice, "Is this all you're going to offer at this time?"

Grosvenor's fingers under the blanket were poised on a button at one side of the bed, ready to press it. He said, "I swear you'll get what you want."

Kent said sharply, "It's out of the question. I couldn't possibly commit myself to such madness. The men won't stand for even a one-year extension of the voyage."

Grosvenor said steadily, "Your presence here indicates that you don't think I have a mad solution."

Kent clenched and unclenched his hands. "It's impossible! How could I possibly explain my action to the department heads!"

Watching the little man, Grosvenor suspected that the crisis was imminent: "You don't have to tell them at this point. All you have to do is promise the information."

One of the technicians, who had been watching Kent's face, spoke up. "Look, chief, this man doesn't seem to realize he's speaking to the Director. How about us working him over?"

Kent, who had been on the point of saying something more, stopped himself. He stepped back, licking his lips. Then he nodded vigorously. "You're right, Bredder, I don't know how I came to start arguing with him. Just a minute while I lock the door. Then we'll — "

Grosvenor warned, "I wouldn't shut it if I were you. It'll set off alarms all over the ship."

Kent, one hand on the door, stopped and turned. There was a set smile on his face. "All right then," he said stiffly, "we'll take you apart with the door open. Start talking, my friend."

The two technicians stepped forward quickly. Grosvenor said, "Bredder, have you ever heard of peripheral electrostatic charge?" As the two men hesitated, he went on grimly. "Touch me and you'll burn. Your hands will blister. Your face — "

Both men were straightening, pulling away. The blond Bredder glanced uneasily at Kent. Kent said angrily, "The amount of electricity in a man's body couldn't kill a fly."

Grosvenor shook his head. "Aren't you a little out of your field, Mr. Kent? The electricity isn't in my body, but it will be in yours if you lay a hand on me."

Kent took out his vibrator and deliberately made an adjustment on it. "Stand back!" he said to his assistants. "I'm going to give him a timed spray of one-tenth of a second. It won't knock him unconscious, but it'll jar every molecule in his body."

Grosvenor said quietly, "I wouldn't try it, Kent. I'm warning you."

The man either did not hear him or was too angry to pay any attention. The tracer beam dazzled Grosvenor's eyes. There was a hiss and a crackle, and a cry of pain from Kent. The light blinked out. Grosvenor saw that Kent was trying to shake the weapon from his hand. It clung stickily, but finally dropped to the floor with a metallic clatter. In evident agony, Kent grabbed his injured hand and stood there swaying.

Grosvenor said with a kind of angry sympathy, "Why didn't you listen? These wall plates are carrying a high electric potential, and since a vibrator ionizes the air, you got an electric shock that simultaneously nullified the energy you discharged, except near the muzzle. I hope it didn't burn you too badly."

Kent had control of himself. He was white and tense, but

calm. "This will cost you dearly," he said in a low voice. "When the others find out that one man is trying to force his ideas – " He broke off and gestured imperiously to his two henchmen. "Come along, we're through here for the time being."

Fully eight minutes after they had gone, Fander came in. It was necessary for Grosvenor to explain patiently several times that he was no longer sick. And it required even longer to persuade Dr. Eggert, whom the young man summoned. Grosvenor did not worry about being found out. It would take a definite suspicion plus considerable research to identify the drug he had used.

In the end, they left him alone, with the advice that he remain in his quarters for a day or so. Grosvenor assured them that he would follow their instructions, and he meant it. In the hard days ahead, the Nexial department would be his fortress. He didn't know just what might be done against him, but here he was as ready as he could be.

About an hour after the doctors had departed, there was a click in the mail-delivery chute. It was from Kent, an announcement of a meeting called, according to the wording, at the request of Elliott Grosvenor. It quoted from Grosvenor's first letter to Kent, and ignored all subsequent events. The printed form ended: "In view of Mr. Grosvenor's past performances, the Acting Director feels that he is entitled to a hearing."

At the bottom of Grosvenor's notice, Kent had written in longhand: "Dear Mr. Grosvenor: In view of your illness, I have instructed Mr. Gourlay's staff to connect your communicator with the control-room auditorium, so that you may participate from your sickbed. The meeting will otherwise be private."

At the designated hour, Grosvenor tuned into the control room. As the image came on, he saw that the whole room was spread before him in sharp focus, and that the receiving plate must be the large communicator just above the massive control board. At this moment, his face was a ten-foot image looking down at the men. For once, he realized wryly, he was going to be present at a meeting in a conspicuous way.

A quick glance over the room showed that most of the department heads were already seated. Directly below the receiving plate, Kent was talking to Captain Leeth. It must have been the end, not the beginning of a conversation, because he looked up at Grosvenor, smiled grimly, and then turned to face his small audience, Grosvenor saw that he wore a bandage on his left hand.

"Gentlemen," said Kent, "without further preamble I am going to call on Mr. Grosvenor." Once more he looked up at the communicator plate, and the same savage smile was on his face. He said, "Mr. Grosvenor, you may proceed."

Grosvenor began, "Gentlemen, about a week ago, I had enough evidence to justify this ship's taking action against the alien intelligence of this galaxy. That may seem like a tremendous statement, and it is an unfortunate fact that I can merely give you my interpretation of the available evidence. I cannot prove to everybody present that such a being does actually exist. Some of you will realize that my reasoning is sound. Others, lacking knowledge of certain sciences, will feel that the conclusions are distinctly controversial. I have racked my brain over the problem of how to convince you that my solution is the only safe one. Telling you what experiments I made happens to be one of the steps which it seemed reasonable to take."

He made no mention of the fact that he had already had to evolve an elaborate ruse in order to obtain a hearing at all. In spite of what had happened, he had no desire to antagonize Kent any more than was necessary.

He continued, "I now want to call on Mr. Gourlay. I am sure you will not be too surprised when I tell you that all this goes back to automatic C-9. I wonder if you would tell your colleagues about it."

The communications chief looked at Kent, who shrugged and nodded. Gourlay hesitated, then said, "It's impossible to say just when C-9 came on. For the benefit of those who are feeling ignorant right now, C-9 is a minor screen that is activated automatically when the dust in the surrounding space reaches a density that could be dangerous to a ship on the move. The apparent density of the dust in any given volume of space is of course relatively greater at high velocities than at low. The fact that there was enough dust around to affect C-9 was first noticed by a member of my staff shortly before those lizards were precipitated into the control room."

Gourlay leaned back in his seat. "That's it," he said.

Grosvenor said, "Mr. von Grossen, what did your department find out about the space dust in this galaxy?"

The bulky von Grossen shifted in his chair. He said without

getting up, "There's nothing about it that we could regard as being characteristic or unusual. It's a little denser than that in our own galaxy. We collected a small amount of the dust by means of ionizing plates with a very high potential, and scraped off the deposits. It was mostly solid, a few simple elements being present and traces of many compounds – which could have been found at the moment of condensation – and a little free gas, mostly hydrogen. Now, the trouble is that what we got probably bears very little resemblance to the dust as it exists outside, but the problem of collecting it in its original form has never been satisfactorily solved. The very process used in capturing it causes it to change in many ways. We can never more than guess at how it functions in space." The physicist lifted his hands helplessly. "That's all I can say now."

Grosvenor continued. "I could go on asking various department heads what they found out. But I believe I can summarize their discoveries without doing anyone an injustice. Both Mr. Smith's and Mr. Kent's departments ran into much the same problem as did Mr. von Grossen's. I believe that Mr. Smith by various means saturated the atmosphere of a cage with the dust. The animals he put into the cage showed no ill effects, so he finally tested it on himself. Mr. Smith, have you anything to add to that?"

Smith shook his head. "If it's a life form, you can't prove it by me. I admit that the closest we got to getting the real stuff was when we went out in a lifeboat, opened all the doors, then closed them, and let air into the boat again. There were slight changes in the chemical content of the air, but nothing important."

Grosvenor said, "So much for the factual data. I also, among other things, performed the experiment of taking out the lifeboat and letting the space dust drift in through open doors. What I was interested in was: If it's life, what does it feed on? So after I had pumped the air back into my lifeboat, I analysed it. Then I killed a couple of small animals, and again analysed the atmosphere. I sent samples of the atmosphere as it was before and after to Mr. Kent, Mr. von Grossen, and Mr. Smith. There were several very minute chemical changes. They could be attributed to analytical error. But I should like to ask Mr. von Grossen to tell you what he found."

Von Grossen blinked and sat up. "Was that evidence?" he asked in surprise. He turned in his seat, and faced his colleagues with a thoughtful frown. "I don't see the significance," he said, "but the molecules of air in the sample marked 'After' carried a slightly higher electric charge."

It was the decisive moment. Grosvenor gazed down at the upturned faces of the scientists and waited for the light of misunderstanding to come to at least one pair of eyes.

The men sat solid, puzzled expressions on their faces. One individual said finally, in a wry voice, "I suppose we're expected to jump to the conclusion that we are dealing with a nebular-dust intelligence. That's too much for me to swallow."

Grosvenor said nothing. The mental jump he wanted them to make was even more farfetched than that, though the difference was subtle. Already, the feeling of disappointment was strong in him. He began to stiffen himself for the next step.

Kent said sharply, "Come, come, Mr. Grosvenor. Explain yourself, and then we will make up our minds."

Grosvenor began reluctantly. "Gentlemen, your failure to see the answer at this point is very disturbing to me. I foresee that we are going to have trouble. Consider my position. I had given you the available evidence, including a description of the experiments which led me to identify our enemy. It is already clear that my conclusions will be regarded as distinctly controversial. And yet, if I am right – I'm convinced of it – failure to take the action I have in mind will be disastrous for the human race and for all other intelligent life in the universe. But here is the situation: If I tell you, then the decision is out of my hands. The majority will decide, and there will be no legal recourse from their decision, so far as I can see."

He paused to let that sink in. Some of the men glanced at each other, frowning. Kent said, "Wait, I have already come up against the stone wall of this man's egotism."

It was his first hostile comment of the meeting. Grosvenor glanced at him quickly, then turned away, and went on. "It is my unhappy lot to inform you, gentlemen, that under the circumstances, this problem ceases to be scientific and becomes political. Accordingly, I have to insist that my solution be accepted. A satisfactory propaganda must be launched, in which Acting Director Kent and every head of a department commits himself to the notion that the *Space Beagle* will have to remain in space the equivalent of five Earth years extra, though we should act as if it were five star years. I am going to give you my interpretation, but I want each head to adjust himself to the notion that he must irrevocably stake his reputation and good name on this matter. The danger, as I see it, is so all-embracing that any petty squabbling we do will be disgraceful according to the time we spend on it."

Succinctly, he told them what the danger was. Then, without waiting for their reaction, he outlined his method of dealing with it.

"We'll have to find some iron planets and set the productive capacity of our ship to the making of atomically unstable torpedoes. I foresee that we will have to spend nearly a year traversing this galaxy and sending out such torpedoes in great numbers at random. And then, when we have made this entire sector of space virtually untenable for him, we depart and offer him the opportunity of following us, this last at a time when he will have literally no recourse but to pursue our ship in the hope that we will lead him to another and better source of food than is available here. Most of our time will be taken up in making sure that we do not guide him back to our own galaxy."

He paused, then said quietly, "Well, gentlemen, there you have it. I can see on various faces that the reaction is going to be a split one and that we are in for one of those deadly controversies."

He stopped. There was silence, and then a man said, "Five years."

It was almost a sigh, and it acted like a cue. All over the room, men stirred uneasily.

Grosvenor said quickly, "Earth years."

He had to keep pressing that. He had deliberately chosen what seemed the longer way to estimating time, so that, when translated into star years, it would seem somewhat less. The fact was that Star Time, with its hundred-minute hour, its twenty-four hour day, and its three-hundred-and-sixty-day year, was a psychological device. Once adjusted to the longer day, people tended to forget how much time was passing according to their older ways of thinking.

In the same way, now, he expected them to feel relieved when they realized that the extra time would amount to just about three years, Star Time.

Kent was speaking: "Any other comments?"

Von Grossen said unhappily, "I cannot honestly accept Mr. Grosvenor's analysis. I have great respect for him in view of his past performances. But he is asking us to take on faith what I am sure we could understand if he actually had valid evidence. I reject the notion that Nexialism provides so sharp an integration of sciences that only individuals trained by its methods can hope to understand the more intricate interrelated phenomena."

Grosvenor said curtly, "Aren't you rejecting rather hastily something which you have never troubled to investigate?"

Von Grossen shrugged, "Perhaps."

"The picture I have," said Zeller, "is of us spending many years and much effort, and yet not once will we have anything but the most indirect and insubstantial evidence that the plan is working."

Grosvenor hesitated. Then he realized that he had no alternative but to continue to make antagonistic statements. The issue was too important. He could not consider their feelings. He said, "*I'll* know when we've been successful, and if some of you people will deign to come to the Nexial department and learn a few of our techniques, you'll know it also when the time comes."

Smith said grimly. "Mr. Grosvenor has this in his favour. He is always offering to teach us how to be his equal."

"Any more comments?" It was Kent, his voice shriller, and edged with triumph.

Several men made as if to speak, but seemingly thought better of it. Kent went on, "Rather than waste any time, I think we should take a vote as to what the majority feels about Mr. Grosvenor's proposal. I'm sure we all want to have a general reaction."

He walked forward slowly. Grosvenor could not see his face, but there was arrogance in the way the man held himself. Kent said, "Let's have a showing of hands. All in favour of accepting Mr. Grosvenor's method – which involves remaining five extra years in space – please raise your hands."

Not a single hand came up.

A man said querulously, "It'll take a little while to think this through."

Kent paused to answer that. "We're trying to get the as-of-now opinion. It's important to all of us to know what the chief scientists of this ship think."

He broke off, and called out, "Those definitely against, raise your hands!"

All except three hands came up. In a lightning glance, Grosvenor identified the three who had abstained. They were Korita, McCann, and von Grossen.

Belatedly, he saw that Captain Leeth, who stood near Kent, had also abstained.

Grosvenor said quickly, "Captain Leeth, this is surely a moment when your constitutional right to take control of the ship would apply. The danger is obvious."

"Mr. Grosvenor," said Captain Leeth slowly, "that would be true if there were a visible enemy. As it is, I can act only on the advice of the scientific experts."

"There is only one such expert aboard," said Grosvenor coldly. "The others are a handful of amateurs who dabble around on the surface of things."

The remark seemed to stun most of those in the room. Abruptly, several men tried to speak at once. They spluttered into angry silence.

It was Captain Leeth who said, finally, in a measured tone, "Mr. Grosvenor, I cannot accept your unsupported claim."

Kent said satirically, "Well, gentlemen, we now have Mr. Grosvenor's true opinion of us."

He seemed unconcerned with the insult itself. His manner was one of ironic good humour. He seemed to have forgotten that he had a duty as Acting Director to maintain an atmosphere of dignity and courtesy.

Meader, head of the botany subsection, reminded him angrily, "Mr. Kent, I do not see how you can tolerate such an insolent remark."

"That's right," said Grosvenor, "stand up for your rights. The whole universe is in deadly danger, but your sense of dignity must be maintained."

McCann spoke for the first time, uneasily. "Korita, if there were a kind of entity out there such as Grosvenor has described, how would that fit in with cyclic history?"

The archaeologist shook his head unhappily. "Very tenuously, I'm afraid. We could postulate a primitive life form." He looked around the room. "I am far more concerned with the evidences of the reality of cyclic history among my friends. Pleasure in the defeat of a man who has made us feel a little uneasy because of his achievements. The suddenly revealed egomania of that man." He gazed regretfully up at Grosvenor's image. "Mr. Grosvenor, I am very disappointed that you have seen fit to make the statements that you have."

"Mr. Korita," said Grosvenor soberly, "if I had adopted any other course than the one I have actually pursued you would not even have had the privilege of hearing me tell these honourable gentlemen – many of whom I admire as individuals – what I have told them, and what I have still to say."

"I feel confident," said Korita, "that the members of this expedition will do what is necessary, regardless of personal sacrifice."

"It's hard to believe that," said Grosvenor. "I feel that many of them were influenced by the fact that my plan would require five extra years in space. I confess it's a cruel necessity, but I assure you there is no alternative."

He broke off, curtly. "Actually, I expected this outcome, and prepared for it." He addressed himself to the group as a whole. "Gentlemen, you have compelled me to take an action which, I assure you, I regret more than I can ever say. Here is my ultimatum."

"Ultimatum!" That was Kent, surprised, suddenly pale.

Grosvenor ignored him. "If by 1000 hours tomorrow my plan has not been accepted, I take over the ship. Everybody aboard will find himself doing what I order whether he likes it or not. Naturally, I expect that the scientists aboard will pool their knowledge in an attempt to prevent my carrying out such a stated purpose. Resistance, however, will be useless."

The uproar that began then was still going on when Grosvenor broke the connection between his communicator and the control room.

CHAPTER TWENTY-SIX

It was about an hour after the meeting when Grosvenor received a call on his communicator from McCann.

"I'd like to come up," said the geologist.

Grosvenor was cheerful. "Come along."

McCann looked doubtful. "I'm assuming you have the corridor booby-trapped."

"We-e-l-ll, yes, I suppose you could call it that," Grosvenor agreed, "but you'll not be troubled."

"Suppose I came with the secret intention of assassinating you?"

"Here in my rooms," said Grosvenor with a positiveness which he hoped would impress any listeners-in, "you couldn't even kill me with a club."

McCann hesitated, then said, "I'll be right up!" He broke the connection.

He must have been very near, for it was less than a minute later that the hidden corridor detectors began to report his approach. Presently, his head and shoulders flashed across a communicator plate, and a relay switch closed into position. Since it was part of an automatic defence process, Grosvenor deactivated it manually.

A few seconds later, McCann came through the open door. He paused on the threshold and then came forward shaking his head.

"I was worried there. Despite your reassurance, I had the feeling that batteries of weapons were pointing at me. And yet I saw nothing." He looked searchingly into Grosvenor's face. "Are you pulling a bluff?"

Grosvenor said slowly, "I'm a little worried myself. Don, you've shaken my faith in your integrity. I honestly didn't expect you to come up here carrying a bomb."

McCann looked blank. "But I'm not. If your instruments show any such – " He stopped. He took off his coat. He began to search himself. Suddenly, his movements slowed. His face was pale as he brought up a wafer-thin grey object about two inches long. "What is it?" he asked.

"A stabilized plutonium alloy."

"*Atomic!*"

"No, it's not radioactive, not as it is. But it can be dissolved into a radioactive gas by the beam from a high-frequency transmitter. The gas would give us both radiation burns."

"Grove, I swear to you that I knew nothing of this."

"Did you tell anyone you were coming?"

"Naturally. This whole part of the ship is blocked off."

"In other words, you had to get permission?"

"Yes. From Kent."

Grosvenor hesitated, then said, "I want you to think hard about this. At any time during the interview with Kent did you feel that the room was hot?"

"W-why, yes. I remember now. I had the feeling that I was going to suffocate."

"How long did that last?"

"A second or so."

"Hmmm, that means you were out probably ten minutes."

"Out?" McCann was scowling. "Well, I'll be damned. That little wretch drugged me."

"I could probably find out for sure just how much of a dose

you were given." Grosvenor spoke deliberately. "A blood test would do it."

"I wish you'd make it. That would prove – "

Grosvenor shook his head. "It would only prove that you actually underwent such an experience. It wouldn't prove that you didn't do so willingly. Far more convincing to me is the fact that no man in his right senses would permit plutonium alloy Pua-72 to be dissolved in his presence. According to my automatic nullifiers, they've been trying to dissolve it now for at least a minute."

McCann was white. "Grove, I'm through with that vulture. I admit I was in a state of conflict, and I agreed to report to him the result of my conversation with you – but I intended to warn you that I had to make such a report."

Grosvenor smiled. "It's all right, Don. I believe you. Sit down."

"What about this?" McCann held out the small metal "bomb."

Grosvenor took it and carried it to the little vault he had for his radioactive material. He came back and seated himself. He said, "I imagine there'll be an attack. The only way Kent could justify to the others what he's done is to make sure that we are rescued in time for us to be given medical treatment for radioactive burns."

He finished. "We can watch it in that plate."

The attack registered first on several electronic detectors of the electric-eye type. Faint lights flashed on a wall instrument board, and a buzzer sounded.

They saw the attackers presently as images on the large plate above the instruments. About a dozen men in space suits rounded a distant corner and approached along the corridor. Grosvenor recognized von Grossen and two of his assistants from the physics department, four chemists, of whom two were from the biochemistry division, three of Gourlay's communications experts, and two weapon officers. Three soldiers brought up the rear, riding, respectively, a mobile vibrator, a mobile heat gun, and a large gas-bomb dispenser.

McCann stirred uneasily. "Isn't there another entrance to this place?"

Grosvenor nodded. "It's guarded."

"What about down and up?" McCann indicated the floor and the ceiling.

"There's a storeroom above, and a motion-picture theatre below. Both are taken care of."

They fell silent. Then, as the group of men in the corridor stopped, McCann said, "I'm surprised to see von Grossen out there. I think he admires you."

Grosvenor said, "I stung him when I called him and the others amateurs. He's come to see for himself what I can do."

Out in the corridor, the group of attackers seemed to be consulting. Grosvenor went on. "What, specifically, brought you up here?"

McCann's gaze was on the plate. "I wanted you to know you were not completely alone. Several executives asked me to tell you they were with you." He broke off distractedly. "Let's not talk now, not while that's going on."

"Now is as good a time as any."

McCann seemed not to hear. "I don't see how you're going to stop them," he said uneasily. "They've got enough power out there to burn down your walls."

Grosvenor made no comment, and McCann faced him. "I've got to be frank with you," he said. "I'm in a state of conflict. I feel sure you're right. But your tactics are too unethical for me." He appeared unaware that he had turned his attention from the viewing plate.

Grosvenor said, "There's only one other possible tactic, and that is to run for election against Kent. Since he's only Acting Director, and was not himself elected, I could probably force an election within about a month."

"Why don't you?"

"Because," said Grosvenor with a shudder, "I'm afraid. The thing – out there – is practically starving to death. At any time it's liable to make a try for another galaxy, and it might very well go for ours. We can't wait a month."

"And yet," McCann pointed out, "your plan is to drive it from this galaxy, and you've estimated that will take a whole year."

"Have you ever tried to snatch food from a carnivore?" Grosvenor asked. "It tries to hold on to it, doesn't it? It will even fight for it. My idea is that when this being realizes we're trying to drive him off, he'll hang on as long as he can to what he's got."

"I see." McCann nodded. "Besides, you'll have to admit your chance of winning an election on your platform is pretty close to zero."

Grosvenor shook his head vigorously. "I'd win. You may not believe that on my say-so. But the fact is that people who are wrapped up in pleasure, excitement, or ambition are easily controlled. I didn't devise the tactics I'd use. They've been around for centuries. But historical attempts to analyse them just didn't get at the roots of the process. Until recently the relation of physiology to psychology was on a fairly theoretical basis. Nexial training reduced it to definite techniques."

McCann was silent, studying him. He said finally, "What kind of future do you envisage for man? Do you expect us all to become Nexialists?"

"On board this ship it's a necessity. For the race as a whole, it's still impractical. In the long run, however, there can be no excuse for any individual not knowing what it is possible for him to know. Why shouldn't he? Why should he stand under the sky of his planet and look up at it with the stupid eyes of superstition and ignorance, deciding vital issues on the basis of somebody's fooling him? The smashed civilizations of Earth's antiquity are evidence of what happens to a man's descendants when he reacts blindly to situations, or if he depends on authoritarian doctrines."

He shrugged. "At the moment a lesser goal is possible. We must make men sceptical. The shrewd though illiterate peasant who has to be shown concrete evidence is the spiritual forebear of the scientist. On every level of understanding, the sceptic partly makes up for his lack of specific knowledge by his attitude of 'Show me! I've got an open mind, but what you say cannot by itself convince me.' "

McCann was thoughtful. "You Nexialists, are going to break through the cyclic-history pattern, is that what you have in mind?"

Grosvenor hesitated, then said, "I confess I was not too conscious of its importance till I met Korita. I've been impressed. I imagine the theory can stand a great deal of revision. Such words as 'race' and 'blood' are particularly meaningless, but the general pattern seems to fit the facts."

McCann had returned his attention to the attackers. He said, puzzled, "They seem to be taking a long time getting started. You'd think they'd have made their plans before they came this far."

Grosvenor said nothing. McCann glanced at him sharply, "Just a moment," he said. "They haven't run up against your defences, have they?"

When Grosvenor still made no reply, McCann jumped to his feet, walked nearer to the plate, and peered into it at close range. He stared intently at two men who were down on their knees.

"But what are they doing?" he asked helplessly. "What is stopping them?"

Grosvenor hesitated, then explained, "They're trying to keep from falling through the floor." Despite his effort to remain calm, excitement put a tremor into his voice.

The other didn't realize that what he was doing was new to him. He had had the knowledge, of course, for a long time. But this was practical application. He was taking action that had never been taken before, anywhere, in quite the same way. He had used phenomena from many sciences, improvising to fit his purpose and to suit the exact environment in which he was operating.

It was working – as he had expected it would. His understanding, so sharp, so broadly based, left little room for error.

But the physical reality exhilarated him in spite of his pre-knowledge.

McCann came back and sat down. "Will the floor actually collapse?"

Grosvenor shook his head. "You're not getting it. The floor is unchanged. They are sinking into it. If they proceed much farther, they'll fall through." He laughed in sudden glee. "I'd like to have a good look at Gourlay's face when his assistants report the phenomenon. This is his 'balloon', teleportation, hyperspace notion, with an idea added from oil geology and two techniques of plant chemistry."

"What's the geology notion?" McCann began. He stopped. "Well, I'll be damned. You mean the way to get oil these days without drilling. We just create a condition on the surface to which all oil in the vicinity has to come." He frowned. "But, just a minute. There's a factor that — "

"There are a dozen factors, my friend," said Grosvenor. He went on soberly, "I repeat, this is laboratory stuff. A lot of things work at close quarters on very little power."

McCann said, "Why didn't you use a little of this trickery against pussy and the scarlet monster?"

"I've told you. I've rigged this situation. I worked through many a sleep hour installing my equipment, something which I never had a chance to do against our alien enemies. Believe me, if I had had control of the ship, we wouldn't have lost so many lives in either of those incidents."

"Why didn't you take control?"

"It was too late. There wasn't time. Besides, this ship was built several years before there was a Nexial Foundation. We were lucky to get a department aboard."

McCann said presently, "I don't see how you're going to take over the ship tomorrow, since that'll involve coming out of your laboratory." He stopped and stared at the plate. Then he said breathlessly, "They've brought up de-gravity rafts. They're going to float over your floor."

Grosvenor made no reply. He had already seen.

CHAPTER TWENTY-SEVEN

DE-GRAVITY rafts operated on the same principle as the anti-acceleration drive. The reaction that occurred in an object when inertia was overcome had been found on examination to be a molecular process but it was not inherent in the structure of matter. An anti-acceleration field shifted electrons in their orbits slightly. This, in turn, created a molecular tension, resulting in a small though all-embracing rearrangement.

Matter so altered, acted as if it were immune to the normal effects of speeding up or slowing down. A ship proceeding on anti-acceleration could stop short in mid-flight, even if it had been travelling at millions of miles a second.

The group attacking Grosvenor's department merely loaded their weapons on to the long, narrow rafts, climbed aboard themselves, and activated them to a suitable field intensity. Then, using magnetic attraction, they drew themselves forward toward the open door two hundred feet away.

They proceeded about fifty feet, then slowed, came to a full stop, and began to back. Then they stopped again.

Grosvenor, who had been busy at his instrument board, came back and sat down beside the puzzled McCann.

The geologist asked, "What did you do?"

Grosvenor answered without hesitation. "As you saw, they propelled themselves forward by pointing directional magnets at the steel walls ahead. I set up a repeller field, which is nothing new in itself. But actually this version of it is a part of a temperature process more related to the way you and I maintain our body heat than it is to heat physics. Now they'll have to use jet propulsion, or ordinary screw propellers, or even" – he laughed – "oars."

McCann, his gaze on the viewing plate, said grimly, "They're not going to bother. They're going to turn their heater loose. Better shut the door!"

"Wait!"

McCann swallowed visibly. "But the heat will come in here. We'll roast."

Grosvenor shook his head. "I've told you; what I did was part of a process involving temperature. Fed new energy, the whole metal environment will seek to maintain its equilibrium on a somewhat lower level. There – look."

The mobile heat blaster was turning white. It was a white that made McCann curse softly under his breath. "Frost," he mumbled. "But how. . . . "

As they watched, ice formed on the walls and the floors. The heater gleamed in its frozen casing, and a chill blast of air came through the door. McCann shivered.

"Temperature," he said vaguely. "A somewhat lower equilibrium."

Grosvenor stood up. "I think it's time they went home. After all, I don't want anything to happen to them."

He walked to an instrument that stood against one wall of the auditorium room, and sank into a chair in front of a compact keyboard. The keys were small and of different colours. There were twenty-five to a row, and twenty-five rows.

McCann came over and stared down at the instrument.

"What is it?" he asked. "I don't recall seeing it before."

With a quick, rippling, almost casual movement, Grosvenor depressed seven of the keys, then reached over and touched a main release switch. There was a clear, yet soft, musical note. Its overtones seemed to stay in the air for several seconds after the basic note had died away.

Grosvenor looked up. "What association did that bring to your mind?"

McCann hesitated. There was an odd expression on his face. "I had a picture of an organ playing in a church. Then that changed, and I was at a political rally where the candidate had provided fast, stimulating music to make everybody happy." He broke off, and said breathlessly, "So that is how you could win an election."

"One of the methods."

McCann was tense. "Man, what terrific power you have."

Grosvenor said, "It doesn't affect me."

"But you're conditioned. You can't expect to condition the whole human race."

"A baby is conditioned when it learns to walk, move its arms, speak. Why not extend the conditioning to hypnotism, chemical responses, the effects of food? It was possible hundreds of years ago. It would prevent a lot of disease, heartache, and the kind of catastrophe that derives from misunderstanding of one's own body and mind."

McCann was turning back to the mounted, spindle-shaped instrument. "How does it work?"

"It's an arrangement of crystals with electrical circuits. You know how electricity can distort certain crystalline structures. By setting up a pattern, an ultrasonic vibration is emitted, which by-passes the ear and directly stimulates the brain. I can play on that the way a musician plays on his instrument, creating emotional moods that strike too deep for any untrained person to resist."

McCann returned to his chair and sat down. He looked suddenly pale. "You frighten me," he said in a low voice. "I regard that as unethical. I can't help it."

Grosvenor studied him; then, turning, he bent down and made an adjustment on the instrument. He pressed the button. The sound was sadder, sweeter, this time. It had a cloying quality, as if endless vibrations continued to throb in the air around them, though the sound itself was gone. Grosvenor said, "What did you get that time?"

McCann hesitated again, then said suddenly, "I thought of my mother. I had a sudden desire to be back home. I wanted –"

Grosvenor frowned, "That's too dangerous," he said. "If I intensified that enough, some of the men might curl up again in the womb position." He paused. "How about this?"

Rapidly, he set up a new pattern, and then touched the activating switch. He drew a bell-like sound, with a soft, soft tinkling in the distant background.

"I was a baby," said McCann, "and it was bedtime. Gosh, I'm sleepy." He seemed not to notice that he had reverted to the present tense. Involuntarily, he yawned.

Grosvenor opened a drawer in a table beside the machine, and took out two plastic headpieces. He handed one to McCann. "Better put that on."

He slipped the other over his own head, while his companion, with evident reluctance, did the same. McCann said gloomily, "I guess I'm just not made to be Machiavellian. I suppose you'll try to tell me that meaningless sounds have been used before to evoke emotions and influence people."

Grosvenor, who had been setting a dial pointer, paused to answer. He said earnestly, "People think a thing ethical or unethical depending on the associations that come to their minds at the moment, or while they're considering the problem in retrospect. That doesn't mean that no system of ethics has any validity. I personally subscribe to the principle that our ethical measuring rod should be that which benefits the greatest number, provided that it doesn't include extermination or torture of, or denial of rights to, individuals who do not conform. Society has to learn to salvage the man who is ill or ignorant."

He was intent now. "Please note that I have never used this device before. I have never used hypnosis except when Kent invaded my department – though of course I intend to do so now. From the moment the trip began, I could have lured people up here by stimulating them in a dozen unsuspected ways. Why didn't I? Because the Nexial Foundation laid down a code of ethics for itself and its graduates, which is conditioned right into my system. I can break through that conditioning, but only with great difficulty."

"Are you breaking through it now?"

"No."

"It seems to me, then, that it's pretty elastic."

"That's exactly right. When I firmly believe, as I do now, that my actions are justified, there is no internal nervous or emotional problem."

McCann was silent. Grosvenor went on. "I think you've got a picture in your mind of a dictator – myself – taking over a democracy by force. That picture is false, because a ship on a cruise can be run only by quasi-democratic methods. And the greatest difference of all is that at the end of the voyage I can be brought to account."

McCann sighed. "I suppose you're right," he said. He glanced at the plate. Grosvenor followed his gaze, and saw that the space-suited men were trying to propel themselves forward by pushing against the wall. Their hands tended to go right into the walls, but there was some resistance. They were making slow progress. McCann was speaking again. "What are you going to do now?"

"I intend to put them to sleep – like this." He touched the activating switch.

The bell sound seemed no louder than before. Yet in the corridor the men slumped over.

Grosvenor got up. "That will repeat every ten minutes, and I've got resonators spread all through the ship to pick up the vibrations and echo them. Come along."

"Where are we going?"

"I want to install a circuit breaker in the main electric-switch system of the ship."

He secured the breaker from the film room, and a moment later was leading the way into the corridor.

Everywhere they went, men lay sleeping. At first McCann marvelled out loud. Then he grew silent and looked troubled. He said finally, "It's hard to believe that human beings are basically so helpless."

Grosvenor shook his head. "It's worse than you think."

They were in the engine room now, and he crawled on to a lower tier of the electric switchboard. It required less than ten minutes to fit in his circuit breaker. He came down silently, nor did he subsequently explain what he had done or what he intended to do.

"Don't mention that," he said to McCann. "If they find out about it, I'll just have to come down and put in another one."

"You're going to wake them now?"

"Yes. As soon as I get back to my rooms. But first I'd like you to help me cart von Grossen and the others to their bedrooms. I want to make him disgusted with himself."

"You think they'll give in?"

"No."

His estimate was right. And so, at 1000 hours the following day, he pressed home a switch that rechannelled the main electric current through the circuit breaker he had installed.

All over the ship, the constantly burning lights flickered ever so slightly in a Nexial version of the Riim hypnotic pattern. Instantly, without knowing it, every man aboard was deeply hypnotized.

Grosvenor began to play on his emotion-educing machine. He concentrated on thoughts of courage and sacrifice, duty to the race in the face of danger. He even evolved a complex emotional pattern that would stimulate the feeling that time was passing at double, even treble, what had been normal before.

The basis laid, he activated the "General Call" of the ship's communicator, and gave exact commands. The main instructions stated, he then told the men that each and every one would thereafter respond instantly to a cue word without ever knowing what the cue word was, or remembering it after it was given.

Then he gave them amnesia for the entire hypnotic experience.

He went down to the engine room and removed the circuit breaker.

He returned to his own room, wakened everybody, and called Kent. He said, "I withdraw my ultimatum. I'm ready to give myself up. I've suddenly realized that I cannot bring myself to go against the wishes of the other members of the ship. I would like another meeting, at which I will appear in person. Naturally, I intend to urge once more that we wage all-out warfare against the alien intelligence of this galaxy."

He was not surprised when the ship's executive, strangely unanimous in their change of heart, agreed that after consideration they could see that the evidence was clear, and that the danger was compellingly urgent.

Acting Director Kent was instructed to pursue the enemy relentlessly, and without regard for the comfort of the members of the ship.

Grosvenor, who had not interfered with the over-all personality of any individual, observed with grim amusement the reluctance with which Kent himself acknowledged that the action should be taken.

The great battle between man and alien was about to begin.

CHAPTER TWENTY-EIGHT

THE Anabis existed in an immense, suffused, formless state, spread through all the space of the second galaxy. It writhed a little, feebly, in a billion portions of its body, shrinking with automatic adjustment away from the destroying heat and radiation of two hundred billion blazing suns. But it pressed tightly down against the myriad planets, and strained with a feverish, insatiable hunger around the quadrillion tingling points in which were dying the creatures that gave it life.

It was not enough. The dread knowledge of an imminent starvation seeped to the farthest reaches of its body. Through all the countless, tenuous cells of its structure came messages from near and far, proclaiming that there was not enough food. For long now, all the cells had had to do with less.

Slowly, the Anabis had come to realize that it was either too big – or too small. It had made a fatal mistake in growing with such abandon during its early days. In those years, the future had seemed limitless. The galactic space, where its form could wax ever huger had appeared of endless extent. It had expanded with all the vaunting, joyous excitement of a lowborn organism grown conscious of stupendous destiny.

It *was* lowborn. In the dim beginning it had been only gas oozing from a mist-covered swamp. It was an odourless, tasteless gas, yet somehow, someway, a dynamic combination was struck. And there was life.

At first it was nothing but a puff of invisible mist. Ardently, it darted over the muggy, muddy waters that had spawned it, twisting, diving, pursuing incessantly and with a gathering alertness, a gathered need, striving to be present while something – anything – was being killed.

For the death of others was its life.

Not for it was the knowledge that the process by which it survived was one of the most intricate that had ever been produced by a natural life chemistry. Its interest was in pleasure and exhilaration, not in information. What a joy it felt when it was able to swoop over two insects, as they buzzed in a furious death struggle, envelop them, and wait, trembling in every gassy atom, for the life force of the defeated to spray with tingling effect against its own insubstantial elements.

There was a timeless period then, when its life was only that aimless search for food. And its world was a narrow swamp, a grey, nubiferous environment, where it lived its contented, active, idyllic, almost mindless existence. But even in that area of suffused sunlight it grew bigger imperceptibly. It needed more food, more than any haphazard search for dying insects could bring it.

And so it developed cunning, special little bits of knowledge that fitted the dank swamp. It learned which were the insects that preyed, and which were the prey. It learned the hunting hours of every species, and where the tiny, non-flying monsters lay in wait – the flying ones were harder to keep track of. Though – as the Anabis discovered – they, also, had their eating habits. It learned to use its vaporous shape like a breeze to sweep unsuspecting victims to their fate.

Its food supply became adequate, then more than adequate. It grew, and once more it hungered. Of necessity, it became aware that there was life beyond the swamp. And, one day, when it ventured farther than ever before, it came upon two gigantic armoured beasts at the bloody climax of a death struggle. The sustained thrill that came as the defeated monster's life force streamed through its vitals, the sheer quantity of energy it received, provided ecstasy greater than it had experienced during all its previous lifetime. In a few hours while the victor devoured the writhing vanquished, the Anabis grew by ten thousand times ten thousand.

During the single day and night period that followed, the steaming jungle world was enveloped. The Anabis overflowed every ocean, every continent, and spread up to where the eternal clouds gave way to unadulterated sunlight. Later, in the days of its intelligence, it was able to analyse what happened then. Whenever it gained in bulk, it absorbed certain gases from the atmosphere around it. To bring this about, two agents were needed, not just one. There was the food it had to search for. And there was the natural action of ultra-violet radiation from the sun. In the swamp, far below the upper reaches of that water-laden atmosphere, only a minute quantity of the necessary short waves had come through. The results were correspondingly tiny, localized, and potentially only planetary in scope.

As it emerged from the mist, it was increasingly exposed to ultra-violet light. The dynamic expansion that began then did not slow for aeons. On the second day, it reached the nearest planet. In a measurable time, it spread to the limits of the galaxy, and reached out automatically for the shining stuff of other star systems. But there it met defeat in distances that seemed to yield nothing to its groping, tenuous matter.

It took in knowledge as it took in food. And in the early days it believed the thoughts were its own. Gradually, it grew aware that the electrical nerve energy it absorbed at each death scene brought with it the mind-stuff of both a victorious and a dying beast. For a time, that was its thought level. It learned the animal cunning of many a carnivorous hunter, and the evasive skill of the hunted. But, here and there on different planets, it made contact with an entirely different degree of intelligence: beings who could think, civilization, science.

It discovered from them, among many other things, that by concentrating its elements it could make holes in space, go through, and come out at a distant point. It learned to transport matter in this fashion. It began to junglize planets as a matter of course because primeval worlds provided the most life force. It transported great slices of other jungle worlds through hyperspace. It projected cold planets nearer their suns.

It wasn't enough.

The days of its power seemed but a moment. Wherever it fed, it grew vaster. Despite its enormous intelligence, it could never strike a balance anywhere. With horrendous fear, it foresaw that it was doomed within a measurable time.

The coming of the ship brought hope. By stretching dangerously thin in one direction, it would follow the ship to wherever it had come from. Thus would begin a desperate struggle to remain alive by jumping from galaxy to galaxy, spreading ever farther into the immense night. Throughout those years, its hope must be that it would be able to junglize planets, and that space had no end. . . .

To the men, darkness made no difference. The *Space Beagle* crouched on a vast plain of jagged metal. Every porthole shed light. Great searchlights poured added illumination on rows of engines that were tearing enormous holes into the all-iron world. At the beginning, the iron was fed into a single manufacturing machine, which turned out unstable iron torpedoes at the rate of one every minute, and immediately launched them into space.

By dawn of the next morning, the manufacturing machine itself began to be manufactured, and additional robot feeders poured raw iron into each new unit. Soon, a hundred, then thousands of manufacturing machines were turning out those slim, dark torpedoes. In ever greater numbers they soared into the surrounding night, scattering their radioactive substance to every side. For thirty thousand years those torpedoes would shed their destroying atoms. They were designed to remain within the gravitational field of their galaxy, but never to fall on a planet or into a sun.

As the slow, red dawn of the second morning brightened the horizon, engineer Pennons reported on the "General Call."

"We're now turning out nine thousand a second; and I think we can safely leave the machines to finish the job. I've put a partial screen around the planet to prevent interference. Another hundred iron worlds properly located, and our bulky friend will begin to have a hollow feeling in his vital parts. It's time we were on our way."

The time came, months later, when they decided that their destination would be Nebula NGC-50,437. Astronomer Lester explained the meaning of the selection.

"That particular galaxy," he said quietly, "is nine hundred *million* light-years away. If this gas intelligence follows us, he'll lose even his stupendous self in a night that almost literally has no end."

He sat down, and Grosvenor rose to speak.

"I'm sure," he began, "we all understand that we are not going to this remote star system. It would take us centuries, perhaps thousands of years, to reach it. All we want is to get this inimical life form out where he will starve. We'll be able to tell if he's following us by the murmurings of his thoughts. And we'll know he's dead when the murmurings stop."

That was exactly what happened.

Time passed. Grosvenor entered the auditorium room of his department, and saw that his class had again enlarged. Every seat was occupied, and several chairs had been brought in from adjoining rooms. He began his lecture of the evening.

"The problems which Nexialism confronts are whole problems. Man has divided life and matter into separate compartments of knowledge and being. And, even though he sometimes uses words which indicate his awareness of the wholeness of nature, he continues to behave as if the one, changing universe had many separately functioning parts. The techniques we will discuss tonight. . . . "

He paused. He had been looking out over his audience, and his gaze had suddenly fastened on a familiar figure well to the rear of the room. After a moment's hesitation, Grosvenor went on.

" . . . will show how this disparity between reality and man's behaviour can be overcome."

He went on to describe the techniques, and in the back of

the room Gregory Kent took his first notes on the science of Nexialism.

And, carrying its little bit of human civilization, the expeditionary ship *Space Beagle* sped at an ever-increasing velocity through a night that had no end.

And no beginning.